RUSSELL A. R

GUNLORDS

THE SAPPHIRE KING

Printed in the United States of America

ISBN:	Softcover	978-1-63871-350-0
	eBook	978-1-63871-351-7

Republished by: PageTurner Press and Media LLC
Publication Date: 08/04/2021

To order copies of this book, contact:

PageTurner Press and Media
Phone: 1-888-447-9651
info@pageturner.us
www.pageturner.us

BY

RUSSELL A. REBALL

"KILL OR BE KILLED, BUT WHENEVER POSSIBLE THERE'S ONLY ONE SURE WAY TO SURVIVE COMBAT............. **avoid it.**"

—U.S. Secretary of Defense, Barry Conan

PROLOGUE:

With daytime drawing near, its massive form moved swiftly through the trees, but it was in no particular hurry; compelled to carry out a mission, yet void of any sense of urgency, the robot was simply doing what it was programmed to do, and that upon itself was beyond its control.

Nothing could stop it, nor would anyone dare to try. Weighing four thousand-six hundred pounds and walking upright on powerful legs, it pounded the earth with each measured step. *Tchwonk. Tchwonk. Tchwonk.*

It didn't speak. Nor did it make grunting noises, or express sounds of exertion as it continued to drive through the dense forest. It was, of course, incapable of all that. But it was hardly silent. Pistons hissed. Springs squeaked. Servos and gears rattled and clicked.

Two robotic arms, each with an integration of links and joints, swung as it strode. The arms were in proportion to its height—it stood just over fifteen feet—but its claws, with three jointed fingers, were abnormally large, like a lobster's claws, big and clunky. They were designed to lift boulders in the diamond mines where the robot had been engineered and its purpose conceived, but that was a long time ago. On this day, they carried the bodies of soldiers in each claw—more accurately, one soldier and a half of one, from the waist up.

The forest came to an end at a desolate road lined by trees on both sides. The machine stopped here a moment, calculated its position relative to its destination, and then made a sharp turn. Heading south now, it passed below a streetlamp mounted to a wooden pole, and continued on toward the bridge, or rather, where the bridge used to be. What remained of the steel truss bridge were the broken ends of I-beams protruding from concrete mounts embedded in the rock ledge over a crevice more than one hundred feet deep.

Here was its destination. Here was where it would deposit the bodies. But there came a sudden alert, a vibration that triggered an audible sensor from which data would require immediate processing.

"Please, don't..."

The machine raised its right arm, where the sound originated, to get a better view of the soldier. Thermal imaging identified it: alive. Unusual. Unlikely, given its sustained damage.

"Talia..."

The robot had only one eye, a spherical lens encased in a glowing blue shell attached to braided metallic synapses (like muscles) that enabled the eye to turn and see what the soldier was looking at.

Down the road, under the spot of the streetlamp, stood a cloaked figure whose face was concealed within the shadow of its hood. The soldier seemed to know who it was, and this time cried out, "Talia, you can stop this!"

The cloaked figure remained still. Silent. Gave no signal. No indication for the robot to cease its program. And so, the robot looked back at the soldier. Was there something more it cared to say? Something perhaps more influential?

No.

The robot positioned both its arms over the edge of the crevice and opened its claws wide. It was nothing personal. The body held in the left claw—the half body—fell free with no resistance. Soundlessly it plummeted. But the soldier still clinging to life held on best he could, so desperately the robot had to shake him loose. Several attempts did the trick. Soundlessly this soldier did not plummet; his high pitched shrill carried to the bottom and was cut short when he landed on the pile of bodies already down there, bodies that the robot had deposited earlier in the evening.

The robot cast its eye over the side to peer below. Satisfied with what it saw, the machine turned and headed back into the woods, back where it came from.

Tchwonk...

Tchwonk...

Tchwonk...

CHAPTER ONE

"The Landlord Project"

Can it be done?

The big question. The only thing that mattered.

The General sat in his chair and clasped his hands upon his desk as he watched the scientists who would provide the answer to that question pour into his office. His desk was too big for the space, like a wide entry door turned sideways. Items on it ridiculously out of reach; a cup filled with pens and pencils, a stapler, and a framed photograph—not of his loving family (he didn't have one)—but of his dog, a mean looking snarling Rotweiler. Befitting.

It was the moment of truth

There were five scientists all together. Four of them were men, dressed in white lab coats, the shortest of whom was the lead scientist. His name was, Doctor Syed Sadeem, he remained in back of the intellectual quintet, quiet and unobtrusive. The spokesperson of the group was a woman. She was thin, wore a dress and heels, but carried herself stately in spite of loveliness. Her name was Doctor Tamika Devon.

There were no chairs for them to sit. They had been given no reason to stay. For a time, Dr. Devon was given a chance to speak. She spewed technical jargon too incomprehensible for a layman's ears, filling the air in the room with words and phrases that made sense only to her colleagues. When the general had heard enough, he raised his hand high in the air as a signal for her to stop.

"Just answer the question," he told her.

She maintained her composure. "Yes, General, it can be done."

And thus came the welcoming news of the malevolent project to be forged for use in the *Second Civil War* in the United States of America: **THE LANDLORD PROJECT;** a top secret undertaking by the weapons division of the United Federal Armed Forces to create genetically enhanced soldiers.

General Christian, the self proclaimed Father of the project, sat back in his chair and grinned. To anyone who knew him, it was a grin that could best be described as devilish.

Dr. Devon proceeded, "If we only had more time..."

"We're out of time," the general conceded.

"There were some setbacks, sir," the lovely doctor wished to express, "some minor, if you will, side effects to the process."

The general sat up straight. "I'm listening."

"Well, for one, the blood vessels in their eyes, sir, quadruple in size and multiply, engulfing the eye in a deep dark red overlay—like a shell—that is almost black."

"Are they blind?" There was obvious concern.

Dr. Devon shook her head. "Their eyes, as well as all their senses, have been enhanced. It's just that they appear, well..."

"Fierce," the general suggested.

She was going to say *freakish*, for lack of a better term.

"Imagine, Doctor, you're the enemy, on the battlefield, and one of our guys comes at you with those black eyes glaring at you, how intimidated would you be—come to think of it—how absolutely terrified would you feel? You might drop your weapon right then and there and run away, yelping like some dog that's been kicked in the ass!"

"I suppose, that is one way of looking at it..."

"Anything else I need to know?"

Dr. Devon held a clipboard in her hands and she flipped to a second page and pretended to read from a chart in order to keep from looking the general in the eye. "There is a drastic rise in their level of aggression; general, so precise it can be measured. We're calling it the Jekyll and Hyde Affect."

The general gave it some thought. "The initial subjects of yours, they were death row inmates, hardened criminals, am I correct?"

"Yes, sir, that's correct."

"Well, then, this setback of yours may be more *psycho*-logical than neurological."

His wishful thinking no doubt. But Dr. Devon knew better.

"And what arrangements have you prepared for these criminals?" the general asked.

"They will have to be put down, of course."

"I agree."

She knew he would, being well aware of his nature; she took a mental note of the gleam in his eyes.

General Christian slapped his hands loudly on his desk and brought the discussion to an abrupt conclusion. Drawing on inspiration, he stated profoundly, "Let's do it." And he thanked all of them for their success and continued cooperation and gestured toward the door for them to leave. They exited without hesitation. But one of them remained, the lead scientist, Dr. Sadeem.

The general fought the urge to roll his eyes. "Is there something you need to tell me, Doctor?" He was, in fact, expecting this.

The scientist approached the desk. "I would like to point out something, general."

"Of course you would," Christian muttered intelligibly.

"We are building a bridge, sir..."

—He was speaking figuratively, of course— "a bridge, that will allow passage into a very dark and dangerous territory; a bridge that, once completed, can not be blocked or blown up. It will allow others to cross—others, sir, that can take advantage of what we have endeavored to create. This presents a responsibility on our part to be wary of what we choose to do from this moment on."

The general responded, "Isn't that what you smart fellas call a milestone?"

The military man got up from his chair and took a step toward the window in his office. The blinds drew dark lines across his face as he looked out. His view was grim. The danger was drawing near. He could see smoke rising from the tops of buildings in the distance and hear the faint sounds of sirens from responding emergency vehicles.

And there was also the crack of distant gunfire.

"You and I seem to keep knocking heads regarding this issue, Sayed." the general said.

"The primary subjects you chose, they're *Gunlords,*" Syed pointed out. "I handpicked them. Soldiers from the 54th."

"We were hoping for subjects less volatile."

The general turned to look at the doctor like he was crazy. "What's the point in that? I don't need cooks, I need killers."

"Oh, they'll be that, sir. They'll be killers all right."

"So what's your problem?" Again, the general looked out the window. "My objective is to end this war. Clear and simple. Whatever means necessary. This senseless slaughter needs to stop. Peace and security must be brought back to this great nation of ours—and to the world!"

"A man by the name of Robert Oppenheimer said that a long time ago."

"What's your point, Sayed?"

Dr. Sadeem took a deep breath. "These Gunlords, once the war is over, what have you planned for them?"

"Are you suggesting I should have them put down like the test subjects, the prisoners?"

"No, sir. I would never suggest anything like that. But you need to take into consideration what may happen if these Gunlords were to join society. They may intermingle with the opposite sex, procreate."

"You make it sound so romantic, doctor."

"They could have children. Their children will inherit their altered gene code. If their children were to have children, they too will have the enhancements. And so on. We would be paving the way to a new evolutionary track for mankind. What do you think the end result of that will be?'

The general gave it some thought and replied, "More better soldiers."

And with that said, Dr. Sayed Sadeem immediately excused himself.

Later that evening, safe in the quiet solitude of his home, the lead scientist contemplated a means by which he could secure the knowledge he possessed and keep the world safe. He felt he had a responsibility. He could come up with only one solution; a solution that would preserve his knowledge indefinitely, perhaps even forever. But it was a difficult one. And the more he thought about it, the more impossible it became to realize.

For he was too much of a coward to kill himself.

CHAPTER TWO

"LIKE FATHER, LIKE SON"

EIGHTEEN YEARS AND NINE MONTHS LATER, J. Hollister Duncan was moving through the trees at an amazing speed, running faster than he ever ran in his life. Faster than he ever thought he could. He felt good—no, magnificent, was the word—and he felt he could go on like this forever and never get caught. The world to his left and right was a blur while his keen eyes remained fixed on a point in the infinite horizon. He was able to control his breathing. He could smell the sweet aroma of the smooth-barked Arizona cypress and velvet mesquite. It was invigorating. He endured no fatigue. No hurtle was too high to scale, nor brush too thick to penetrate. He was unstoppable. Then suddenly, he had an awareness of something, something he wished he had been aware of sooner: he was all alone!

"*Ugh...*" he grunted.

He reached out with one hand and hooked onto the nearest tree to turn himself in the opposite direction. He stopped and looked around. Where was Uncle Billy? *Shit*! He cursed himself for thinking his uncle could possibly keep up.

The two of them had successfully outrun the storm—the gunfire, the shouts and the vehicles crackling through the forest in hot pursuit—and Hollis felt good about it. The two of them were safe, at least for the moment, from immediate harm. But now Billy was nowhere in sight.

Don't let them catch him, son.

The words of his mother; her voice filling his head, speaking to him from the kingdom of the dear departed. He could picture her now, looking down at him from that place and shaking her head in disappointment.

They will torture him, son. If you get away, they will make him talk, force him to give information about you, and about your father.

"I am my father's son," Hollis thought aloud, looking up at the sky. How could his mother forget that by his very nature he was destined to ruin expectations and diminish the hope and decency of good people? "I am the son of a Gunlord."

Hollis ran back to where he had last saw his Uncle Billy. Not very far. About three hundred meters he found the man lying on his back in the thick brush, lying there with his eyes open and staring up at the midday sky.

"Are you resting, Uncle?"

Billy's eyes shifted slightly toward his nephew. Calmly he replied, "Waiting for the next bus to pick me up."

Hollis crouched down. "I'm sorry, I got carried away."

"I'm done with all this. I quit."

"What do you mean, you quit?"

"I'm not built like you, kid. I can't keep running like this. I'm just going to lie here and wait for them to catch me. Besides, all they really want is *you*, not me."

"And when they catch you, what do you suppose they'll do, help you to your feet and thank you for the challenge?"

Billy sighed.

"Get your ass up, Uncle. I mean it. Get your ass up...or I'll carry you."

"I won't let you."

"We'll see about that."

A bullet cut through the vegetation. It buzzed past Hollis' head and the young man dropped to his chest. "Sons-a-bitches," he spat, "how the hell did they find us so fast?"

"One of us must have been tagged..."

Another round struck a tree near to Hollis' head. He could go no lower.

"Listen to me, kid," Billy urged. "They will shoot me. They won't mean to kill me. Just to wound me. Enough to make me stop, because they will expect you to come back for me." Billy sat up and grabbed Hollis by his shirt collar. "Prove them wrong. Save your own ass."

"I'm not leaving you."

"Well, then, you're a fool." Billy said, and he released Hollis' collar. "I've been called worse."

"What are you going to do, you're going to fight them?"

"Couldn't be more than eight of them. I can take'em."

"Sure, only eight…with guns."

Hollis' keen senses could hear them coming, and determine how far off they were. He could smell them, too, coming from every direction, got a sense they were surrounding them. He knew of them; a bunch of yahoos from the Eight Brigade, a rogue unit of lawless country boys, no doubt, out to make a name for themselves by capturing a high profile target. That was all they were. Not a unit of any significance.

Hollis made two fists. His teen-aged hands were thick, like mallets, and every bit as useful to clobber someone. And then he stood up.

The next crack of gunfire was meant to keep him down. He ignored it. He stood up straight and dug his feet into the ground.

He wasn't afraid.

He was prepared to make a clear example of the first one to come within reach. The others, if they didn't get the message, were going to pay a hefty price for their ignorance—an arm and a leg, and not necessarily in that order.

In the minutes that followed, J. Hollister Duncan put up a good fight. He had no intentions of killing any of them, but he was not about to be lenient. The soldiers from the 8th Brigade were given an exercise in humility; just what occurs when a Gunlord's son gets backed into a corner.

Hollis took to the first one like a wild animal, knocked him out with one pulverizing punch and then flipped his body up into the air with almost no effort. His body ended up dangling from a tree limb up above where he hung like a dish towel.

One by one they came at him, and for awhile Hollis struck them down. He cracked ribs. Knocked out some of their teeth. Tore so much flesh his hands were stained red with their blood. But when their strategy changed, he was eventually overwhelmed. They started coming at him from all sides, seemingly all at once, and even a strong boy such as Hollis had his limits. They beat him to the ground.

While they pummeled his face with their fists, Hollis laughed. As they shouted things into his ears, such things as *traitor*, *mercenary*, *murderer*—things he could not deny—he still continued to laugh. His spat his blood in their faces. They managed to get him to the ground, but were unable to keep his arms still. And then one of them said something, something so terrible it caused Hollis to stop laughing, and stop struggling. In that moment they took advantage and clubbed his thick skull with the butt of their rifles until he was unconscious. Fortunately for Hollis he was worth more alive than dead.

"You're just like your father..." they had said to him, "a *monster*."

"Fear has always been different for me than for most men. There is a certain kind of thrill in hunting down something that has no misgivings whatsoever for hunting me down as well. If a man cannot appreciate that, then he should not be a hunter, nor, for that matter, a soldier."

— Excerpt from an interview with big game hunter, Sir Edmond Winthrop; Printed in *The London Herald;* June, 1912.

CHAPTER THREE

"BRAVO COMPANY"

THEY WERE DOOMED FROM THE START.

It was called Razorback; the M-CAV-A2 multi-purpose combat vehicle; weighing in at over 40 tons, armor plated and equipped with a 50 caliber machine gun turret. With its rear compartment, it was designed to carry twenty-two soldiers "safely" to the front line. But it was much too big and sluggish, impractical, and had a track record that proved its delinquency on the battlefield. And here, now, was one of them crippled on the side of a long desolate road that seemed to go nowhere in every direction. The chief mechanic of Bravo Company, Sergeant Percy, who had warned command of the vehicle's poor maintenance record, declared its condition terminal and later wrote in his report: *They just don't make a war machine worth a damn anymore.*

Percy's feet were sticking out from the undercarriage of the M-CAV when Lieutenant Lewison came to check on his progress. With a firm kick of the bottom of his boot, the Lt got Percy's attention. "Are you asleep under there, sergeant? What's the status?"

"Everything's gone ka-put," Percy replied.

"Is that a joke?"

"Let me set it up for you, sir; what happens to the gears inside a transfer case when the rear axle gets bent?"

Sergeant Percy crawled out from under the M-CAV. His face was scruffy, wrinkled and the grease on it looked like war paint. His hands were caked with grease also, and he offered his hand to Lewison for an assist. Lewison turned away.

"Just tell me what you need to fix it?" the Lieutenant asked.

"A magic wand."

Percy got up on his own. He began to walk away. Lewison followed. "Someone needs to get on a radio and request another transport."

Lewison looked at him like he was crazy. "You know where we are. Making a call isn't possible here—this is the *UEB*, for Christ's sake!"

The UEB. The Uri-Etzel Belt. An eighty mile wide band of scorched earth. It began before the war, a year-long bombardment of cosmic gases from a collapsed star from some distant galaxy that left the region ion-charged. No communication in or out.

For anyone unfortunate to have to pass through it, it was called *Dark Alley*.

Bravo Company was stranded smack dab in the middle of it.

Lewison kept following after Percy. Percy stopped abruptly and Lewison nearly walked right into him. "Try this, get these guys out and split them up among the remaining vehicles, so we can move on."

"Mix the prisoners in with the enlisted? I should suggest that to the Captain?"

"I wouldn't."

Lt. Lewison began rubbing the chin of his boney face. He did that when he was nervous, which was often. Always dressed accordingly, with his uniform pressed and clean, he now looked out of place—like an official on some public relations mission ordered to make a battlefield observation. He hated the dust and kept having to wipe off his uniform.

"The first thing we need to do is get off the road."

That remark came from First Sergeant Fitz. Fitz was the voice of reason, who took over for Percy in the matter of what to do next.

Lieutenant Lewison was grateful for his participation.

He was Top, but to the enlisted men and women who revered and trusted him, he may as well have been called *Pop*. A big man, with a deep voice, the fatherly NCO was the go-to man when the solution to a problem was simple common sense. As an added credit to his character, he had seen more action in combat than anyone else in Bravo Company, perhaps as much as anyone in the whole battalion.

Fitz went on to advise Lewison. "Make sure everyone's armed, sir.

Marauders are rogue gangs that hang out in isolated areas like this. There have been reports of Marauder activity in this section of Dark Alley and I don't want our people picked off like fish in a barrel."

"Do you think they would dare?"

"They're crazy. They might try anything."

Lewison asked, "What about the prisoners inside the M-CAV, Top?"

Fitz made a face. "That's going to be an issue. That M-CAV is going to turn into an oven by midday, and those guys inside will start to smell like cooked meat."

Lewison agreed, but approaching the Captain about it caused him to start rubbing his chin again.

Captain Radigan, the lead commander of Bravo Company; what could be said about him? He was physically fit with a chiseled face; the front man on a poster to be seen in a recruitment office. Being the son of a wealthy corporate executive with political ties, he spent the duration of the Second Civil War in the humble confines of a TRADOC facility in Alabama, where he served as a drill instructor. *Those who can't do, teach*, as he believed, and while he longed to command his own unit and prove his worth, his superiors kept him down, ordered by their superiors to keep him safe. The saying goes: you can list the steps needed to hammer a nail into a block of wood, but until you've hit your thumb, you've never learned anything. He nagged his superiors to let him get his hands dirty, but his superiors were too aware of how often Radigan might whack his thumb at the expense of his troop. **But** the war was over now. **And** the country was in relative peace and at an acceptable level lawlessness, so they eventually gave in and granted Radigan a company of his own, more so to shut him up. Bravo Company; a unit of no more than seventy-five men and women whose commander recently had the luxury of dying in his sleep. And they presented Radigan with a simple detail, to transport prisoners to a more secure location, all in the hopes that he would prove them wrong.

Unfortunately, future events would provide the truth—that they were right.

It had been twenty minutes since Lt. Lewison spoke with Fitz, and now he had news to report.

"You better tell me something good," Radigan growled to Lewison as the man approached.

"First Sergeant Fitz sent a platoon to recon the area, sir. What he found was a town some three miles from here called, Oliveri. It's a ghost town, I'm sure. Remote places like Oliveri, were evacuated for the safety of the residents during the war. Sergeant Percy, from the motor pool, recalls that a civilian detachment, the 36th Signal Corps, occupied that town near the end of the war. They were a communications unit. No doubt they've gone on, but they may have left some equipment behind. Often units like those didn't bother to dismantle the towers. It was too much trouble. If we can get to the town, with one of our portable generators, we can get power to one of those towers to boost our signal, so we can call for a replacement vehicle. There's just one problem..."

Radigan made a face. "Of course there is."

"Only one access road leads to it, sir, and the bridge to cross a deep crevice has been demolished."

"Demolished?!"

Lewison began rubbing his chin. "Yes, sir. The 36th may have been responsible for that. You see, if the town was too riddled by combat and no worth to repopulating it, they would seal it off, to keep local riff-raff—like Marauders—from establishing a stronghold."

"So, what's the plan?"

"We send a platoon of men on foot, dragging the generator with them. There has to be some other way into the town, a back entry that's not accessible by vehicle."

"How long is that going to take?"

"No more than a few hours, sir, I would guess."

"Fuck," Radigan muttered and stepped away to avoid striking Lewison. "And what about the prisoners?"

"Well, that's fortunate news; Top located an abandoned school two clicks southeast of here. We can store the prisoners in a makeshift holding cell inside the school and set up a temporary camp on the grounds until our guys come back."

"Fine, do it," Radigan barked.

Lewison saluted and then did an abrupt about-face. He was two steps away when the captain called him back.

"I want *Fourth* Platoon to go," the captain said.

The Lieutenant's reaction was a clear objection to that. "A problem?"

"Captain, they don't call this Dark Alley for nothing. There could be Marauders in the area, and might see Fourth Platoon as an easy target."

"They wouldn't dare attack a United Federal Force," Radigan argued. "Begging your pardon, sir, but Fourth Platoon isn't..."

he searched for the right word, "*equipped*...to handle that sort of aggression. Now, *First* Platoon is older, more battle hardened. They should—"

"Nonsense." Radigan was insistent. "This will be an easy detail for Fourth Platoon. They need to get their feet wet and earn some respect from the rest of the company." Radigan harbored sympathy for the fourth, perhaps identifying with them. "That's an order, Lieutenant. See to it."

Lewison responded sharply, while rubbing his chin, "Yes, sir."

A moment later, when Lewison told Fitz the news about sending Fourth Platoon instead of First, he was scolded. "We may as well be marching those greenhorns off a cliff," the first sergeant told him.

"What did you expect me to say, Top?" Lewison replied apologetically. "The captain had his mind made up."

Fitz began pacing.

"Besides," Lewison added, "those boys will be fine. The Captain's right. No Marauder unit would have the balls to fuck with us."

Fitz shook his head. He was furious. "Marauders are fucking stupid, not ballsy, Lieutenant. They shoot first, and then if they decide it was mistake, they run away like friggin' cowards."

"I'm just passing the order, Top. You do whatever you think is right." This time it was the Lieutenant's turn to walk away.

Fitz watched him leave, tagging him a look like he wanted to give him the finger.

Fourth Platoon was Bravo Company's newest recruits. Having served in Boot Camp together, it was Captain Radigan's bright idea to keep them together, instead of blending them in with the more seasoned veterans of the company. As a result of his leadership program, he hoped these young men and women would evolve into a more cohesive fighting unit. They stood now in formation while the rest of the platoon watched from a distance as officers and NCO's maneuvered into their formal positions. First Sergeant Fitz was over-stepping his bounds by addressing the platoon personally. They were an eager looking bunch.

"All right, people, quiet down!" Fitz had to say it twice, like they were children. "I said, listen up! I'm only going to say this once." He did a slow pace at the front line. "Number one; you get to the town. Two; you get power to the radio tower—if there is one. And number three; when you are done, you haul your asses back here on the double." He looked at their young and innocent faces, studied each and every one of them, in case he saw any doubt. "You don't go looking for trouble. You do what I just told you. Is that clear?"

They responded *Yes, Top*! in unison.

He grinned at them like the proud old man. And in a moment, they were ordered to depart.

Fitz stood vigil. Standing in one spot with his arms folded, watching as Fourth Platoon headed out, first into the nearby canyon, and then out of his sight when they turned at the first bend.

He remained there, staring for quite a few minutes longer.

He didn't know it, but it was the last time he would ever see them alive.

CHAPTER FOUR

“The Ruby Queen”

Talia had come to see the Queen.

She never appreciated the long journey, and the climb up the jagged rocks to the ledge where the Queen was lodged came as a bit of a challenge for her, but she hadn't seen the Queen in several days, so the effort was worth it.

At about halfway up she paused to rest her eighteen year old muscles. A convenient jagged piece of rock jutted from the wall and was well suited for her to sit upon. She took in the view. At this height she could see the tops of the pines, like a lake of green that spread below her for hundreds of square miles. She marveled at the strange shaped rock formations that surrounded this immense forest patch and saw a hint of the open plains beyond it. If she had to be trapped anywhere in the world, this diverse region of New Mexico was more than she could ever ask for.

She inspected the flowers she had brought as a gift for the Queen. They were yellow tulips she held in a side pouch of the pink colored pack she wore on her back.

Talia felt sad about their condition, they were beginning to wilt, but she knew the Queen would understand that they never could have survived the journey without taking a toll.

After her rest, Talia resumed her climb. With her legs muscles still aching, she managed to climb almost to the top, to a point where another flat section of rock jutted from the wall; this one was quite large, like a protruding shelf if viewed from the ground. Here was where the Queen lived.

Talia didn't have to announce herself. The Queen could always tell when she was coming. The Queen possessed magical powers of awareness. The Queen had lots and lots of magical powers.

Talia rested the flowers at the base of her Majesty's massive form and then took a step back. "Good morning, my Queen," Talia said, formally announcing her arrival.

IT IS NOT GOOD MORNING, MY DEAR. IT IS THE AFTERNOON.

Talia clocked herself in the head, feeling silly for not realizing. "Yes, of course," she admitted gleefully, "it *was* morning when I left to come here..."

THANK YOU FOR THE FLOWERS, MY DEAR. THEY ARE BEAUTIFUL.

"Momma picked them out," Talia admitted as she inspected a bleeding scrape she had gotten as a result of the climb. "I wanted to bring the purple colored lilacs, but Momma said they weren't ready, whatever *that* means."

I WOULD HAVE THOUGHT THEM BEAUTIFUL AS WELL.

Talia smiled. All proud of herself. Little things like that meant so much. She felt appreciated.

DO YOU HAVE SOMETHING ELSE FOR ME, MY DEAR?

"Oh... oh, yes, my Queen."

Talia dutifully unfastened the backpack from her shoulders and unzipped the main compartment. She removed an oil can. It was one of the old kinds with a spring trigger mechanism to draw out the ointment—what she liked to refer to as medicine—to administer to the Queen. Her Highness was stricken so terribly by a condition.

All that rust. So awfully painful looking.

Talia began to administer the ointment, and she knew how pleased the Queen was with her for doing so. By the time she was done, there was not a drop left in the can.

THANK YOU, MY DEAR. YOU ARE SO KIND.

Again, Talia smiled, feeling so proud of herself. "You're quite welcome my Queen." And she bowed subserviently.

SUCH A SWEET YOUNG LADY. I WISH THERE WERE MORE LIKE YOU.

In the next few moments, Talia sat on the ground beside the Queen, and the two appreciated each other's company in silence. They listened to the chirping birds in the forest below. Some of the birds even landed on the Queen and Talia and the Queen laughed about it.

I HAVE SOMETHING TO SHARE WITH YOU, MY DEAR.

"What is it, Your Highness?"

WE ARE GOING TO HAVE VISITORS SOON.

Talia made an odd face. "You mean, *people* are coming? Are you sure?"

I DETECTED THEM.

Talia knew what the Queen meant by that, and suddenly there was no doubt.

Talia's eyes darted back and forth as her mind began to piece together all that she could imagine. "My Queen, do you think…do you think the Prince is with them?"

IT IS QUITE POSSIBLE, MY DEAR. A PRINCE COULD BE AMONG THEM. A PRINCESS SUCH AS YOU DESERVES A MAGESTICK MATE.

Talia sighed greatly. This was good news.

A thought crossed her mind, and she asked, "Where is the King?" And the Queen replied:

HE HAS GONE TO GREET THEM.

CHAPTER FIVE

"THE PRISONERS"

Like animals...

Had they been recognized as prisoners than perhaps they might have at least been treated like humans. Instead they were driven like cattle.

In contrast to the dark camouflage uniforms the soldiers were wearing, the day-glow orange body suits the prisoners had on were beacons; and for good reason, if one of them tried to escape, they were a clear target to be viewed in a gun sight.

The middle school where they were to be held was an old decaying brick structure that looked to have been abandoned for decades, perhaps long before the Second Civil War even started. As they were escorted in, J. Hollis Duncan recognized the smell, like so many of the dives he had sought refuge in the last couple of weeks, before he was caught. He and his Uncle Billy, and the eighteen others prisoners, were guided through the school's main hall, prodded past empty classrooms and finally held at a thick steel door marked, of all things: FALLOUT SHELTER.

Yeah... Hollis thought, *here it is, all right*, and keeping his expectations low, prepared for an assault on his senses in this dwelling underground. He followed his fellow inmates down a flight of concrete stairs, through a narrow hallway made of cinder block walls, all the while thinking he was being thrown in a medieval dungeon.

Bravo Company had set the shelter up in advance. The demoralizing space was barely illuminated by the light of a half dozen lithium charged lanterns. What could be seen as the prisoners poured in were three rows of five field cots, not enough for the lot of them; some were going to have to sleep on the damp floor. Upon each of the cots was a plastic bottle of drinking water. Conveniently, at each corner of the room was a bucket—on the floor, next to each bucket, a roll of toilet paper. No questions needed.

Hollis stood back with his uncle, patiently waiting their turn, while the rest of the prisoners scurried pathetically to claim their own space in the cramped quarters. One of the largest of the prisoners was nicknamed *El Toro*. He was three times the size of Hollis or anyone else held captive down here. This hairless bull had a montage of ugly and suggestive tattoos that lent no doubt to the deplorable depths he had risen from, or to the degree of his maliciousness nature. El Toro was a captured Marauder who had lines carved on each of his forearms that signified all the people he had killed. He gave Hollis a firm shove out of his way as he moved to claim a cot furthest from the crap buckets.

Hollis had an urge to confront him, but Billy cautioned his nephew with a determined look for him to keep a cool head. Billy was always looking out for him.

They were given less than a minute to orient themselves.

"This place smells like piss and rat feces," Hollis announced irritably. "We've stayed in worse, kid, so relax and try to deal with it."

"Easy for you to say, Uncle, you don't have the same sense of smell as I do." When the minute was up, a voice blasted through the cramped confines.

It was Bravo Company's commander, Captain Radigan. "All right you prisoners, listen the fuck up...!" *Inspiring...*

Hollis thought, if this chapter of his life had a villain, Radigan was surely it. "Take a good look around, you pieces of shit. This is going to be home for awhile." Radigan seemed to know just what to say and exactly how to say it. "It ain't pretty. Nope. And it ain't too comfortable neither. But if you think things can't get any worse, try me. Give any of my men trouble, and you'll find out just how much worse it can get. I don't have the patience to deal with any of your bullshit. My job is to get each of you to Fort Bradley. I can do that in one piece…or several. It doesn't matter to me.

So behave yourselves. Obey the orders my men give you. And let me say this again... do *not* give me or any of my people a problem."

Hollis noticed that El Toro was going around collected the bottles of drinking water for himself. Who the hell died and put *him* in charge? Hollis turned to Billy, who was able to read his mind:

Oh, yes… there was going to be a problem.

CHAPTER SIX

"DARK ALLEY"

THE TROUBLE BEGAN AT 21:30 HOURS. Just one half hour after Fourth Platoon departed the camp bound for Oliveri, all communication with them was lost. There was some cause for concern, of course, but the company was not put on alert—not yet—they were in Dark Alley, after all. The blackout was likely due to the unstable electromagnetic presence in the region; in fact, it had been anticipated, which was why Fitz gave the platoon strict instructions to fire up a flare once they surfaced from the narrow passage through the canyon and before they advanced further into the north woods.

But after an hour passed, well... the first sergeant stood outside the CP staring up at the night sky wondering why it was so dark. Where was the flare?

Being a man few words, the phrase Fitz shot to Lewison with his eyes was as precise as a sniper's bullet: *I told you so.*

In a matter of seconds, the company was put on alert. It was time to send a search party.

And worse...time to wake up the captain—who'd chosen to take a nap—and dare to inform him of what happened.

Launching a drone was the captain's first order of business. He ordered Sergeant Percy to retrieve the six prop, low altitude combat drone from one of the cases in the supply truck; called *Thunderfly*, it had a 5.56 caliber machine gun turret mounted to its belly. Two miniature drones, each the size of an M249 magazine, flew in advance of the Thunderfly, as reconnaissance. Radigan's hope was that the drones would catch up to the lost patrol, and that the images relayed from the drones would uncover that Fourth Platoon had simply gotten lost in the woods, and that their neglect to launch a flare was further example of their ineptitude.

In the CP, the officers kept watch of their progress on the display monitors. As predicted by Fitz, who advised that sending the drones was a waste of valuable time, the images transmitted from the drones went dark shortly after they flew out of the canyon.

Insult to injury: Thunderfly would have to be recovered. It cost the taxpayers four million dollars.

Plan B. First Platoon was assembled; twenty-eight of Bravo Company's most hardened troops (the ones Fitz recommended to be sent in the first place) and sent into the canyon in the hopes of tracking down Fourth Platoon and sending them back to base with their tails between their legs. Their mission served a dual purpose: once Fourth Platoon was secure, they were to proceed to Oliveri and enable the com link.

"I'm picking up some kind of weak signal," reported Corporal Reynolds, the second squad leader of First Platoon. Reynolds was a smart one. Top of his class at Christian Military Academy, he was a faithful strategist.

"I've got it, too," Sergeant Hennessey confirmed. Hennessey was leader of first squad. Not as book smart, but his combat experience made him an invaluable asset. "Coach, are you picking it up? It's a steady beep. It's getting louder now as we move north."

The coach was Staff Sergeant Walters. His proven qualities as a platoon leader got Bravo Company out of numerous jams during the latter years of the Second Civil War. His greatest trait was that he could think and make decisions on the fly. Something else made him unique; he was the only soldier in the company who was married. "All squads, hold your positions and keep quiet," he ordered.

First Platoon had come out of the rock canyon, maneuvering quickly without a hitch. Their next phase of the journey had them advancing through the woods. They had gotten this far without losing contact with command. The darkness hung like a black velvet curtain. Visibility was barely arms length. Dark Alley was a poor choice to execute an attack, for either side.

A voice communicated in Walters' headset, that of Specialist Chang, speaking from the command post. He was without constraint. "It's an ICS warning beacon." Chang was the young Asian man at the field radio. He was the last minute replacement for the lead com tech who went with Fourth Platoon to get the transmission tower working in Oliveri. Chang was more technical savvy than your average soldier, with an extended knowledge in automatronics.

Walters already knew what the sound was and had reason to believe some of the others did, too.

An ICS (Independent Conduct Spur) was a device implanted under the skin and attached to the spinal cord, designed to manipulate the adrenal gland to keep the body healthy and strengthen the immune system, but its side effects were more highly sought; sensory awareness and heightened muscular strength. Quite simply, an ICS turned cowards into conquerors. Intended for use by those who were severely disabled and less so by professional athletes, such as *Battle Bowl* players, they were strictly forbidden for soldiers to use.

They had the adverse affect of making them *too* aggressive and thus dangerously unpredictable. Imagine a drunken warrior so willing to give his life? "Someone from Fourth Platoon may have been wearing one," Fitz hastily admitted to the Captain. "That sound is an ICS warning beacon, informing its user that the batteries are going dead."

It was beyond Radigan's comprehension why someone under his command would feel the need to be equipped with such a device. His response was in character, "Something that makes a noise like that on the battlefield doesn't make him better…it makes him and all those around him a *target*!"

Fitz agreed, but the pressure Radigan put on Fourth Platoon to perform to his level of acceptance had left at least *one* of them with no choice. Now was not the time to debate it.

On the large monitor mounted inside the command post, the officers were able to track the movement of First Platoon via the feed from the helmet cams, designated: SSG Walters and his three squad leaders: SGT Hennessey, SGT Reynolds and third squad leader, a female, CPL Laura Hammond. Four images displayed on the screen at once.

Everyone kept a close watch. The platoon was advancing beyond the point where communication was lost with Fourth Platoon.

Captain Radigan snatched the mic out of Chang's hand. His words were intended for Walters. "Unit One, this is Bravo Command, trace the signal to its source, but approach with caution. It could be a trap."

Lightning shattered the night sky. Bolts touched down in the distant horizon like the spiny fingers of a demon playing the piano. Thunder shook the ground beneath everyone's boots.

It began to rain, and the hiss of it through the trees was a constant distraction. "Command, say again your last. Over."

Walters waited a moment. There was no reply. He repeated himself.

Nothing. Dead air.

It could be a trap. That was the last thing he heard the captain say.

Walters snapped his fingers and signaled his squad leaders to gather close. "My radio's blacked out. I've lost contact with command. Can any of you reach them?"

Sergeant Hennessey shook his head. Reynolds remarked, "I can't even talk to my own squad. And my nite-vision goggles have crapped out, too. It's like someone just cut the power off on us."

Corporal Hammond asked, "Coach, do you think someone out here has the capability to jam our equipment?"

Walters shook his head. "I doubt it. It's probably just ion interference. Let's not forget where we are." He noticed something about Hammond. There was a green light emitting from her helmet cam. He asked her, "Are you still transmitting, corporal?"

"I'm getting a loss-of-transmission indicator on my HUD, sarge," she reported.

She had a gruff sounding voice, like someone who smoked a lot of cigarettes, "but I suppose my cam is still recording. What do you want me to do?"

"Nothing. Be aware. Maybe command is still receiving an image from you."

Hammond was equipped with an older model helmet cam, one used by her great uncle who swore that it gave him luck during his service in Afghanistan.

Walters took a deep breath. He felt the pressure of not making the same mistake as Fourth Platoon. "Each of you, pull your people in. Keep them close. We'll use hand signals and flashlights from here on."

"Back to basics, aye, Coach?" Reynolds cajoled.

Walters wasn't in the mood. "Move your squad north," he told the sergeant. "Locate the source of that ICS and report back to me."

"Roger that," Reynolds replied, and motioned to his squad to keep moving.

Back at the CP, Captain Radigan and the others stood watching the only view available to them on the monitor. There was no sound, but a clear enough display of Hammond's point of view; she was doing a good job looking around, keeping notice of everything, as if she knew someone may be watching.

The low pitched beep of the ICS had changed its tone to a dull sounding hum, making it less traceable. It led Reynolds and his squad to a sudden break in the tree line, but not before they came upon the wreckage of the Thunderfly.

The drone was lying in the bushes. Everyone gathered around it, peering down upon it like it was a fallen comrade. Its lights were out. It was dead.

One of Reynolds' men explained, "It goes into emergency hover mode when it loses a signal. By default, it rises to about fifty feet or so and then hovers there waiting for the signal to be reestablished. I suppose it ran out of fuel and dropped."

Reynolds made a face. It didn't look to him like it just dropped. It looked painfully obvious, like it had been snatched out of the sky and then stomped on by something big—big as an elephant!

First Sergeant Fitz moved away from the monitor in the CP and approached Sergeant Percy. Percy was seated in one of the chairs at the field desk. "What do you know about that unit you said occupied Oliveri during the war?" he asked.

Percy sat up. "The 36th Signal Corps? They were scum."

"Anything more helpful?"

"Most civilian detachments, they were untrained, undisciplined. They didn't even do any *real* fighting. I doubt the 36th was an exception."

"That being true, why would the Federal Forces hire them in the first place?"

"They were cheap." Percy shrugged. "Planted in the middle of nowhere to keep watch of the movement of rebel Americanists during the war; when they saw something unusual they sounded the alert. That's about it."

Fitz thought about it some more. "And what ever happened to them?"

"I'm not exactly sure about the 36th—but if they were any good, they joined a local Federal force, or… if they sucked... they simply disbanded."

"And if they didn't disband, could they still be out here?" Percy made an odd face. "Why would they be?"

Fitz's remark caught the attention of Captain Radigan who stepped closer. "What are you getting at, First Sergeant?"

"I'm not getting at anything, Captain," Fitz replied curtly, "I just want to be sure we're the only ones out here."

Someone was approaching, moving through the trees slowly. Staggering, as if drunk, it was Sergeant Reynolds, and the first thought on Walters' mind was that he'd been injured. "Are you all right?" Walters asked him. "Where's the rest of your squad?"

Reynolds was breathing heavily. He jerked his thumb over his shoulder. "They're back there, at the clearing."

"What clearing? Where?"

Reynolds looked upwards, as if he was talking to God, speaking hopelessly. "I found Fourth Platoon."

"Alive?"

Reynolds hesitated, and then he subtly shook his head. "They couldn't be." Walters grabbed Reynolds by his BDU collar and shook him. "Snap out of it, Rey. Take me to them."

Reynolds muttered, "You're not going to believe this…"

As much as Walters could see in the dark, the clearing was about half the size of a football field. But this was no ordinary clearing. It was an almost perfectly formed square, and by his proclamations, its corners were precise right angles. And it was fresh. Like it had been done only hours ago. The timeline was eerily coincidental.

What sat in the middle of this clearing was something even stranger.

Horrifying. There was a cube, in about six foot dimensions; seven layers high, made up of bodies—*Fourth Platoon*'s bodies.

It seemed unreal, like a stack of rubber dolls squished together; each body so grotesquely misshapen due to their combined weight on top of one another, they scarcely looked human anymore. No need for a formal count, at a cold glance all twenty- eight of them were there.

What was the message? The intent?

It seemed ritualistic.

"No shell casings on the ground," Hennessey pointed out. "Can you see that? The ground is clean. Those kids never got off a shot. Whoever they were…or whatever *it* was that attacked them must have completely shocked the shit out of them."

Walters clamored into his headset again in the hopes of reaching command, just in case they were able to receive his transmission. He described what he saw in as restrained a tone as he could muster. In the meantime, his other two squad leaders, Sergeant Reynolds and Corporal Hammond were addressing their people, ordering them to spread out, keep quiet and out of sight.

Hennessey approached Walters. Walters was staring at that grotesque cube like he was expecting it to do something.

"We need to fall back, Coach," Hennessey told him. "Our equipment is pounced. We're blind and deaf out here. We should go back to the canyon and try to reconnect with command, maybe wait until sun up. Things might look a whole lot different then."

Reynolds approached and stood between them. "Sun up isn't for another three hours, Hen." He related to Walters, "A lot can happen in that time, Coach."

"What do *you* suggest?"

Reynolds breathed in deeply. "Risk one man. Send him out there, into that clearing and—"

"Are you insane?!" Hennessey argued.

"Goddamn it, Hen, keep your voice down," Walters turned back to Reynolds.

"Go on."

Reynolds continued. "There may be someone alive in that mess. Buried in there. We need to find out what happened. If we don't, we won't know what we're up against."

Walters turned to Hennessey. "It makes sense, Hen."

Hennessey shook his head. "No, it doesn't. Listen to me, that pile could be booby-trapped. This clearing could be the blast radius. That ICS beacon may have been an attempt by our enemy to lead us here."

"Well, maybe you should stand back where it's safe, Hen," Reynolds insinuated.

"Fuck you, Reynolds, I'm trying to save lives here."

"So am I."

Hennessey and Reynolds: they were the best two men Walters could have advising him. Both made sense, in spite of their opposing views. It was up to him, the platoon leader, to make the final decision. It was never easy. "Get me Specialist Donohue, the sniper," Walters said. Hennessey grunted with frustration. Walters continued, "I want someone who can crawl out there undetected and gather intel."

"You're making a mistake, Coach," Hennessey pleaded. "Just get him, Hen."

"What are they doing?" Captain Radigan asked.

As before, all eyes in the CP were glued to the only image on the monitor. Without sound, First Sergeant Fitz could only suppose. "It looks like they might be sending someone out into the clearing. That's Specialist Donohue. He's putting on his Kettric suit. It conceals his thermal image from infra red detection."

Radigan turned away from the monitor. "Who the fuck would amass a pile of bodies like that?"

"I still think it could be Marauders?" Lieutenant Lewison said.

"No," Fitz adamantly argued, "even if they did this by *accident*, they wouldn't make a neat pile like this. It has to be the work of someone else."

Radigan moved toward the open flap of the CP, presumably to get a breath of fresh air. No one blamed him. Fitz joined him.

"Captain," Fitz kept his voice low, "we need to get word to First Platoon and send them back here."

"You talking retreat? No, we need to get to Oliveri."

"I understand that, sir, and we will, but right now we need to gather our forces and prepare for an attack. Whoever did this to Fourth Platoon has to still be around here, and I'd say they're a significant threat, wouldn't you?"

"Staff Sergeant Walters is capable of coordinating his men and then getting to Oliveri. Once they turn power on to that transmitter, we'll call for support."

First Sergeant Fitz shot another one of his looks, this time to Radigan, but it was not the pinpoint accuracy of a sniper this time, rather it was the wide-eyed shotgun blast of *are you fucking kidding me*?

"Give your weapon to your squad leader, "Walters instructed Specialist Donohue.

Donahue didn't like the sound of that, he didn't like being unarmed, but he did what he was told. He removed Kettric suit from his ruck sack and began to put it on.

Walters instructed, "I just need you to crawl out there to Fourth Platoon and gather whatever intel you can, then crawl right back here."

"Don't touch them," Hennessey stressed. He was still convinced the pile was a booby trap.

"As much as my equipment works, Specialist, heat image sensors are indicating nothing alive out there, but we need to know for sure. If someone is alive out there, keep them calm. Tell them help is on the way. Tell them they'll be all right. Lie to them."

"And remember," Hennessey reiterated, "don't touch any of them."

"That's enough, Hen."

Walters patted Donohue on the shoulder and sent him on his way. It may have been a mere hundred feet of distance to cross, but at ground level that pile of bodies looked to Donohue like it was miles away.

"What if he turns up nothing?" Hennessey muttered to Walters. "Then we proceed with *your* plan; we fall back and wait til daylight."

PFC Sapatos, from Hennessey's squad, was positioned farthest north on the left side of the clearing. Some fifty meters beyond his position he could see an odd shape that stood out among the trees that were in line there. It looked unnatural, metallic possibly, with its side shiny and reflective when the lightning flashed again. Maybe it was just the rain glistening off the surface of a boulder. But then...

it moved. Or at least, he thought it did. It was so damned dark he couldn't be sure of anything.

He moved closer, to investigate. No point in sounding the alarm unless he was one hundred percent sure.

And then he saw, yes... indeed... It *did* move.

CHAPTER SEVEN

"THE ATTACK ON FIRST PLATOON"

It had known there would be others; even with its limited capacity for awareness and consideration. Here was the evidence. Here they were. And in the same manner as before, it prepared a course of action…

The soldiers of First Platoon watched from the side lines as Bravo Company's sniper, Specialist Donohue, made his way toward the center of the clearing, crawling on his stomach in the dark. In the last few minutes he had gone about halfway. The stack of bodies, consisting of Fourth Platoon, loomed just ahead; six layers high and four men deep, it was like a tower, and the blood that drained to the base of this gruesome tower was a moat. As he continued to advance the salty taste of their blood touched his lips, though he did not waiver. His mission was critical.

Donohue was no stranger to the atrocities of war. Prior to this revolting task, and two years before he joined the military, he'd seen a considerable share of death as a junior in high school. Each day, after class, he hopped a bus waiting just outside his home town and earned some cash disposing of dead bodies. The *Meinsar* virus was still claiming victims throughout the countryside and the bodies needed to be gathered and burned. Donohue dragged bodies from CDC flatbed trucks and tossed them into the fire pits. Some of those bodies were not even in body bags, because there just weren't enough bags for the many victims the virus claimed. Children were the hardest to deal with, and he had to develop an emotional detachment. This should have hardened him to his current task and enabled him to go on without distraction. But as he came to the base of the stack, and the remembrance of his ghastly after school job poked into his mind, he was suddenly aware of why this was different. Here were the misshapen and bludgeoned faces of people he recognized, not those of strangers. Here were the cold lifeless stares of those twenty-eight men and woman from Fourth Platoon he had conversations with, argued with, and at times even spoken ill of. Their mouths agape, as if about to say something.

Whispers from ghosts. A warning:

Go back before it's too late.

Being this close was a sobering reminder to the specialist how much easier combat was to experience through the scope of a high powered rifle from hundreds of meters away.

Don't touch any of them. The words of Sergeant Hennessey. But Donohue had no intention. None whatsoever.

The ground was suddenly too moist and slick for him to manage. To gain ground he pulled on things like the roots of trees protruding from the soil. Maybe another eight feet left to go before reaching the base of the pile. His hands were trembling. Once, while reaching blindly, his hand gripped something smooth and pliable, he nearly jerked his hand back because he knew right away that it was someone's foot. A *bare* foot. The boot and sock removed, perhaps blown off. He expected some resistance when he tugged on it, to move it out of his way, but that was when he realized it was an entire leg, by the looks of it *twisted* off at the point where the upper thigh connects to the pelvis. Slender and smooth, with a thorny vine tattoo around one ankle, it had to be a woman's. Fourth Platoon had two women in its ranks. Donohue pictured them both.

"Is anyone alive here?" he asked, his voice barely above a whisper.

The ICS warning beacon was off. Its batteries dead. The space was stricken with the sound of the rain trickling down each layer of the bodies, a crimson waterfall.

Donohue swallowed hard and posed the question again—a little louder this time, but not much.

Silence still. A part of him was grateful for that. What might happen, he pondered, if one of them were to hear him and respond, and start crying out in terror. No amount of training would have prepared him for that. And although he would never admit it to anyone, he hoped they were all dead.

He didn't ask the question a third time, he simply turned toward the tree line and started back. The quicker, the better. Crawling out here was a waste of time and a careless risk.

"Movement—twelve o'clock!" Sapatos shouted. In the quiet of the night his sudden outburst resonated like a high yield explosive.

Trusting what he saw, someone in the ranks took immediate action and fired a flare. There was a *woosh* and a *pop* and less than ten seconds later the sky was ablaze with light.

The thing emerged from the mist. A dark metallic figure as tall as the trees.

Staff Sergeant Walters drifted forward, taking a commanding position to see it more clearly. "Hold your fire, people!" he ordered. He didn't want to commit his men to firefight—that may have been the mistake Fourth Platoon made.

What appeared in the clearing was far beyond anyone's

expectations. Its movement was astounding. It bounced as if on springs, seemingly defying all laws of physics; something so large—so heavy looking—should not have been able to move this way. From one end of the clearing to the next, its extraordinary dance had everyone's head panning left to right. It would land firmly, causing the ground to tremble, and turn artfully without any loss of momentum to seek firm purchase elsewhere.

At about fifteen feet tall, it was a monster. Pistons, Gears. Pipes. Carbon fiber hoses and fluid lines. Imposing and fierce looking. It made a series of pulsating sounds, like the release of pressure from some broken down oil burner...

PSSSSSST. KONK. BZZZT. BLURP. PSSSSSST...

From a dual exhaust port on its back spewed blooms of white vapor that had such a pungent odor it could trick the mind into thinking it was toxic.

An M135 minigun mounted on each of its shoulders left no doubt, it was deadly.

Above the waist, upon a pivotal platform, was one half an oval shield of thick armor to protect the inner components; a steel block that was presumably its source of power—its motor.

And at its center, extending from a thick arm of braided cables, a shining entity encased in a glowing bowl of sapphire blue. This was its eye.

First Platoon looked at each other baffled. For all at once, it stopped.

It stood in the center of the clearing and just sat there, hissing and puffing, with its arms held out from its sides in a gorilla-like stance. Such an abrupt lack of motion it seemed somewhat more disturbing. It remained just a few feet from the stack of Fourth Platoon's bodies. Walters' eyes shifted from it. Preparedness was crucial. He snapped his fingers. He had to do it several times to peel Sergeant Hennessey's fixed gaze. "Hen, which of your men is the fastest?" he asked.

Hennessey was stunned by the question, but then he answered, "Private Jackson.

Jack Rabbit, we call him. Why?"

Walters looked around to see if there were any more of these malicious looking machines. The one here looked dangerous enough. "Find Jackson," Walters told Hennessey. He struggled to maintain his composure. "Someone has to report what's going on here, in case we don't get the chance. Send him back to command on the double. He's our message in a bottle, you get me?"

Hennessey nodded—he got it—and keeping low, he took off toward his squad.

Reynolds came at Walters aggressively. "All due respect, Coach, but what the fuck are we waiting for?"

"A clear sign."

"Of what?"

"Of that thing's hostility."

"Those guns aren't clear enough?"

"I meant its *intent*. Stand down, Sergeant." Walters took a breath. "Once we start shooting, that's it. There's no going back. Now, look at it," he ordered Reynolds, and guided his attention. "Take a real good look at it... and consider what *we* have to combat it? Small arms?"

"We have the *numbers*," Reynolds argued.

"This ain't Vegas, Reynolds. How many casualties do you think we'll suffer before we bring it down? If it's waiting for us to fire the first shot, how stupid would we be not to be patient?" He forced the debate to a close and began spouting commands. "I want you to pull second squad back. Have them form a second line behind first squad, here. I don't want them getting caught in a cross-fire in case the shit hits the fan. Go on." He had to push Reynolds to get him started.

Walters looked out at the center of the clearing. The robot hadn't moved. The sapphire crowned shiny eyeball of the thing seemed to be staring directly at him, as if it knew precisely who was in charge.

Walters stood tall, and wondered... *what are you waiting for?*

Soon the question was answered.

The sapphire crowned eye shifted noticeably. Walters turned his head in the direction of its line of sight, to see that it was looking at Private Jackson. Following Hennessey's orders, the trooper was leaving the scene. The mini gun barrels atop the shoulders of the metal monster re-positioned themselves and began to spin. In an astonishing display of might and ferocity, Jackson's legs were cut out from under him and he fell with hardly a cry out. The iron monster had seen—or rather *detected*—the movement of the soldier as an attempt to flee and aimed to stop him.

"DESTROY THAT MACHINE!" Walters cried out. His voice echoed through the woods.

There came a hail of fury. Shots started firing from virtually every direction.

Walters' expression changed. In that moment he saw the sapphire eye shift back to him, and the guns turn toward him. Before he could draw his weapon and shoot first, he was sprayed by rounds that quite literally tore him to shreds. Reynolds, who was standing nearby, was struck by a wave of the staff sergeant's blood and shattered bits of flesh.

Walters was gone. Gone as if he had been thrown into a blender. Another commander surfaced.

It was Hennessey. He moved along the southern line, behind his squad, to instruct them. "Concentrate your fire on those mini guns," he shouted. "Take them out!"

The next act of the machine's aggression was an obvious retaliation. Rounds tore through Hennessey's BDU jacket as he dove for cover behind the thick trunk of a tree.

He was injured and bleeding badly, but he was still conscious and well aware how lucky he was.

Reynolds's men, the men from Second Squad, who had not yet fallen in line with First Squad on the south end of the clearing, dropped to prone positions and fired their rifles through the low lying brush while rounds from Third Squad passed over their heads from across the clearing.

The war machine was being pelted by torrential outpour of lead, but it seemed to have no noticeable affect. A rocket from someone's shoulder launcher detonated near to the beast's steel hoof. The steel beast stammered, but regained its balance in an instant. It was a stout and coordinated war machine. The men of Bravo Company were prepared for combat against a human adversary, but not this, no... not this autonomous *gun engine!*

Clearly, they would need more than bullets and low yielding explosives to take it down. The upper body rotated on its torso, positioning the mini guns to fire independently of one another, thus allowing for an even wider range of fire, the likes of which had not been seen by man since the Second Civil War when *Terra-Dusters*, driven by Landlords, roamed the battlefields.

As each of the men from First Platoon were taken out, less and less of the shots were being fired. Replaced by the gunfire were the terrible sounds of the wounded and dying. In time, confusion and disillusionment would ignite fear, and while the triumphant course for the machine could no longer be ignored, panic was sure to spread through the remaining ranks.

From his concealed position, Hennessey witnessed the machine do something clearly diabolical—so purposefully fiendish—it shocked him with an acute awareness.

It—this *thing*—was not merely a drone performing a task programmed into it.

No. It possessed cunningness, and carried with it a will to conquer all.

"I'm going to kill you, muther fucker…" Hennessey thought aloud. As preposterous as it sounded, even to himself, he had chosen his words carefully.

"… *kill* you!"

What the machine had done was this:

In the midst of crossfire from three different directions, it scooped three men off the ground and pressed them tight to its chest, thus creating a human shield no member from First Platoon would dare shoot through.

There was an abrupt cease fire.

When the men held within the robot's grasp tried to break free, the machine squeezed them tighter.

Some of Walter's men managed to keep their heads, though only a few weren't taking hits or ducking for cover. First Platoon was a courageous brotherhood.

The war machine went after Hennessey now. It approached the tree where it last saw him. But Hennessey kept hidden, moving ever so slightly to remain out of its line of sight. With just one eye to see and only one free arm to grasp, it was difficult for the gunengine to capture the sergeant, and so it sought an easier target elsewhere, perhaps determined to get Hennessey later.

Hennessey breathed a sigh. He looked around for a soldier nearby who could help him carry out his plan. Private First Class Vertelli was crying out in agony; he'd been shot and what flesh hung from both his tattered sleeves could scarcely be considered hands anymore. So Hennessey searched for another; one with at least *one* useful hand to throw a grenade. He settled on Specialist O'Sullivan and called out to him.

O'Sullivan was inserting a fully loaded magazine into his rifle when he heard Hennessey call out, "Soldier—get your ass over here!"

O'Sullivan made his way toward Hennessey, crawling on his stomach.

And Reynolds, who had been recovering from the shock of Walters' body virtually *exploding* right beside him, joined Hennessey behind the thick tree trunk. It would have been poetic justice for Hennessey to point out their last conversation, but now was not the time. "I've noticed something," Hennessey addressed. "With all its side stepping and jockeying around, it keeps its back toward the northern side, protecting it. I think we have an opportunity." He unclipped an incendiary grenade from the harness across his chest. He slapped the grenade into the palm of O'Sullivan's hand, checked the proximity of the assaulting war machine, and said, "We might have a chance to take it down if we can strike it hard from behind."

The gunengine was seeking out targets, pulling out men from the brush where they were hiding and then mashing them with its free claw.

Hennessey went on. "Our grenade launchers might penetrate

that back plating, knock it free and expose its power unit. But we'll need to get close."

"That won't be easy," Reynolds admitted.

"O'Sullivan, here, will distract it with this incendiary grenade. It might blind it long enough for us to maneuver into position." To O'Sullivan, Hennessey said, "Wait for one of us to reach the tree line. I'll signal you, and then you toss it." He thought to himself... *sixty seconds, that's how long it should take.*

O'Sullivan looked unsure. "But the ground is wet, sarge, it might not catch."

"The flash," Hennessey insisted, "it will be enough—it *has* to be!" He turned to

Reynolds, "Work your way up the line where Third Squad is. Keep up with me on the opposite side. If we're lucky—and God help us if we're not—we can hit that mutha' together, a one-two punch right up its iron-clad ass!"

"Sarge?"

"What is it, O'Sullivan?"

"Why the fuck is this thing attacking us? What did we do?"

"I don't know, Specialist, I don't have a fucking clue."

Hennessey and Reynolds loaded their grenade launchers. The M240A2 grenade; in the proper placement the ordinance could flip a jeep. This wasn't Vegas, he reminded himself, but still hoped he could beat the odds.

"Nice knowing you, Reynolds," Hennessey remarked. "Yeah… good luck to you, too, Hen."

The two sergeants took off in opposite directions.

The heavy clunk of the war machine's footsteps were drawing near to O'Sullivan. It was still searching, shooting its light beam from the spotlight atop its shoulder. There was a lot of smoke now and it was getting harder for it to make things out.

Sixty seconds…

It wasn't a long time, but it felt like an eternity to Hennessey. As he moved past the remainder of his men positioned along the west side of the clearing he had an eerie sense of that monster's sapphire eye following his course and perhaps at any moment figuring out his plan.

Fifty seconds... He was counting to himself. At forty he noticed the machine was no longer firing its miniguns. *Out of ammunition?* He looked out into the clearing. The men had succeeded in taking out the guns. The guns dangled from their mounts.

Atta-boy, men!

If Walters was still alive, he'd be proud. *Thirty seconds...*

Without weapons now, the robot took to a different tactic, brute force. And it proved to be as equally skilled at killing in this manner. Those men still alive let loose with cries that sounded more horrible and more painful than when they were hit with rounds, for now they were being stomped on, grabbed by the machine's free claw and smashed against trees.

Ten seconds...

Less of the men were firing their rifles at this point. Most were merely hiding, because it was clear that if you fired at it—you died; it would zero in on you specifically and attack.

Sensing no need for the human shield, the robot tossed away the three men held to its chest. It was free to attack with both claws now.

Three.

Two.

One.

Hennessey had reached his point when, without giving the signal to O'Sullivan, he heard a distinct *pop...ping* sound. The incendiary grenade makes that sound.

Hennessey stopped and took a safe position and spotted Reynolds on the other side of the clearing darting from the tree line. Reynolds hadn't chosen to wait for the signal either, he must have seen an opportunity and took it.

Everything after that happened so fast.

The war machine was standing still, only a few feet from the pile of bodies of Fourth Platoon when the incendiary went off with a blinding flash. Its claws rose to shield its eye, the way a living thing would react. It made a sound. *Pssst.* Hennessey's eyes shifted. He watched Reynolds run towards it. Its instinct to defend itself was uncanny, the way it crossed its mechanical arms to shield its body as Reynolds raised his grenade launcher to fire at it *point blank.*

Reynolds was standing just a few feet from it. He fired, but the grenade ricocheted off one of the claws and exploded without having any affect. He was thrown back by the concussion.

The war machine recovered and then went after him.

Hennessey gasped, not out of fright but out of frustration and disappointment. He witnessed the machine move into the tree line where he presumed Reynolds was. He could not see it any longer—it was too dark over there, and he was in the wrong position—but he could hear it stomping its feet and there was the crack of tree limbs.

Someone on the other side cried out, "Reynolds run—it's right on top of you!" More shots were fired, obviously to protect Reynolds. The monster made a different sound now: *Eeyaawwnk.* The kind of sound an angry elephant makes. Squeaks and clangs were logical, even the high pitched roar of an internal engine could be expected, but how these sounds were being emitted was anyone's guess.

Someone else shouted, "Reynolds is dead!"

Hennessey heard a hellish cry out of pain. He was sure it was Reynolds. He stood up and saw Reynolds being twisted into the ground, the robot behaved the way a man does when he extinguishes a lit cigarette with the tip of his boot.

The pitiful fire from O'Sullivan's incendiary fizzled out.

The war machine stepped back into the clearing, lending itself to be easily tracked.

The flare had long since gone out, too.

This was Hennessey's only chance. The last chance he was sure the platoon had.

Madness drew him from his position. His adrenaline surged. Emerging from the tree line, he charged like a bull until... suddenly his feet felt like lead and he was straining to breathe. He was only halfway into the clearing. He didn't want to admit what his subconscious mind was inflicting upon his body to keep him from carrying out this suicidal maneuver. He managed to make it to the pile of Fourth Platoon's bodies. He kept out of the machine's line of sight. So far so good. When the gun engine got close, he kept stepping around. He readied his grenade launcher to fire into the beast's back. But when he ran out to fire, it detected him, and turned to face him at the last second. He looked the war machine right in the eye, thought of Reynolds, and aimed at the center of it. That angry elephant sound echoed across the sky, but this time it was coming from another direction, like there was another one—a *second* one—somewhere close by.

Hennessey's actions, those of a dying man, were quite desperate in nature. In the dark and at such close range, he fired the launcher in the hopes he might have some affect. The last thing he saw before the grenade detonated on impact and everything for him went black, was the steel beast's eye…closing shut.

There was so much smoke, PFC Laura Hammond couldn't be sure of anything. This thick gray mass—the result of O'Sullivan's incendiary grenade—was like a curtain and prevented her from seeing past it. It just hung in the air, fixed. Several seconds passed and she grew positive that the beast had been immobilized.

But then… She heard it. *Tchwonk.*

And she watched as the few remaining troopers in her platoon tried to flee.

Psssst. Ka-thunk.

A dark shadow moved within the smoky mass, and she could tell it was still alive, and still capable of killing. It went after those that had fled, caught them, and quickly eliminated them. No one stood a chance of getting away. It was quite clear to Hammond, too, that there would be no survivors left to tell what had happened here.

She breathed deeply, considered her next step, and then moved into the smoke.

With its squeaking thick coils and oil bleeding shock absorbers, the beast centered itself in the clearing. Its upper body pivoted slowly on its mid section. It was scanning. When it spotted Hammond coming towards it, it stopped.

She was unarmed. Intentionally, she held out her hand, palms up, to show her surrender to it. She wasn't prepared for the end, but her instincts as a warrior took over for her. This, she convinced herself, was what she was supposed to do. This was her role in this horrible situation. In her dazed state she was somewhat aware that her helmet cam was still functioning, recording at the very least; it would provide evidence of what had happened here for command when—and hopefully not *if*—it was recovered.

She walked straight up to the machine that had just wiped out her entire platoon; stood a mere foot away from it, more frightened in this moment than she had ever been in her life. Trembling with fear, and while listening to the terrible sounds of the last two men dying nearby, she took a deep breath and held it. She knew it was her last.

This is the enemy, she was thinking.

Get a good look at it, she urged her commanders in the subconscious state of her mind.

Learn how to defeat it. Avenge us!

The iron claws, weighing in at a hefty five hundred pounds each, were pitched to the left and right of her. They were no good for grasping but ideal for mashing.

Hammond closed her eyes tightly and pictured the faces of her parents, looking so proud of her on the day she graduated from the military academy; and then of the boy she had a long time crush on in High School; and finally, Scraps, her chubby pet beagle sleeping peacefully on the pillow of her bed, waiting for her to return home.

The claws of the war machine clapped together with the might of two diesel trains colliding head-on.

CHAPTER EIGHT

"AFTERMATH"

No picture. Nothing. Just static. And it left no room for misinterpretation. The battle was over.

None of the officers in the CP uttered a word. They just stood staring at the monitor. They were in shock.

It… that… mechanized *thing*… for whatever reason for wanting First Platoon to be wiped out, had succeeded, its thirst for their annihilation quenched.

The hum of the computers and communications equipment; the loose canvas flap rattling in the wind; the wind itself—all of it seemed to have an amplified pulse. When a ballpoint pen slipped from someone's trembling fingers and landed on the hardwood field desk with a bang there a unified sigh in the tent.

Captain Radigan looked this way and that, his body making small jerky movements. He looked like a squirrel caught in traffic. In a moment, he began to move, pace...so slowly...possessed by a seemingly uncontrollable impulse. He muttered unintelligibly and then picked up a field chair and threw it violently. It spun in the confines of the tent toward Lt. Lewison; and although Lewison had time to duck, he stood there and let the chair hit him as an effort to appease his commander's violent outburst. None of the others would have denied him his tantrum either, but to play it safe they kept out of his way.

First Sergeant Fitz, who had stepped out momentarily during the attack to put the unit on alert, returned just as Radigan went to grab a second chair. "Captain!" he shouted, immediate assessing the situation. "Sir... Second and Third Platoon are formed outside. They're fully armed and ready for your order, sir."

"Order for *what*, Top?" Lt. Lewison asked, rubbing a sore shoulder.

Fitz ignored him. Keeping his eyes on Radigan, he pressed, "We need to strike back at it now, sir. It's damaged. We saw its guns were taken out. If we wait another second, we may lose the opportunity."

Captain Radigan wouldn't respond, but at least he put the chair down.

Fitz kept on. "If the enemy has the resources to construct this thing it stands to reason they have the means to repair it!"

"No," Radigan said, and his lips parted to say something else, but no others words came out.

"No, what, sir?" Fitz looked around. They all shrugged. "What's our next move, Captain?"

"I'm thinking."

Like most battle hardened soldiers who had worked their way up the ranks to senior NCO, this First Sergeant did not care for officers, especially those presently standing around him, those he was convinced had been '*molded from cookie cutters in a classroom*'. His only admiration for any of them was that they got paid more than he did. *Yes, sir* and *No, sir,* was the extent of any conversation he cared to have with them.

Captain Radigan was no exception.

Fitz approached the Captain. The captain, in the meantime, had retreated to side of the tent and was doing something with his survival knife. He kept the knife in a sheath at his hip. When Fitz went to his side he saw what the commander was doing. Radigan was slicing his hand, causing blood to pool in his palm. "Captain," Fitz said, keeping his voice low. "What are you doing?"

"I said, I'm thinking," Radigan calmly replied, and made a fist and winced.

Fitz took a deep breath. "If you won't send the platoons out then we need to, at least, send a small detail to recover the wounded. Some of our guys could still be alive."

"A rescue mission?" Radigan interjected. He shook his head. "Too risky—no, wait! You're right. If there is anybody alive out there they might be wounded and not thinking clearly. Their instinct may be to head back here. They'll give away our position!"

Fitz's face stiffened.

"Sir, that's not what I'm saying..."

Captain Radigan was losing it. He was losing it faster than any of his superiors back at battalion would have ever predicted.

Fitz had to take careful consideration now. "I think what we need to do is..." he kept his voice low, but made himself perfectly clear. "We need to get you and the other officers out of here. I'll assign an armed detail to go with you. I'll have them top off your FSV. A full tank will get you as far south as Las Cruces. You'll be out of Dark Alley. You can re-establish contact with Battalion Headquarters and call for help."

"Out of Dark Alley?"

"Yes, sir."

"With my tail between my legs?" Radigan's expression looked distant.

Fitz had seen this before. The look on Radigan's face had a textbook clarity; the commander was trapped in a whirlwind of pure fear and confusion.

Radigan shook his fist at Fitz and shot a stream of blood across his face with the self-induced cut from his hand. "Nobody bugs out, you hear me!"

"Sir, you need to calm down..." Fitz wiped the smear of blood off his face.

"I am in charge here—not you!"

Fitz didn't know what to say. He turned to look at the others in the tent. Each of them looked helpless. No one else was ready to stand up to the captain. "All right, then. But what are we going to do now? What's our next move, Captain? We better do *something*."

Radigan nodded. "Establish a perimeter around the camp. Take Second and Third Platoons and set up guard mounts. I want men in the high ground in that canyon, ready to sound the alarm in case that metal fuck makes its way here. You got that?"

That made sense to Fitz. He nodded. But he was getting the sense that Radigan was treating him like a buck private whose commander had no confidence in his skills or guidance. Little did he know. Fitz was prepared to do whatever it took to get them out of this mess, all in spite of Radigan.

Fitz turned to exit. Before he stepped through the open flap of the tent, Radigan called him back.

"Do you think they knew about this?" Radigan asked him.

"Who knew, sir…and about *what*?"

"Battalion, you idiot—who else? Do you think they knew, when they sent us out here, that we would encounter this thing?"

Again, Fitz's face stiffened. "To what end?"

"To try and prove that they were right, that I wasn't ready to take command of a unit?"

"You would have me believe, sir, that Battalion would risk the lives of our men to…*prove a point*?" Fitz shook his head in disbelief, and then he exited without being properly relieved.

With Fitz gone, those that remained were sheep.

"Lieutenant Lewison!"

"Yes, sir."

"I want all this..." He waved his arms and referred to everything in the CP. "All this equipment here relocated. This tent provides zero protection. I want it all inside the school."

"I'll get right on it, sir."

"We have dossiers on the prisoners, don't we?"

Lewison looked confused by the question. "Yes... sir, we do."

"Get them to me."

Lt. Lewison moved to exit.

"One more thing. Before we left HQ, bound for Fort Bradley, Battalion gave us satellite recon photos to guide us through Dark Alley. Where are they?"

Lewison looked confused again. "You said we didn't need them. You told me you were familiar with the location and could get us through without them. Do you remember, sir? Do you remember saying that?" He sounded like he was pleading for mercy.

Radigan took a long breath, but did not relent. It was a strained effort just for him to remain calm. "Pray Lieutenant—pray on your all mighty God that you did not leave them behind, and get them to me, on the double."

Lewison began rubbing his chin. "Yes, sir."

Now Radigan turned to Corporal Chang. He stood over the young man and put his cut hand on the boy's shoulder. "Review all the footage recorded by Corporal Hammond's helmet cam," he said to the nervous specialist, who began to feel the warmth of the captain's blood seeping through his BDU jacket. "Analyze it. I want an extensive report on every inch of that war machine. I want to know who made it. Who sent it.

How it ticks. And most importantly, how we can destroy it. Is that clear?"

"Yes, sir."

Radigan released him and stepped back. He was beginning to feel a sense of awareness and self-assuredness.

Fuck them, he thought.

Fuck them all.

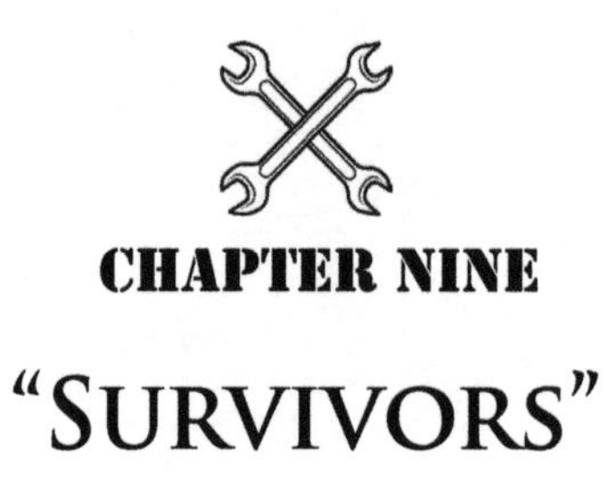

CHAPTER NINE

"SURVIVORS"

It began to make a second pile, next to the first, of bodies it had collected from the woods.

The sniper watched with his keen eyes…

The robot could carry two, sometimes three, bodies in a single claw if it squeezed them tight enough. If the bodies were in pieces—for example, if just the upper half or maybe only the legs had been collected—the machine would go back and retrieve the rest. It was efficient. It got everything. The weapons, the helmets and even the boots, if they had fallen off. But it lumbered as it walked, dragging its feet. Limping, sort of, like it was wounded. First Platoon had given it a lesson, that perhaps for the first time in its artificial life it had come to realize it was not invincible. The miniguns, broken by gunfire, lay impotently upon its shoulders. Oil leaked from joints like a hemorrhage of blood. Like some weary soldier, the machine left its post with its detail unfinished. It drove into the woods… stomping and dragging off toward some mysterious place.

Specialist Donohue sighed, relieved, but he still had to be careful. Dawn was beginning to peel away the layers of the night sky and that threatened to expose his position. He controlled his breathing so as to not show his warm breath to cool air. It was getting harder to remain undetected. He did not know the limits of how well this killing machine could see with its mechanized eye. For now, darkness was his friend. His ally. But his ally was soon to abandon him. Maybe just one more hour left to go before daylight would point him out.

In the absence of a clear explanation, Donohue tried to come up with some reason as to why he was still alive and all the others in his platoon were dead or dying. The simplest reason made the most sense: he posed no threat; having surrendered his sniper rifle to his squad leader before he ventured into the clearing, the iron monster simply left him alone.

For a long time he lied there on his back, sinking into the mud while listening to the moans of the few around him fade until they had finally died. In the end, there was just one. He recognized the voice. It was Sergeant Hennessey.

It was the oldest trick in the book, Donohue thought, for the enemy to provoke someone into coming to the aid of another in the hopes of exposing them. Donohue was hesitant to venture out. He had convinced himself that anyone in his position would be doing the same thing; staying put. Waiting for reinforcements to arrive, to simply *survive,* but he couldn't help but feel ashamed. He felt like a coward.

When the fear that crippled him finally loosened its hold, Donohue sat up and looked around. The steel monster was nowhere in sight, but he didn't feel safe. He had an unsettling feeling that the beast was lurking nearby, ready to pounce. He noticed that only about a dozen of First Platoon bodies had been stacked. There were a dozen more left to make the pile complete.

The war machine might very well return.

"Sergeant Hennessey?" he said with a controlled whisper.

He began to crawl toward the sergeant. He saw the man about a hundred feet away.

"Who's that?" Hennessey replied. "Is that you, Petrozzi?"

"No, sarge, it's... Specialist Donohue."

Hennessey sighed. He was lying on his stomach, his arms tucked underneath him. His face was in the mud. "Donohue. Oh, Jesus. I forgot about you. How bad were you hit?"

"No. No, sarge, I wasn't hit. It never had me in its sights."

Hennessey mustered the strength to shift his body sideways to observe Donohue as the boy crawled towards him. Fifty feet from away at this point. "How did you manage *that*?"

Donohue crawled right up to him. One good look and Hennessey came to realize the answer to his question. "It never had you in its sights because it never knew you were there. It couldn't *see* you."

"What do you mean, sarge?"

"Your suit, kid. That Kettric suit you're wearing. It conceals your body heat— your *thermal infra-red image*."

Donohue never considered that.

"That might be how it identifies targets, in the dark at least. If you want to stay alive, Donohue, don't even think about taking that suit off."

Donohue poked his head up like a submarine periscope and looked around. "It may be gone for good, sarge. What's our next move?"

Hennessey examined his wounds. Next move? He came to the

conclusion he was incapable of making *any* moves. So much blood soaking through his uniform. He couldn't move his legs. Breathing and talking was about the only thing he could manage, and he had no idea how much longer he would be able to do even *that*.

"Why do you think it attacked us?"

"The billion dollar question," Hennessey responded. "Who even knows, kid. I certainly don't have a clue."

"You know, I was thinking…maybe it was something left over from the war. You know, maybe it was something the Americanists whipped up to aid them in battle, and then they just forgot about it. The war ended, but this thing was never turned off. And it's been bouncing around these woods for all these years, looking for Feds to kill, because it thinks the war is still on."

"You thought of that all by yourself?" Donohue shrugged, slightly abashed.

Hennessey snickered. "First of all, the Americanists never had anything like this. And second, if they did… it never would have worked so well. No, kid. This thing is the product of some diabolical genius."

Donohue laughed.

"I'm not joking. Whoever they are, they sure as hell hate us."

"Yeah…no shit about that."

For a few moments, they lied in silence, each listening to the other breathe, until Hennessey said, "I can't reach my canteen. You have to help me."

Donohue retrieved the sergeant's canteen from the utility belt around his waist. When he raised it to the man's mouth hardly a drop came out. The canteen had been pierced by a minigun round and drained dry. "Donohue," Hennessey instructed, "you have to find me some water. Look around for someone else's canteen. If I don't get some water soon, I'll die."

"I'll be right back," Donohue assured him. "Help is coming. It'll be daylight soon. You'll see, sarge, everything will be all right. The First Sergeant won't abandon us. And Captain Radigan is already sending the other platoons to come get us. You'll see."

Hennessey let out a laugh as Donohue crawled away toward another body to get him water, because he knew all the things Donohue was saying were false. Help was not coming. Not now. Not anytime soon. And after this, sending more soldiers was quite simply...stupid.

"Don't die on me, sarge, okay?" Donohue called back. Hennessey responded under his breath, "I'm not promising."

CHAPTER TEN

"Damage Assessment"

SEVERED CONNECTORS TO FOLLOWING LOGIC GATES...

- LN Junction to diode (lower chassis)
- 250W brick diode on left front leg ARMAMENT FAILURE...
- check valve in Gun 1 and Gun 2 needs replacement
- range finder and DMS in Gun 2 out of service CONVENTIONAL CURRENT FLOW DISRUPTION, INCLUDING MODULATION FROM UPPER CARRIER ASSY REQUIRES ATTENTION.

SHUTDOWN EMINENT...

SHUTDOWN EMINENT...

SHUTDOWN EMINENT...

The tektronic main control was running a series of diagnostic checks, a report that was a long list of "illnesses". The list seemed endless.

Their violence was great, but *its* violence was greater. The beast had won, but it did not favor the outcome. Damage indicators throbbed. It strained to move, growing increasingly difficult as more fluid was lost. Although it could run faster than any man, it could not calculate with any certainty just how long.

It was aware that others may attempt to track it. What came as result of this awareness was a rational course of action—it fled.

It learned that it could be harmed, so it sought refuge.

CHAPTER ELEVEN

"The Asset"

Had it only been an hour?

After all that happened, it felt to Captain Radigan like it had been *days*. Weeks even, since the MCAV broke down and they were stranded, and *years* since the whole tepid task to transport prisoners had started. He wished he could go back to the beginning of August, three months ago. He would have been wise to battalion's shenanigans and made a different choice that would not have resulted in the deaths of more than fifty of his men.

At the end of the Second Civil War, while the country remained divided and recovering from a stricken economy, Colonel Schwaiger and his 8th Brigade were given orders by the Secretary of the Defense of the Western States of America, to prevent the flow of human traffic and secure the southern borders of West America, from New Mexico, across the desert flats, to El Paso. Since the end of the war, in 2059, and while tensions overseas between China and the Unified Country of Korea were escalating, there was a sizeable migration of Asian citizens crossing into the Americas from Mexico.

Colonel Schwaiger was tasked with rounding up the illegal aliens for organized deportation. His 8th Brigade, consisting of four battalions, each with six platoons, covered the border from Nogales to Sunland Park, except for a narrow gap of about eight miles on the southwestern corner of New Mexico, just south of Columbus. The assistance of someone willing to follow Schwaiger's strict orders was needed. The nearest mobile combat unit in the area was conducting maneuvers outside Tucson. It was a newly formed company of troops; a mixture of hardcore vets and new recruits, whose leader, Captain Radigan, was a former West Point instructor who had no formal combat experience. Expecting an eagerness to be recognized by his more seasoned peers, Schwaiger presented the offer to Captain Radigan. But their alliance proved difficult. Radigan agreed to aid the colonel with his border patrol, but failed to follow his specific instructions. When, after three months, Schwaiger had gotten word from his trusted scouts that Radigan had not captured a single soul trying to enter into West America, it was suspected he was allowing them to slip through, when in fact, it was much worse. When questioned by Schwaiger, Captain Radigan replied adamantly: "When I catch someone trying to cross the border, I order them to halt. They usually don't. So, I order my men to fire a round six inches above their head. If they still don't, I give the order to shoot six inches *below* their head. The job gets done."

His method for dealing with trespassers, as he called it, was a virtual blood bath that stretched across the eight miles he was ordered to cover. Colonel Schwaiger didn't bother to ask him what he was doing with the bodies. He immediately dismissed Radigan, but did not fully relieve him of his duties. Instead, he allowed the captain an opportunity to redeem himself. With nearly twenty-five prisoners amassed by his nearby Fourth Battalion, Schwaiger presented Radigan with new orders: to transport his prisoners *safely* to Fort Riley, Oklahoma, where they would be surrendered to General Gutter. Safely was stressed, implying that if the captain had failed him again, he would be forced to account for the irresponsibility of his actions.

Only ten of the prisoners were Asian refugees. Three were

Mexican born. And the rest were either escapees from a Mexican prison (drug smugglers mostly) or American felons trying to escape incarceration by fleeing the country.

None of them could be trusted. A few could be useful.

And one in particular might very well hold the key to Captain Radigan's plan and the fate of his ill begotten company.

There was a steadiness to his walk, and his boots tapped with a rhythmic clarity on the concrete steps leading down to the sub floor of the school. Radigan was not alone. Fortunately for him, the First Sergeant tagged along, and a muscle bound soldier who carried a loaded 12 gauge at port arms. In the air was the unpleasant odor of damp concrete mixed with the smell of urine. When they reached the foot of the stairs, and came to the entrance to the fallout shelter, two men posted there snapped to attention and saluted. Radigan failed to acknowledge them. His focus went immediately to the issues with the door. It had a large crack through the center of it and it looked to have been hastily repaired. "Why are there chains on this door, Private? What happened here?"

The guard on the right still held his hand up in salute. "Something happened a short while ago, sir..."

"They tried to escape?"

"No, sir. An altercation." The guard put his hand down. "A fight, sir, between two men. One of them was thrown at the door. It involved that huge one called the Bull."

El Toro. Everyone knew that creep. "He threw someone into

this door?"

"Not exactly, sir. Someone threw *him*. Tossed him head first. He's recovering now upstairs in our makeshift infirmary."

Radigan turned to Fitz, who shrugged inconsequently. It was hard to imagine anyone being strong enough to send a three hundred pound Mexican flying.

It was Fitz, not the guard, who provided the answer. "Uh, sir... I have a feeling it was that one hundred and sixty pound kid we came down here to see."

The inner room had an assaulting smell; it hit Radigan like a slap in the face, the stench of twenty men in desperate need of a shower. Hardly the place the commander wished to be in; given the choice, he would rather soak the place in gasoline and toss a lit match to it. He stood at the entrance, waited for his eyes to adjust to the dim light, and then headed in. There were three lanterns burning low here in the two hundred square foot space. The prisoners were all sleeping; their snores were a jackhammer chorus.

They had organized themselves since the last time he was down here. Some of the cots had been collected and organized close to the walls, so as to create an open space in the center of the room. The dozen or so cardboard boxes of canned food stuff that had been left behind when the school was abandoned years ago were laid out to form either play tables where decks of playing cards were strewn or as room dividers for those prisoners wanting their own space. Evidence of the fight; some of the cots had been thrown into a heap against the block wall with pieces on the floor. Where the light from the open door fell upon the floor was an almost perfectly round blood stain. A scenario played in Radigan's mind of the tattooed Mexican giant attempting to impose his rule.

How it actually played out was this:

Hollis was playing cards with Uncle Billy when his sensitive ears caught the sound of distant gunfire. He was able to decipher that it was military small arms and conveyed to Billy that Bravo Company might be in trouble.

"I can hear something else, too..."

"What is it?"

"I'm not sure."

Billy shouted to everyone in the room. "Hey, everybody, shut the hell up a second!"

Hollis strained to isolate the mysterious sound. Billy could tell by the look on his nephew's face it was something strange.

That was when El Toro interrupted them. "Who the fuck has a death wish?" He looked like he was ready to pound a poor soul into the ground. Even a fool would have surely kept his mouth shut.

"Back off, big guy," Billy said to him, "we're trying to hear something."

El Toro laughed, raised both his arms and cracked his knuckles loud enough to break Hollis' concentration. "I don't want to hurt you, Toro," Hollis warned him, "so back off."

"You don't want to hurt *me*? Puta madre, *everybody* wants

to hurt me!"

Hollis made an irritated face. He got up from the box he was sitting on and gave El Toro an open hand slap across his face that turned the man's head sideways. El Toro stood shocked a moment; no doubt the slap was ten times harder than he would have ever expected. Before he could turn his head back around, Hollis jabbed two fingers from his left hand up into the soft flesh under El Toro's jaw and got a firm hold of the three hundred pound man, like the firm grip of handle on a suitcase. El Toro tried to cry out, but his jaw was pinned shut. "All right, mister," Hollis began," I've had about enough of your bullshit. Now, I want my water bottle back. And my uncle wants his, too."

El Toro tried to pry Hollis away with his hands, but his hands were ineffective. Hollis told him, "Keep you hands to yourself."

El Toro wouldn't, so Hollis slapped them down with his free hand.

"And I want *your* water bottle, too. And if you get thirsty, you come crawling to me on your hands and knees—and beg me for it! You understand?" Hollis manipulated El Toro's skull to go up and down. "Nod, like this, if you understand."

The Bull raised his hands again to try and free himself.

Then Hollis made his eyes turn Gunlord black, and he got real close to El Toro's face. Nose to nose. And he said, "You must be losing your concentration."

El Toro looked terrified, like he was staring into the evil eyes of El Diablo.

Hollis let go of El Toro's jaw and shoved his body to the ground. "El Toro..." he muttered disdainfully, "they should call you *pig*!"

One of the prisoners in the room began clapping his hands. Soon all of them were applauding.

Hollis turned to them in a flash. "Shut up!" he cried. They were abruptly silent.

"Who the hell do you think you are?" he shouted at them. "You think we're in this together? Fuck no!" He stared at them. His eyes were back to normal now, but they looked at him like he was inhuman. "The reason some of you are in here makes me want to puke! Your mothers must be real proud!"

No one made a sound.

Hollis returned to the playing table and sat down. Billy was still seated across from him.

"Did I make an impression?" Hollis asked.

Billy made a face. "You demonstrated some real restraint this time... except that part about their mothers."

"Too much?"

"A tad."

El Toro got to his feet. Possessed with the foolish urge of a man driven insane, he stammered drunkenly toward Hollis, unveiled a hunting knife he had concealed somewhere on his body, and lunged. Hollis was knocked to the floor, suffering a minor cut through the soft tissue of his bicep. The card table was flipped. The force caused Billy to fall backwards.

What transpired next was a demonstration of a Gunlord's fury.

The guard referred to it as an altercation. But that was a gross understatement.

"Where is he?" Captain Radigan asked.

First Sergeant Fitz pointed. "The guard says he's in the corner."

Lit by a single lamp resting on a box between two cots was inmate number zero- one-three: Jacob H. Duncan (he went by his mother's maiden name); 19 years old, wanted for questioning for an incident that involved the death of his team leader in combat. The young man was lying on his side, his face to the wall.

Radigan stepped up to his cot. Using his foot, he dragged one of the boxes close so he could sit down.

Fitz stood by his side, ready, in case the boy got tricky.

The muscle bound guard with the shotgun remained posted by the door.

The Captain got comfortable. He folded his legs and slapped the folder he had brought with him onto his lap. "Wake up, Jacob, I want a word with you."

The prisoner remained still.

Time was critical. Childish bullshit like this was unacceptable. To get things started, Fitz kicked the cot hard enough to raise it above the floor. "I'm sure he's awake *now*, Captain."

Radigan began, "You and me haven't been formerly introduced.

I'm Captain Radigan, unit commander of Bravo Company, Eighth Brigade."

Hollis casually glanced over his shoulder, and sized up the captain in a sum of two seconds. *He wants something from me, of course*, he thought, *and he's going to drag it out*, *instead of getting right to the point*.

Hollis rolled back over.

"I'm talking to you, Jacob. That is your name, isn't it?

A voice spoke up, from a cot just next to his. "Call him by his middle name— it's Hollis."

"Who are *you*?" Radigan asked.

"I'm his uncle," the man answered.

Radigan posed to Fitz an 'it figures' look and then opened the folder on his lap. "When I was handed your military OPF, here... Hollis, I thought someone had made a mistake. I don't care how much trouble you got yourself into, or what sort of name you hoped to make for yourself, the fact is, a nineteen year old should not have a file this thick. This is the file of a career soldier."

He paused before continuing. Still no reaction from the prisoner.

"Some of your accounts in the military are described in here, but not in detail. A good portion of text has been redacted, blackened out. I'm familiar with Operation Witch Hill. Twenty-seven men were deployed, but only one man made it out alive. You served under Captain Gordon Cutter. Son of General Mason Cutter. The General is eager to get his hands on you, Hollis—*both* of his hands, around your throat."

"It was not my fault," Hollis moaned.

"Well, you can tell him that when I hand you over to him."

Radigan referred back to the folder. "Cutter, the son, found you—*found* you, it says here, like you were some treasure to be had—in some town called, Hidden Pond. You demonstrated some extraordinary physical behavior that got his attention and made him want to recruit you into his elite squad." Radigan chuckled evilly. "Now, knowing a bit about Cutter's character, I should say that his recruitment tactics are akin to kidnapping." Radigan turned over some pages in the file. "But enough about Cutter.

What I'm interested in is your father and his biological relation to you.

"Your father was Sergeant Jacob Dillinger. He fought as a Gunlord in the Federal Armed Forces during the Second Civil War. His brother was Colonel Hack Dillinger.

They were both *Landlords*. Hell raisers, if the stories are true. Cold blooded and ruthless as any creature that walked on two legs.

"Now, I've never known a Gunlord—particularly a *Landlord* Gunlord—to breed, let alone pass on his skills. It's no secret, Landlords are killers. Your father killed a lot of people. He turned on his own unit of Gunlords, did you know that? Hack was never anyone's favorite, but it's one hell of a thing for you to be killed by your own brother."

When Hollis finally spoke, he said, "Why are you bothering me?"

Radigan clapped the folder shut. "I'm hoping you inherited more than your father's inability to work with others. I need someone with Gunlord skills to do something for me."

"Your men chased me and my uncle through the woods for miles—"

"It was Schwaiger's men, not mine."

"—and then they fired shots at us. When they caught up to us, they beat us until we were half dead. And if that wasn't enough, they dragged our unconscious bodies by our feet through the mud and rocks back to their base, scraping our skin almost to the bone."

Radigan pointed out, "If it were *my* men, Mister Dillinger, it would have been your corpses we were dragging back to our base."

"So now..." Hollis rolled over fully to face Radigan. "Give me one good reason why I should care to do anything for you?"

Radigan's face broadened with the smile of a crooked politician. "Because if you do what I tell you... I'll let you go."

All the snoring in the room ceased. The sudden silence was jarring. It seemed all those pretending to be asleep were suddenly awake and aware of the conversation.

"You'll set me free?" Hollis asked.

"I didn't say that," Radigan told him, and clarified, "what I said was, I'd let you *go*. You won't be free until you're held accountable for your actions. But you stand a better chance of getting away, and finding somewhere to hide. At least I won't be handing you directly over to Cutter…for what it's worth."

Hollis thought about it. "What do I have to do?"

"Run an errand."

"That simple?"

"No, stupid. If it was simple, I'd do it myself; I wouldn't be sitting here in a basement that smells like piss and talking to you."

"Take the deal, kid," the First Sergeant coaxed. "What have you got to lose?"

"What about my uncle? No deal unless you let him go, too."

Radigan turned his head back and whistled to the guard by the door. The muscle bound guard approached with a rucksack and emptied the contents of it at the foot of Hollis' cot. It was a military uniform, complete with boots and a cap.

"Your uncle gets cut loose once you've done what I ask. Now, put that uniform on. This guard will escort you upstairs where you'll be briefed. I want you in my command tent in fifteen minutes. If you make me wait, the deal is off, and I'll come back down here and pick someone else. I'm sure I can find another prisoner here who will risk their life for a chance at freedom."

"I'll do it, sarge!" a voice called out in the dark.

A tall lanky Hispanic man swooped in. "The name's Ramirez!" He was all too eager and even saluted.

"I'm a captain, you asshole" Radigan responded. "And as a prisoner, the honor of saluting me has been taken from you. But I like your enthusiasm. I'll be getting to you soon enough."

Soon enough? First Sergeant Fitz wasn't sure what that meant. He shrugged it off.

Radigan stood up and turned for the exit. Fitz waited a moment to judge Hollis' reaction, and when he was sure of Hollis' cooperation, turned and followed the captain to the door.

"Fifteen minutes Hollis," was Radigan's last words. The door slammed shut... and almost broke apart again.

When they were gone, and the sound of their footsteps heading up the stairs confirmed they were out of ear shot, Billy sat up in his cot. He said to Hollis, "that captain is a no-good, lying, scoundrel. Don't believe a fucking word he says."

"Now you tell me..."

"He aims to get you killed, Hollis, make no mistake about that. This mission, whatever it is, is a suicide one."

"Keep talking, uncle, I'm almost convinced..."

Billy sat up and moved in close toward Hollis. First, he checked the proximity of the guard by the door, and kept his voice low. "You're going to listen to what this captain has to say, and you're going to act like everything is fine—like he's got your complete cooperation—and then, as soon as you get the chance you're going to shoot like a bullet out of here. You're going to head south and get into Mexico, like we planned."

"Splitting up was not part of the plan."

Billy made a face. "You'll get where you need to go without me as an anchor. Besides, these clowns aren't going to hold me. I've got some skills of my own. When their backs are turned, I'm gone,too."

Hollis examined the uniform lying on his cot. At a quick glance it looked like it would fit, like the captain knew all along he would agree to do this. That sort of confidence in the captain was already troublesome. He got up and began to strip off his orange jumpsuit. "I swore I would never put a military uniform on again," Hollis said to Billy sullenly.

Billy understood why. But there was more to it. "Listen to me, Hollis, shed that uniform as soon as you can. Run naked, if that's what it takes."

Hollis had begun to put on the uniform. The mere feel of the fabric against his skin was loathing to him.

"The Captain would never order you to wear it," Billy stressed, "unless he expected to find you *dead* in it."

Hollis rolled his eyes. He started to put the boots on.

Billy told him, "I want you to head south. Get to Las Cruces, like we planned. There's a bar on the beach called, Las Hombreras. The owner is a guy by the name of Tina—"

"Hold on. A *guy* has the name Tina?"

"*Lou* Tina. Tina is his last name, smart ass, now pay attention... he'll set you up with a new ID badge, so you'll get past checkpoints. He also knows where your father is."

Hollis sighed. "I take it, he owes my father a few favors?"

"He owes your father his *life*," Billy replied.

“Three minutes,” the muscle bound guard marked at the door. He was checking his watch.

Hollis stood tall and put his cap on. “How do I look?”

Billy responded forlornly, “Like a target.”

CHAPTER TWELVE

"CLOSE EXAMINATION"

"What do you want to hear first, Captain, the good news or the bad news?"

Captain Radigan had just passed the through the door of the Principle's Office inside the old abandoned school. The question came from Specialist Chang, who was seated behind a desk in there held together with little more than rust and flaking paint with his equipment spread out on top of it. Light streamed in from the outside floods and cast lines on the look on Radigan's face, it was clear he was in no mood for riddles.

Chang sat up in his chair immediately, abashed.

"Just tell me where it came from, soldier," the captain said wearily. His arms hung straight at his sides. He looked tired and worn out.

Chang apologized and said, "That's the bad news. I don't know. We may *never* know." At present, there was an image of the fighting robot frozen on his computer monitor. Radigan positioned himself to get a better view of it. Chang manipulated the image with his keyboard to show some closer details. "There is a marking on the machine that indicates who owns it, or rather, who *used* to." Chang pointed specifically.

"Look here, sir, on its arm—it reads: Sapphire Engineering Corp."

"In what language?"

"Russian, sir. The core of it—its basic structure, that is—is that of a Russian *Monotok*; a mining drone. It's been altered, obviously. The legs are different. They've been replaced with these agile jumpers. The guns, of course, aren't standard issue. They're good old U S of A

Army issue. Someone upgraded it for combat."

Radigan interjected with a sigh, "But the Russians have no interest in this area.

And they wouldn't be stupid enough to attack a Federal Armed Force, especially on American soil."

"They wouldn't," Chang agreed, "at least not…willfully." Radigan cleared his throat. "Are you getting at something?"

"Are you familiar with the term, *furrow*?"

Towns evacuated along the DMZ during the war; happened so often they came up with a word for it.

"Furrows, yes, I know."

"Taking into account the lack of security in Dark Alley, suppose an organization— a gang, or mob boss—decided to stake a claim in this area to strengthen their empire, using a furrow as a home base. It's been done before. If they planned to stay awhile, they would need some way of securing their investment. They might want something to protect themselves and their assets from, say Marauders, who might try to take it from them. Someone with enough money and perhaps unlimited resources could fabricate a monstrosity like this to guard their perimeter."

"A guard dog."

"You get the idea."

"Is that the *good* news?"

"Sir?'

"When I came in here you said you had good news and bad news..."

"Oh, well...yes, sir, that is, I mean...we have to consider the possibly that we just ran into this thing by accident. We weren't targeted. We just happened to be in the wrong place at the wrong time, and we're not at war with anybody."

"You're wrong, specialist," Radigan corrected. "Very wrong. We *are* at war.

Someone put us there."

"Yes, sir."

Radigan's agitation drew Chang's attention. He grew cautious of the man as he moved slowly around to the side of the desk, well within striking distance. Chang also took note that Radigan had removed his survival knife from its sheath and began tossing it from one hand into the other. The sharp blade glistened in the dim light.

Specialist Chang referred to the monitor in an effort to lure the captain's attention elsewhere. "A Monotok functions solely on a set of instructions programmed into it, sir. It doesn't think on its own. It *can't*. A mining drone doesn't have that capability.

They're not that sophisticated. Come to think of it, that may be why it formed that pile of bodies, it was collecting samples—performing a basic task. You see, these drones work in pairs; one is programmed to do the drilling, while the other makes piles of rocks for the human miners to sift through. Once we discover this Monotok's fundamental initiative, we can trick it, find ways around it."

"To defeat it?"

Chang was about to reply when a knock came on the door. The Captain barked, "Who's there?"

"Corporal Kline, sir."

"Enter."

Corporal Kline was a soldier from Headquarters Platoon. He stomped into the office and saluted, presenting a folder to Radigan at the same time. "These are the satellite pictures you requested from Lieutenant Lewison, sir. He said you might find them interesting."

Radigan stabbed his knife back into its sheath and snatched the file out of Kline's hands. He rifled through them immediately. There were about a dozen photos; aerial shots taken from a satellite in orbit above the Southwest, and this region of Dark Alley. One of the photos was of particular interest to him. His eyes became very narrow and he tilted his head upwards at the ceiling.

"Also, sir...," Kline said, "the prisoner is up from the basement. He's in the CP waiting for you."

Radigan was still too deep in thought to care. "That'll be all, corporal."

"Yes, sir."

Kline saluted and did an about-face. Radigan and Chang were alone again.

Radigan asked, "How smart would you say this thing is?"

“Smart, sir?” Chang chuckled. “That would imply it had some awareness, which it surely doesn't.”

“You find that funny?”

Chang had to be especially careful now. “It's efficient, sir, of that we can agree on.”

“I need to know its ability to solve problems and adapt.”

“To be certain of its AI limitations, well...it would have to be tested.”

“That means we need test rats.” Radigan's mind began to picture twenty of them, all in a room directly below him.

He looked directly at Chang and said, “I want you to study the data some more. I need you to figure out how we can take this thing down. I need a knock out punch.”

“I've tried to find its weakness, a pattern in its behavior that would give a hint as to how we could take it down. I never found it. Suffice is to say, if we keep hitting it with bullets it's bound to break.”

“Not at the expense of any more of our men.”

It was a noble statement, even for someone as arrogant as Radigan to say. “If we had a tank, armed with an M700 plasma weapon—” Chang stopped himself before continuing on, certain that Radigan had zero interest in wishful thinking. “Everything has an Achilles heel, specialist,” Radigan assured, and sounded oddly pleasant. “*Everything*. Your job here is to find it.”

“I've watched this recording at least a thousand times. How many more times do you think I should look at it to draw the same conclusion?"

Captain Radigan grinned audaciously. He leaned in towards the young man and whispered, "Do you want to hear the good news or the bad news?"

CHAPTER THIRTEEN

"There Are Two"

With First and Fourth Platoon having met their fate, the culmination of Bravo Company's fighting force was cut in half, but the sixty-two that remained were a significant body; stout and highly trained. At this moment, however, their lack of restraint had them degraded to the corps of an angry mob.

They were in the front parking lot outside the old school; full attendance, with the exception of two guards posted inside the school to secure the prisoners and the handful of soldiers on the main road ordered to watch over the convoy vehicles. The atmosphere was tense and of course it was not without reason. Everyone was shouting all at once, voicing their opinions at the top of their lungs and it sounded nothing more than just noise. They weren't just angry. Standing in front of the formation was First Sergeant Fitz, and he knew his people well enough to see it clearly; beneath their will to shed blood to avenge their fallen, they were saddened by their loss, confused as to why it had happened, and weary of their own future.

Fitz raised his hands up into the air. "At ease, people! I understand your frustration! Quiet!"

One of the soldiers was pacing behind the formation, muttering something with such passion it seemed he was going mad. Fitz caught him before he went too far. "Miller!" he shouted. "Stand fast—or I swear I'll shoot your kneecap!'

The pacing man came to a stop, and he took a deep breath to calm himself.

Fitz hadn't seen these soldiers this crazed since the war, and back then they were all a lot younger, and a lot more naive.

Someone in the back row exclaimed, "We need to strike back now, Top! We're wasting time standing around with our hand in our pockets! You know how it works; before the enemy has time to regroup, we hit them hard with all we've got."

They were all willing to lay down their lives to avenge their fallen comrades, but Fitz had to confess, "That time's has passed, Jules. Expecting us to retaliate, our enemy—whoever they are—has already regrouped and by now, has reinforced their defensive line."

"We should have acted faster!"

Fitz agreed, but he had another thought. "What if there is more than *one* of those machines out there?" He added, "We don't know fully what we're up against. Sending all of you in, half-cocked, may be the death of you all. But I will tell you this: Captain Radigan is planning a strategy as we speak. And when he's ready to initiate it, we won't hesitate."

Another soldier dared to speak out. "The Captain's scared!" All eyes turned to him.

He went on. "He's scared, that if we leave to attack the enemy, no one will be left here to protect him."

There was some truth in that, but Fitz did not want his men losing faith in their command. He said, "What do I always say? Anyone?" The First Sergeant looked in the ranks for someone to recite his creed. His eyes fell on Sergeant Percy. "Percy?"

Percy stepped up like a kid called to the head of the classroom. "Strength and courage," he recited, "are no match for the wisdom of knowing when you're in over your head."

"That's right...and we just may be in over our head." The men seemed to settle down after that.

Fitz snapped his fingers to usher his platoon sergeants close. They clustered in a single bounce. Staff Sergeants Becker and Longfield; both polished veterans. Fitz kept his voice low. "I want a hole dug. A pit. At the entrance to the canyon. Fifteen feet deep, just as wide, and as deep."

"A trap?" one of the platoon sergeants asked.

"Probably not," Fitz answered, "but if that thing tries to attack us here, the pit may slow it down. In any case, I want our guys keeping busy and not standing around talking and thinking too much. You understand me?"

"I got you, Top," Becker assured, "we'll get right on it."

Fitz turned his attention to Percy. "I need a favor from you..." He took Percy by the collar and tugged him away from the group. "I need you to do something for me, something the Captain can't know about."

Percy's brow furrowed. "What's wrong with the Captain?"

Fitz made a gesture. "He's recovering right now, from a blow to the head."

"What do you mean?"

"You know...that imaginary hit from a sledgehammer that every commander feels when they realize they fucked up. Don't worry about him. I can handle him. What I need from you is a vehicle, a fast one with a good radio."

"The Skip; it's small, but it performs."

"And I need two men from your Headquarters Platoon. Preferably two that won't be missed."

Percy asked, "Do they have to be able to shoot straight?"

"I need them to *drive* straight," Fitz stressed. "They'll take the Skip and drive out of Dark Alley and make that distress call we should have made before sending First Platoon to their deaths."

Fitz wasn't proud conducting business behind the commander's back, but he knew what he had to do, and he was willing to except the consequences of his actions.

"Don't beat yourself up about that, Top," Percy said, trying to ease the first sergeant's guilt. "It wasn't your call. Besides, no one could have known this was going to happen."

"Just do what I tell you, Percy. And do it ASAP."

"Do what?" Captain Radigan asked as he abruptly approached.

Fitz was caught off guard, but he was quick to recover. "Just informing Sergeant Percy to make sure the vehicles are all topped off, in case you change your mind about leaving."

Radigan's face tightened. "I told you, Top, nobody is bugging out. This is our play to execute and no one is going to take our field, you get me?"

"I got you, sir," Fitz assured him, and as always, he fought the urge to roll his eyes. He began to wonder if his lack of enthusiasm for whatever the Captain said was giving the commander signals that he disapproved of his orders.

Percy departed with a wink.

"Walk with me, back to the CP," Radigan ordered Fitz. "I have something I want to show you."

They left the parking lot and headed up the small incline toward the Command Post at the top of the hill, walking side by side. The wind was blowing exceptionally warm. In Radigan's hand was the folder of SAT photos given to him by Corporal Kline, in the principle's office. He took one photo out and handed it to Fitz. Before Fitz could focus on it, Radigan announced, "There are *two* of those mechanized mother fuckers."

Fitz stopped dead in his tracks.

An aerial photo, taken at dusk, showed mostly vegetation; trees and bushes and a partial mountain range, and even that was overgrown and difficult to make out. But in the upper right hand corner of the photo was something different, a landing spot for two objects that were slightly out of focus but clear enough to make out. Robots. Almost identical, except one was blue and the other red.

"They're simple mining drones that someone had the bright idea to attach weapons to," Radigan began to explain. "At one time, they were programmed to dig for diamonds in the northern part of Siberia, in those areas where the air was too contaminated with radiation."

Fitz remarked, "They're a long way from home."

Radigan went on. "As I understand it, they are deployed from an IKOVV cargo chopper. The chopper takes them over their designated drop point, and then releases them. They descend in parachutes. Now take a close look at this photo. The blue one—the one that attacked our guys—it landed in one piece. But the red one, you see... one of its legs broke off. It landed hard on this cliff ledge. I'm guessing its parachute didn't open. We're in luck with that one."

Fitz squinted to examine something specific in the photo. "That red one looks equipped with rocket launchers, Captain."

"Easy, Top. It doesn't matter. That robot can't move."

"Sir, it doesn't have to be mobile to be a threat. Those could be long range missiles. Hellfires maybe. I suggest we assemble a team to—"

"Hold that thought, First Sergeant," Radigan interrupted and flipped a second photo into Fitz's hand. "Take a look at *this* one."

The second photo was a shot of Oliveri, the nearby town, from high altitude. "This town was supposed to be abandoned. It may be hard for you to see, but take a good look at what's on the streets of that town. Tell me what you see." Fitz muttered with disbelief, "People."

"Fuckin' aye. Oliveri is *occupied*. And I have a feeling in my gut, like a twisting knife, that those people are responsible for the attack on our men."

"How old are these photos, Captain?"

Radigan shrugged. "Three weeks? Three months? Who knows? There's no date on the photographs. Battalion could have had them left over from the war for all I know."

That seemed to make a difference to Fitz. He passed them

back to Radigan and shook his head. "If they're that old, sir, we can't rely on them."

"But we have nothing else to go on."

Fitz thought about it. He couldn't argue the fact. "All right, then, sir...what do you want to do?"

Radigan breathed deeply. He had a response ready and wanted to make it clear. "We need to get to that town and take those people out."

"Okay...okay, sir...say you're right and those people are responsible for the attack on our men, and we need to take them out... how do you plan on doing that with that war machine as their first line of defense?"

Radigan grinned. It was an evil grin. He said, "By using the prisoners as bait."

CHAPTER FOURTEEN

"BRIEFING"

Jacob Hollister Duncan stood in the doorway to the school library, now home to the Bravo Company command post. His hands were bound behind him with handcuffs. There were no books inside the room, only empty shelves; the only reason Hollis knew it was the library was because of the sign above the door. Remnants of the old school were strewn about. Tattered posters of kids reading books still hung on the walls. An old banner stretched across the width of the room, above the windows read: GOOD THINGS ARE GOING TO HAPPEN. Hollis hesitated before stepping in to observe the chaotic scene.

"This is Bravo Company, 8th Brigade, calling on all frequencies. Is anyone reading?" clamored a radio tech into a microphone. Another soldier behind the radio was frantically checking the connection of wires to the back panel. Apart from them, an officer was seated on a field chair with his head buried in his hands, rocking back and forth. *Were those tears rolling down his face*? Hollis couldn't tell. And in the center of the tent, standing over a field table with a map spread across it, were two more officers, their expressions so grim it was like seeing combat surgeons standing over their dying patient.

The guard assigned to Hollis nudged him further in with the butt of his rifle.

Hollis took only one step, so the guard nudged him again, twisting the butt of the rifle into Hollis' spine this time. Hollis wanted to clobber him. He could have easily dealt with him, turned and dropped him with one swift punch to the throat, but he kept his cool, all for the sake of his uncle still being held in the fallout shelter—Captain Radigan's dungeon.

Hollis heard the buzz, clicks and winding motors of a robot come from behind him. And he heard someone say to him, "Out of the way, soldier!" Hollis was taken aback, being addressed as a soldier sounded strange, but then he remembered he was wearing someone's woodland camouflage uniform. He *was* a soldier... for now.

Hollis and the irritating guard who liked to use his rifle as a cattle prod parted ways to allow the robot to pass between them. The four foot tall motorized contraption drove on two sets of treads and entered the library. No one seemed to react surprised by it, but the lieutenant at the field table put himself directly in the path of it. Above his breast pocket was the name, Lewison.

"What the hell is this?" Lewison shouted.

"It's *Nickels*, LT," a man answered. The man had come up from behind the robot holding a tablet as a control device. He was in charge of the robot.

"I know what it is, corporal," Lewison said, "my question is, what is it doing in here?"

The M55 explosive ordinance disposal bot (nicknamed *Nickels*) weighed only about 60 pounds. It had a slim cigar shaped body with one three-point manipulator. At the end of its slender neck was attached a soldier's combat helmet, complete with a helmet cam. It looked funny, but was no joke.

"Now, hear me out, LT..." the EOD operator said as he maneuvered the robot to an open spot in the room.

"Make this quick, corporal."

"I was lucky to find an old helmet cam similar to the one Corporal Hammond wore and fasten it to the top of his head. What I have in mind is, we strap six pounds of C4 to Nickel's belly and send him into those woods looking for that war machine. I can rig a lever that can activate a detonator."

"I'm listening," Lewison said.

"We can monitor Nickels' every move with this tablet. We'll be able to see when that war machine comes close. And when it does, we hit a switch and—*boom*! It's lights out."

"What about the radio interference? The same thing that happened to the Thunderfly can happen to Nickels."

The EOD operator made a face. "I know, sir, that's a problem. But you see, Nickels is mostly constructed of lead, the same material that makes him impervious to an electro magnetic pulse. The remote signal will be an issue, but I'm thinking we send a guy in with Nickels. A volunteer. As long as he maintains a close proximity, the signal shouldn't be lost."

"How close does this volunteer have to be?" Lewison asked. The EOD operator made another face. "Real close."

"How close?"

"About a hundred feet?"

Lewison shook his head. "So basically, this volunteer gets blown up too?" The EOD operator shrugged showing some regret. "It's a kink, I admit..."

"Work out the kink and I'll submit your suggestion to the captain," Lewison told him. "For now, get that thing out of here. The last thing the captain wants to see in his command post is another robot."

"Yes, sir."

As quickly as they arrived, the EOD operator and his mechanized pet were gone.

The timing was perfect.

A few seconds later, Captain Radigan entered the library. The First Sergeant followed behind him.

"*Atten-tion!*" Lewsion shouted.

"As you were," Radigan instructed and passed through to the far side of the room.

"Remove his cuffs," Fitz ordered the guard, passing a glance to Hollis. "Are you sure, Top, this prisoner can run like hell," the guard advised. "Just do it."

Fitz looked deep into Hollis' eyes for reassurance. In a moment, the guard did what he was told.

There was a brief discussion amongst the officers in the room. Radigan was giving the low-down on some recent details. When he was finished he turned to Fitz and gave him a nod. Lieutenant Lewison was given a folder.

Fitz stood between Hollis and the officers at the field table. He said to Hollis, "This is Lieutenant Lewison, he's going to tell you everything you to need to know about what you're expected to do. Pay close attention."

Lewison moved to the forefront of the group and Hollis got a better look at him. The LT had a neck too slim, it seemed, to be able to support his unusually large head, and his bulging eyes were startlingly unnatural. For the next few seconds, before Lewison had a chance to open his mouth and speak, Hollis couldn't decide whether this officer had crawled out from a hole in the ground, or arrived in a saucer from deep space.

Lewison must have gotten the drift by the way Hollis was looking at him, he merely shook his head and looked away. Perhaps it was the way *everybody* looked at him. In a squeaky voice that suited him, he began, "Are you familiar with the term Monotok? It's Russian?"

Hollis shrugged. "It's a drink, no?" He looked around at everyone. "Keep it brief, lieutenant," Radigan said.

Hollis took note of the captain's position. He was standing back, toward the corner, hiding in the shadows. Probably for affect. Hollis could feel the weight of his glare and the caustic sear of his thoughts. The man stood with arms folded across his chest.

"A Monotok is a robot used for mining." Lewison coaxed Hollis closer to the table. Hollis proceeded hesitantly. A photo was lying on the table. It was a still shot taken from the data from a soldier's helmet camera. Slightly out of focus, because the subject in the photo was moving; it was a shot of a robot for war in the volatile state of attacking soldiers from Bravo Company. It was enough to make even the son of a Gunlord's jaw go slack.

"Little more than an hour ago, this Monotok—armed to the hilt—attacked two of our platoons. They were en route to the nearest town to access a radio tower there to boost our signal here, in order for us to reach Battalion and request a transport vehicle to replace the one that had broken down. There were caught off guard. All fifty-three of them were killed."

That accounts for the distant gunfire I heard, Hollis thought, and supposed, too, the cause for the weeping officer he noticed with his head still buried in his hands.

He leaned in to get a closer look at the photo and in amount asked, "Correct me if I'm wrong gentlemen, but since when are guns standard issue for a mining robot?"

No one appreciated the young man's lightheartedness.

Lewison said, getting right to the point, "We need you to finish the job our platoons started."

"Are you kidding?" Hollis asked, looking over at the Captain. "If two of your platoons couldn't stop it, what affect do you think I'll have?"

Lewison's response was immediate. "We don't want you to stop. Hell, we don't even want you to engage it at all. All we need for you to do is to sneak past it, get into the town and get power turned on to the radio tower. That's all. We'll do the rest."

Now I get it, Hollis thought. Of course. They need someone

expendable. And who more expendable than a prisoner? He wasn't really surprised. His uncle was right and had warned him about it... this was a suicide mission.

Lewison referred to the map spread across the field table. The edges of the map were torn. It looked old, like maybe it had been taken from one of the classrooms inside the school. No major landmarks visible, or specific references, but there were notes recently handwritten. "This is where we are," Lewison said, pointing to a spot on the lower portion of the map. "Up here is your destination, the town of Oliveri. A distance of about five and a half miles. The terrain will be a challenge. Your journey begins through this narrow canyon, which opens into a patch of woods. Stay to the right once you're out of the canyon. This area here..." Lewison dragged his index finger past a red circle drawn with a marker. "This is where our men were attacked. I recommend you stay clear of it. Just keep right, move along the base of this ridge. Continue north, another two miles, and you will come to a paved road. Turn left. Take that road straight into town. You'll have to make your way across this crevice somehow, the bridge is out." Lewison paused. "Are you listening prisoner? Are you paying close attention?"

Hollis looked around again. "Is there going to be a test?"

"The things I'm telling you just might save your life."

Hollis stared at Lewison a long moment. He doubted if the bug-eyed lieutenant truly cared whether he lived or died.

Hollis turned toward the captain. "Is it too late to change my mind?" Radigan ignored him.

Hollis was kidding, of course, but no one was appreciating his sense of humor.

Lewison went on, "The tower is mounted on the roof of a building in the center of town." He removed another photo from the file in his hands and placed it over the photo of the war machine. "This is a satellite photo taken of Oliveri at dusk. If you look closely, you'll notice that the power is still on. Notice the streetlamps, their lights are on."

Hollis did look closely at the photo, and he saw something else besides the streetlamps. "What about those people?"

"What people?" Lewison asked.

"The ones in the photo—look here, the ones standing in the street?"

Lewison did not look at the photo. He passed a look to Radigan and then said, "There's a chance you may encounter a civilian element in the town."

"What if they try to stop me?"

The captain spoke out just then, "Deal with them."

"Deal with them?" Hollis wasn't exactly sure what that meant. "That sounds pretty sinister. You care to be specific?"

Radigan stepped out of the shadows and addressed Hollis directly, "You do whatever you have to do. You get that tower turned on. You do what I would expect from any Gunlord."

Hollis sneered. He did not appreciate the implication.

Lewison continued where he left off, "The equipment was left behind by the 36th Signal Corps, a civilian detachment. It's a common IPO-T2 system. You may be familiar with it. We'll send you with a set of instructions just in case."

Lewison passed a look to Radigan. "Is there anything I left out, sir?"

Radigan shook his head and turned away from Hollis. "We've wasted enough time already."

"When does my uncle get released?" No one answered right away.

"I said, when does my—"

"I heard you."

"Well?"

"The sooner my men have established communication with Battalion command, in El Paso, the sooner I'll know you succeeded. That's when I'll order your uncle to be released. Once you re-connect with him, I strongly suggest you keep heading north. Get as far away from Oliveri as possible, and don't make any attempt to come back here." Radigan stepped closer to Hollis. "Oliveri will be ground zero once I call in for an air strike, and every inch of those woods will be scorched earth."

"Do I get a weapon?"

Radigan chuckled. "Now *that's* funny. The answer is no. The bare hands of a Gunlord's son will be all the protection you'll need."

First Sergeant Fitz threw in his two cents. "This robot is not something you want to mess with."

"I wasn't planning on it, but thanks for the advice."

Once more Hollis looked around at everyone. He could judge by their silence this briefing was over and so he asked, "When do you want me to leave?"

Radigan replied, "A half hour ago."

Hollis laughed, because he thought that was funny. No one else did.

CHAPTER FIFTEEN

"THE RABBIT'S FOOT"

THE SKY HAD BEGUN TO LIGHTEN as dawn approached, though it was still pretty dark out. The entrance to the canyon looked even darker, like the gaping mouth of a hungry dragon. Hollis stood staring at it. Two rows of chem-lights had been tossed on the ground, adding to the affect of a runway to Hell. He did not feel fear though. He had been bred to resist that emotion. He was confident in his strength and sure of his speed and his ability to maneuver without being detected. His father had taught him. His plan was to do what they said. Stick to the east, they told him. He would be safe. *Safe*. That was a laugh. But no matter. He had every intention of staying out of harms way. No urge whatsoever of encountering that metal monster and soldier grinder. He was sure of one thing, this robot was more than any single Gunlord could handle.

A few paces in toward the canyon Hollis could see metal stakes driven into the ground with string connecting to each one of them, as if a significant portion of ground was being marked for excavation. *What was Bravo Company planning on doing?*

Hollis turned to look up towards the top where the school sat. He saw the captain and his first sergeant looking down at him, no doubt eager to see him leave. They did not lend him a pistol, but they offered him a canteen. He removed it from his utility belt and took a healthy swig of water. When he was finished he was ready to go.

"Hey, hold on a second!" called one of the two guards posted at the canyon entrance.

As the guard approached him, Hollis made a fist in anticipation of trouble. It was a habit.

"Are you afraid?" the guard asked.

Hollis fastened the canteen back to his belt and replied, "Are you taking a survey?"

"My partner and I were trying to figure out why a kid like you would risk his life for a bunch of grunts he doesn't even know. *He's* betting you're going to head south the first chance you get to save your own ass."

Any other time, Hollis thought, it would have been a safe bet. But Hollis said, "Your captain has my uncle locked up, so... I really don't have a choice."

The guard looked over at his partner, and then back to Hollis. "I want you to have this." He planted something into the palm of Hollis' hand. It was hairy and it was warm, and at fist Hollis thought it was a dead mouse.

"It's a rabbit's foot," the guard told him. "It's for good luck."

"Yeah," Hollis replied coolly. "I know what they're for." He tried to give it back. "I just met your captain...you're going to need it more than me."

The guard put up his hands, refusing to take it. "If you do what the commander asks, and succeed, you can consider it served us both." And with that, the guard turned and went back to his post.

Hollis simply tucked the rabbit's foot in the chest pocket of hihs uniform and began his trek into the canyon. He started out slowly. And then after a few seconds, he took off in a full on sprint. The gaping mouth of the hungry dragon swallowed him.

It was as if he just disappeared.

"And there he goes," Captain Radigan muttered.

"And here we stand," First Sergeant Fitz croaked, "pinning our hopes on the son of a Gunlord."

"I'm not pinning our hopes on that freak," Radigan responded, "in fact; I don't give him a snowball's chance in Hell of making it as far as the bridge."

Fitz looked nonplussed at the captain. "I don't understand, sir, what was the purpose of the briefing, if you thought it was for nothing?"

"Well... in case, by some miracle, he actually *does* make it."

Fitz suddenly realized the poor boy was set up to fail from the start, which is why he brought up the question, "The course you sent him on, that was your idea?'

"Yep."

"You deliberately sent him into the path of that robot. Why?"

Radigan shook his head in disbelief, thinking Fitz should have already known why. "It's a guard dog, you know, this war machine?"

"One way of looking at it, I suppose—a particularly vicious one."

"No, I mean it simply," Radigan said. "I talked with Specialist Chang who convinced me that this thing is just following a programmed set of instructions, that it can be easily tricked."

"*Specialist* Chang," Fitz commented, "the kid who filled in for PFC Sapatos when he went with First Platoon? Sir, that boy can't be sure of *anything*!"

"He's a smart kid. He has me convinced."

Yeah... he sure has, Fitz thought. "Sir, whatever you think he's figured out... to put it bluntly... is just a guess. We don't know what our enemy wants, exactly. Or why this machine even attacked us in the first place. In fact, there's only one thing we know for certain—if we send a man to Oliveri, he's liable to get killed."

"We're going to trick it," Radigan insisted. In his hands he held a list of the prisoners currently held in the fallout shelter. He forced it into Fitz's hand and said, "Give this to Lieutenant Lewison. Tell him I want one prisoner sent out every half hour, each on the same course as that Gunlord's son. East. If it's a guard dog, I intend to train it, by tossing it a biscuit, one every half hour from the same direction. When I'm convinced it's safe, I'll send a team of our men into Oliveri from the *west*, to get the job done right."

Captain Radigan started to walk away. "One, every half hour, First Sergeant, that's an order."

"History will not reflect kindly on your tactics, Captain."

Radigan paused and turned back. "I'm aware of that, Top; you can remind me of it... if I ever run for President."

CHAPTER SIXTEEN

"PLAN B"

Private First Class Hargrove and Specialist Clemmons did not sign up to be heroes. If asked why they joined the FAF they would be honest and say they needed money for college. Both had different plans beyond that of a career in the military.

Suddenly everything changed.

They were called into action. Lives were at stake now; lives of men and women, who were once strangers but had grown to be their brothers and sisters; they were depending on them.

Sergeant Percy approached the vehicle. "Are you guys ready?" he asked.

The Skip was a big-wheeled, low profile vehicle—a military grade dune buggy—that was quick and reliable.

Hargrove sat in the rear to monitor the radio. His seat faced the back. Above him, mounted on a pole was the 50cal machine gun loaded with a belt of armor piercing rounds.

Clemmons was behind the wheel.

Percy handed Clemmons a map. "Stay on this road until you reach the Interstate, about twenty miles. It takes you a little out of your way, but it's safest. Once you're out of Dark Alley, call Battalion on the secure band. You're call sign is, *motorcade*."

"Motorcade," Hargrove repeated. "Got it."

"Say it again."

"*Motorcade*."

Percy pointed to the dashboard. "Your GPS should kick-in

once you get close, Clemmons. Watch for the signal."

"After we make contact," Hargrove asked, checking the connections to the radio, "what do we do then? Should we head right back here?"

"No," Percy replied curtly. "You stay until reinforcements arrive, and then escort them back here." He added forlornly, "hopefully we'll still be alive."

"What if we encounter trouble?" Clemmons asked. Percy quipped, "steer around it!"

They all had a laugh about that, and then Percy gave the gesture for them to get rolling. "Move out," he ushered, "before I have a mind to jump in there and go with you."

A full tank of fuel. Gauges indicating a go for take-off.

Clemmons pressed the ignition button on the floor with his foot and the Skip roared to life like a lion. "We'll be back with the cavalry, sarge, don't you worry!"

Percy simply smiled and took a step back. He slapped the fender of the Skip like he was smacking the rear of a horse.

And the vehicle galloped off.

PART TWO

CHAPTER SEVENTEEN

"SERVICE STATION"

His eyes closed, the farmer can hear the air as it blows across his fields. So soothing, it is like listening to the gentle plucking of the strings of a classic guitar. He can smell it, too. When he opens his eyes, he sees the hills in the distance at the peak of sunrise. To him, nothing can be more beautiful or peaceful.

Most mornings for Buck Rowe Baker were like that. However this morning, two things were different:

First, there was a pungent odor coming from one of his fields. From his angle on the back porch and the tall row of hedges kept whatever it was out of his direct line of sight, but the smell of it was unmistakable. He would deal with that in a moment.

The second thing was that his dog, Lady, was barking, barking like a mad dog. The old droopy-eared hound held a stance in front of the barn. Her tail was not wagging, it was tucked low between her legs, which usually meant trouble.

Buck carefully placed his steaming mug of coffee on the porch railing. Dressed in his bathrobe and flip-flops, he made his way warily across the yard. He stopped a few feet from the barn when he saw that the metal hasp and padlock used to secure the doors had been torn off. The pieces were lying on the ground. And the barn door itself was partially open. Turning to his dog, he whispered to it what he was sure it already knew, "we have an intruder."

Buck's first thought was that it could be Marauders. In the past, those vile rogue militants from Mexico had sought refuge after being attacked and demanded that he accommodate them. They forced themselves into his house and treated him like a slave, making him feed them and administer first aid to their wounded. They stayed longer than they should have... and lived to regret it.

Buck rapped on the barn door, so as not to surprise anyone inside. Marauders were a 'shoot first' type. After a moment, he ventured hesitantly through the doors.

"Is anyone in here?" he called to the darkness.

He heard the squeals of mice and the flutter of a barn owl's wings in the rafters.

His eyes had not adjusted yet, but the loose boards along the wall allowed enough sunlight to peek in, revealing something enormous hiding in the corner. The top of whoever it was—or rather, *what*ever it was—touched the high loft. At its center, a blue light began to glow, charging up as if it was awakening, and that light drew brightly upon Buck's astonished face.

A little while later, farmer and robot were outside the barn. Buck was using a garden hose to rinse the robot clean, while the robot stood idly by, content with the farmer's chore. Buck washed away the splatter of blood on its surface and dislodged bits of flesh snagged in its joints. A grotesque pool began to form at the robot's feet.

"You have to be careful who you pick fights with, my big friend," Buck remarked. He yanked a small piece of fabric with one hand that had lodged within the jagged creases of the robot's arm. He knew right away who it belonged to, a federal soldier. Like this piece of fabric, federal uniforms had a distinct camouflage pattern.

"You can slay a room full of Marauders and no one would bat an eye..."

The robot lowered itself so Buck could get the hard to reach spots. "But..."

The robot shifted gears to lower itself even further, and spread its arms to their full length to increase the farmer's efficiency.

"Kill someone who might someday be missed, well, that could make things complicated."

The Sapphire King had been severely damaged. While it was crouched, Buck could see evidence of a fierce fire fight. Pock marks from bullets. Carbon streaks and scorched panels from explosives. "I can fix these leaks," Buck offered assuredly, "and patch these fluid lines, too, but those guns of yours, well... they're finished."

The miniguns hung like broken lanterns down the King's back. Buck broke free from his task to go back into the barn and retrieve a pair of bolt cutters. When he returned, he cut the broken weapons loose. They fell in the blood stained mud.

"You're tough," Buck announced. "You can take a beating, no question about it. Someday, though, you will meet your match. Everyone does. You might want to think about staying out of sight... next time."

The King made a sound; a *click* of some sort that Buck took as a response.

Message understood. The robot was learning.

"Now, come with me," Buck made a gesture. "There's something I need to show you." He shifted his weight off his bad hip and pointed a shaky finger across the yard, near the base of the old rusted silo. "Over there." Where he used to park his tractor was a concrete slab covered by an aluminum awning. Lying across that slab was something covered in a blue tarp and tightly tied together with thick rope.

They moved away from the blood soaked ground and towards the slab. Buck wasn't getting along too quickly, but the Sapphire King showed his respect by never getting too far ahead of the old farmer.

At the slab, Buck pulled loose the slipknots and removed the tarp. What he exposed was the leg of the Ruby Queen that had been severed upon landing on the rock ledge when the great lady's chute did not open.

"I was able to pull some parts off my old harvester and get them to fit. The U- joints were especially useful. As for the rest, I might be able to machine them from scratch, but that'll take time. When I'm all done she may not be as pretty as she once was, but at least she'll be able to walk again. I'm not going to be able to work on her where she is. There's just not enough room on that rock ledge. So, I'm going to have to get her here somehow. I'll figure something out. The thing we need to do first is to keep the rust from spreading..."

The two of them were on the move again.

They crossed to another part of Buck's farmstead where a fifty-five gallon metal drum hung from a steel hook inside the legs of a tripod made of 4x 4 wooden posts. Vinyl tubing ran from the drain plug at the base of the drum to where a large turn valve had been fashioned out of an old Ford hood ornament.; a valve easy enough for the clumsy lobster-like claws of this former mining robot to manipulate.

"The drum is filled with linseed oil. This will protect her exposed parts from the bad weather. You set it just right and it will drip down. It's like what doctor's call an IV." Buck gave the Sapphire King a long hard look. He doubted the robot understood what the device was for, or if, after Buck disassembled it, it could manage to reassemble it at the cliff ledge. "Just take it to the Queen, she'll know what to do with it."

The Ruby Queen was the smarter of two, Buck had come to realize. She had a clearer comprehension of the English language—and Russian, too, he found out. She had a background knowledge of almost anything mechanical, which Buck discovered during the many hours he spent with her on that rock ledge trying to repair her.

"When you take this back to her, I want you to keep to the woods. Stay off the main road. Stay out of sight. And most of all... behave, will you, don't go looking for trouble?"

More clicks. "Thank you."

Buck spent the next hour servicing the Sapphire King's minor repairs. He replaced or patched the leaking lines, tightened any loosened bolts and lubricated all of its moving parts. Later, he used nylon straps to securely fasten the five gallon drum of oil to the King's back and used a net for all the IV accessories to be slung over its shoulder, like a back pack.

"Get these to the Queen as soon as possible," Buck instructed.

When the robot tuned to leave, Buck saw more of the shears and pock marks from bullets, and it reminded him that the King may have been lucky not to have been taken down. Obviously these federal soldiers were not adequately armed, and the King had the advantage. "I do hope you got them *all*..." Buck thought aloud to himself. The thought crossed his mind of what he might find in the field. He got a whiff of that pungent odor again—that smell of death—and got a gruesome picture in his mind of what was waiting to be found out there. "Because if just *one* of them got away from you, they might potentially give away the secret of you and the Queen's existence."

A short while later, while Buck stood watching as the Sapphire King departed into the woods, Talia appeared on horseback at the end of Buck's long gravel driveway. She made her way up, whistling to get his attention. The white and black spotted horse was once Buck's. He had given it to her to make the long travel easy between his farm and the town of Oliveri.

Buck maneuvered into a better position to greet her.

"Where is he going?" she asked, referring to the King. She wore a wide brimmed cowboy hat and removed it to swat flies.

"He's gone off to see the Queen, my Princess," Buck ceremoniously responded. And he bowed to her, knowing how much she would appreciate it.

The young lady winced. "What's that awful smell?" she asked, looking towards the field.

Sparing Talia the revolting description of whatever spectacle awaited him, Buck simply said "Why, Your Highness, I suspect your King left me a treasure."

Without as much as a slight reaction to what Buck said about a treasure, the young woman took exception to a trivial point. "He is not just *my* King, Mister Baker, he's *your* King, too!"

"Yes, of course, Talia," he replied, sensing no point in arguing.

Buck changed the subject. "My wife used to say, 'Buck, you could sleep through a tornado, even if it ran straight through our living room.'" He approached Talia, and patted the horse on its neck. "I don't know what happened last night—I don't think I *want* to know—but the King was beaten up pretty badly. Did you hear any commotion?"

"Is he okay?"

Buck chuckled. "He'll live."

Talia shook her head. "No, Mister Baker, I'm sorry, I didn't hear anything."

Buck tried to read her face, to see if she was lying. He couldn't tell. "So, what brings you all the way out here to see me?"

Talia put her hat back on. "I came here to tell you what the Queen said."

"Go on."

"She said we would be getting company. I thought it might be..." Her voice trailed off.

"You thought it was the townspeople returning?"

"No," she replied immediately, "I've lost all hope of *that*."

"Then what?"

"I was hoping it was my prince."

Buck looked in the direction of his field, where the smell was coming from. He pictured there, just out of his view, a stack of dead bodies. All the blood he washed off the robot, and all those pieces of flesh; if there was a prince among them still alive, he was sure that man was in no condition to reveal himself.

The bodies would have to be destroyed. If they were Federal Armed Forces, like he suspected, each of them had homing devices implanted under their skin. Burning them was the only way to destroy them completely.

"Go on back home, Your Highness," Buck said, taking her hand and patting the back of it in a fatherly manner. "And when you get back, you keep an eye out for any strangers that might wander into town. You tell the others to keep a watch out, too, you hear?"

Talia nodded. "Should I worry?"

"Never. Now, you go on."

The young woman turned the horse. She kicked her heels in and prompted the animal toward the end of the driveway, but before she got too far she pulled back on the reins and stopped. "Mister Baker..." she called, "you never told me why you stayed?

Why you didn't leave Oliveri with the rest of the town?"

Buck smiled warmly. It was not the first time she had asked him the question. He wondered if she was expecting a different answer this time. His answer was the same. "Somebody had to stay behind and keep a watch over all of you."

And he added under his breath, too low for her to hear, "somebody *normal* that is."

Satisfied, Talia kicked her heels once more and rode out of sight.

CHAPTER EIGHTEEN

"THE ROAD TO OLIVERI"

The billboard read, SUNFLOWER ESTATES. A LUXURY OASIS OFF THE BEATEN PATH, ONE MILE WEST, OFF COUNTY ROAD 6. WHERE DREAMS ARE MADE. Upon it was drawn a picture of what Sunflower estates had to offer, a brick-faced two story colonial style house set back on a manicured property. In the forefront stood a family of four; Dad, Mom, teen-aged daughter and young son. And their trusted pet, a spotted spaniel. The board was overgrown with vines almost completely concealing it, and the picture so very faded from years of neglect that if Hollis hadn't almost walked straight into it he might have just as easily walked right past it.

He looked at it now, thinking of the last thing his uncle had said to him, *you look like a target.*

Until that moment he had been doing what he was told, keeping to the east. But it did not take a man with limited knowledge of military tactics to see that this was not the safest course to take. The further he walked, the less ground cover there was. He might be seen by the enemy; if the enemy was out here somewhere, likely they were watching and waiting for others to forge their way.

One mile west, the sign said. Hollis began to wonder if Sunflower Estates could provide him with an opportunity. If in this so-called luxury oasis he might be able to find a disguise, it was a worthwhile detour.

In a moment, he was heading there.

Sunflower Estates was a displaced loop of deteriorating homes, some in mid construction phase. Nature had reclaimed most of what

Hollis could see here. Where once was a paved road, now weeds grew tall through all the cracks. The onset of the Second Civil War, like it had in most places throughout the country, hindered Sunflower's development. Here, there was not a soul in sight, and there hadn't been anyone here for many many years. Hollis moved through the neighborhood intently, choosing a house that looked the most intact—the one with that lived-in look to it. The mailbox he came upon first at the curb had the number 3, and the name stenciled upon it read: The Johnsons. This house looked the part. He made his way to the front door. No sense in knocking. He placed his hands flat against the thick wooden door and utilizing only a fraction of his Gunlord strength, gave a push. The door broke off its hinges and tipped backwards into the foyer, clapping loudly on the ceramic tiled floor.

He had no intensions of hanging out, but the urge to explore was too hard to resist. The living area to his immediate left was well preserved. The furniture was intact. A sofa. Two recliners. A rustic looking stone fireplace. There was the smell of a wild animal that had taken residence here. The carpet was littered with rat turds. Above the mantle was a framed portrait of The Johnsons. Nothing like the billboard. Mister Johnson was a chubby corporate type, in a three-piece suit that looked two sizes too small, with a head so wide it could fit two faces. Misses Johnson was bone skinny, with so much make-up she looked like a circus clown, and all that jewelry around her neck and dangling from her ears, it must have been a strain to keep her head up. They had only one child, a teen-aged boy who clearly refused to smile when the portrait was taken.

His scowl forever reminding those who came to visit, *I don't want to be a part of this family.*

Hollis looked around some more, just another minute or two. He saw more of the remains of the Johnsons; there were open food containers on the kitchen counter and three place settings on the adjacent dining room table, evidence to conclude that they must have had to leave in a hurry. For a moment Hollis pondered the event that shook them and forever changed their lives.

But enough. It was time to move on. Time to get what he came for.

Hollis ascended the staircase in the area between the living room and dining room. At the top of the landing were three bedrooms to choose from. The master was first door on the right.

Once there, he noticed the king sized bed still had linen, though some animals had made a nest out of it. He went to the closet, opened the bi-fold doors and saw what he had to pick from. There were plenty of clothes still on the hangers and he smiled inwardly. A red cotton flannel. Denim jeans. Perfect. If these were Mister Johnson's, they would fit loosely. Fine by Hollis.

He shed the uniform without hesitation, leaving it as a pile on the floor, and slipped immediately into the civies. There was a mirror behind the bedroom door and he checked himself out. He looked rather like a little boy whose father gave him his clothes to try on.

So what...

At least, he thought, he was no longer one of *them* anymore—no longer a target.

Before he left the room he remembered the rabbit's foot in the chest pocket of the BDU jacket, but when he went to retrieve it, he noticed something, it was hot to the touch. Very strange. He shook it, and sensed something loose inside. It rattled. He crushed it a bit. Not quite the feel of a rabbit's bones, so he pressed his thumbnail into it and managed to pry a piece of it apart. He exposed a tiny circuit board with a blinking green light.

"Good luck, my ass," he muttered.

This was a tracking device... no doubt orchestrated by Radigan himself to reward a man his freedom for risking his life, only to have it taken away in the end. Hollis wasn't mad at the captain for trying. It was an ingenious double-cross. What Hollis was mad at was that he fell for it.

He tossed the device on the bed. In the event they set out to track him, the trail would end right here.

Hollis took a final look at his reflection in the mirror, and then it was time to get back on course. Before he exited the house he checked the refrigerator downstairs for a bottle of water, was unlucky, and then proceeded out the back door.

He was heading east again.

CHAPTER NINETEEN

"POOR BASTARD"

SERGEANT HENNESSEY WAS DEAD.

He had bled out, living only long enough to watch his last sun rise before closing his eyes forever. With dead bodies all around—severed limbs and crushed body parts—Specialist Donohue sat alone, sole survivor in a nest of gore.

He collapsed onto his back and lied there looking up at the clear blue sky above the tree tops. The warm moist air blowing in swept away the sulphuric smell of the gunpowder. Under any other circumstance this would be a nice day, but as it was now, he could barely wrap his mind around the world of shit that had befallen him. There was no understanding it. No reason for it. It simply should not have happened. This was going to take years of therapy to get over. He found humor in that and laughed. But now what? What was he going to do?

Help was not coming. He accepted that. Even a fool such as Captain Radigan would not risk any more of his people. It made sense, then, to try and make it back to camp. Donohue realized he was their only source of intel; the only one left who could tell them what had happened. Besides that, going back was his best chance of surviving. But guilt would not allow him the comfort of that sanctuary. The Captain needed to know what happened first hand, sure, but going back would be an injustice to those who had given their lives. And so... it did not take Donohue long to decide what needed to be done. He would carry on with the mission, he would proceed to Oliveri—crawl on his belly if he had to—and do whatever it took to get power turned on to the radio transmitter.

There was a sound.

Donohue held his breath and listened. Footsteps running through the forest, crackling through the bushes, *getting closer*. He carefully popped his head up, just enough to see what it was. It was a man. He was running across his field of view, but then suddenly the man stopped. The man held still at the edge of the clearing. It was the pile of bodies in the center that drew his attention; so jarring a sight, it would have caused anyone to stop dead in their tracks.

Donohue whistled to get his attention, realizing the fatal mistake he may have just made. He did not want to attract attention to himself. But the coast seemed clear, for now. The figure turned to him, stood frozen a second, and then walked over. Donohue gave him a hand signal to keep low, but the man didn't seem to get it. Long hair sticking out the cap he wore. Face unshaven. And there was even a certain look about him that gave him away. "You're one of the prisoners, aren't you?" Donohue asked as the man stopped in front of him.

There was no change in the man's expression. He simply nodded. "What's your name?"

"Juan Ramirez," the man said, his accent thick. He kept turning back toward the pile of bodies, as if they were calling out his name.

"Are you trying to escape, Ramirez?" A reasonable question.

"Hey, look at me," Donohue insisted, snapping his fingers to get his attention, "do they know what happened here?"

"Wha... what *did* happen here?" Ramirez asked, his voice tremulous.

"What the fuck you *think* happened here—we were attacked!"

"If he knows what happened, hombre, he did not tell me." Ramirez admitted, "your captain made a deal with me. He said he would let me go if I got to the town and…" Turning to the bodies again, his voice trailed off.

Donohue kept snapping his fingers. "Hey, c'mon...focus. Did he expect you to turn power on to the transmitter? You know how to do that?"

Ramirez shrugged.

Donohue winced, irritated. "Of course not." It was then that he noticed something dangling from the upper button of the BDU jacket Ramirez was wearing. It was a rabbit's foot.

"You have to go back." the sniper told Ramirez.

"No. No way. I'm not doing that!" Ramirez exclaimed.

"Shhh. Keep you voice down." Donohue looked around instinctively for the enemy. Still no sign of them. If they were close, they might have heard Ramirez's voice. "Listen to me, what I need you to do is more important."

Ramirez didn't seem to be paying attention. He just could not keep his eyes off that pile of bodies in the clearing.

Donohue got more annoyed. "Hey, weren't you in a gang or something?

Shouldn't you be used to seeing shit like this?" Ramirez replied sullenly, "I stole cars."

Donohue made a face. "Well, this is your chance to redeem yourself. I need you to go back to the camp and tell Captain Radigan that his platoons were attacked by an automated war engine of unknown origin. It wiped us all out with the exception of me, Specialist Donohue, the sniper from First Platoon. Tell the captain that I'm proceeding to Oliveri on my own and that I'm going to get power turned on to that radio tower."

There came a moment of clarity: the absurdity of giving this important task to a stranger—a prisoner, no less! Donohue had to think twice about it. After a moment— and in spite of his reservations—he came to realize he had no choice. "Will you do this?" he asked.

Ramirez nodded confidently.

Donohue added as encouragement, "You might even get a medal when this over."

Ramirez grinned as he turned to leave. He liked the sound of that.

Eager to be a hero, Ramirez hurried back in a full sprint. In no time at all, and a few hundred meters shy of the canyon entrance, he paused to catch his breath. He was hunched over and the rabbit's foot dangled in his face. He kissed it for good luck and stood up straight. The path ahead would lead him directly back to Bravo Company. He was about to proceed when a glimmer of something caught his eye; a reflection perhaps, flashed high upon the canyon ridge.

A second later, a 7.56 mm round from a long range rifle passed through his skull and he was dead. His body tensed and then fell backwards.

Poor bastard.

CHAPTER TWENTY

“THE JUMP”

"I can do this," Hollis said to himself.

He was looking across the chasm, gauging the distance and calculating how much energy it would require for him to get to the other side; how fast he would have to run to leap seventy feet. He opened a closet in his mind and retrieved a memory. Not so long ago, General Cutter tested his skills, measured his strength and speed that classified him as superhuman. It was a joke that spread throughout the ranks of his Gunlord unit— *Cutter's Superhero*—that gained him neither respect nor admiration, only alienation.

Hollis knew he wasn't a superhero. Superheroes never got hurt. They didn't make wrong decisions. They had good luck on their side. No, Hollis reaffirmed…if indeed he was a superhero, he was a failure at it. If he got hit in the face, his nose would bleed. If he tripped while running too fast, he was liable to break some bones. And luck? Well, he had plenty of *bad* luck. His current situation was proof of that.

He stood at the edge of the cliff, confident being out in the open in the civilian clothes he was wearing. What evidence remained of the bridge that had once stretched across this seemingly bottomless pit was little more than ten foot long pieces of metal bars and wooden planks that protruded from the opposite side. It would make a nice landing platform, as long as it sustained the impact of his jump.

Again, he thought about his luck.

A man would have to be crazy to think he could leap across that.

Hollis took a deep breath and walked back from the canyon edge, about a hundred feet, turned and held his focus on the broken extension of the bridge on the other side. His eyes darkened to

Gunlord black, the way they did when he grabbed hold of El Toro and tossed his greasy ass clear across the room and through the door. He could feel the energy surging within him.

Before he took off he wondered what would happen if he didn't make it and he fell. No one would ever know, or to think—or even *care* enough to look for his body down there at the bottom.

Uncle Billy would assume I took his advice and ignored Radigan's orders and went south, to Mexico, to join my father.

With that thought in mind, Hollis knew he had to make it. He just had to. He launched himself like a rocket and built up so much speed in such short a distance that by the time he got to the edge of the precipice he was practically flying.

In the air, he felt a divine assistance in the form of a back draft that increased his propulsion. He was truly a rocket now, and before he realized it—he crash landed. The extended part of the bridge bounced like a springboard. The steel cross slats that made up the structure were easy for him to grab hold of and he clung to them desperately. He thought he had made it safely, but then the slats began to come undone. The rusted bolts snapped and in a millisecond Hollis was plummeting. He managed with one hand to grab hold of a firm piece of metal and hang there with his face pointing downward into the chasm. In that moment he caught sight of something horrible. Down at the bottom were the rotting remains of soldiers; dead men still dressed in their uniforms and lying in a heap. There must have been about twenty of them. And by looks of how rotted their corpses were, they had been down there for a while.

He twisted his body to enable him to reach up. Like a ladder, he climbed the steel slats that were still intact and made it to the top. Once he reached solid ground he collapsed, rolled onto his back and looked up at the clouds, thanking God. He remained there, recovering for several minutes until his breathing turned normal and his eyes became the crystal blue his mother often told him reminded her of an angel.

"You did it," uttered a voice. At first, Hollis thought it was a voice in his head patting him on the back for what he had just done. But then, he heard the clapping.

Someone was applauding him.

Hollis rolled over and turned his head up to see behind him. The voice belonged to a boy, about eight years old, standing a few hundred meters away in the middle of the road beside his bicycle. Astonished that the boy had snuck up on him, Hollis regarded him a moment.

"You look like you could use a drink of water," the boy said in the comfortable tone of a child. He reached into the basket that was attached to the handlebars of his bicycle and retrieved a clear plastic bottle. He held it out to Hollis. Hollis didn't move. He just kept looking at the boy.

The boy was a strange looking young fellow. He wore a full feathered war chief headdress, the kind that Native Americans used to wear. His clothes looked crudely handmade from the skin of some animal, stitched together with thin leathered straps.

Authentic if not for the modern white T-shirt and blue denim shorts Hollis could see underneath.

The boy shrugged and put the bottle back in the basket. "I watched you from over there." The boy pointed toward the woods. "I didn't think you were going to make it—but you did! You're the only one who has ever made it across."

Hollis kept silent. He sat up and regarded the boy a moment longer.

The kid was skinny, but not malnourished, with dark eyes and long hair in a pony tail tucked under the headdress. Not a feral kid, that is, he looked clean, the kind of kid that had been cared for by someone. In his travels, Hollis had seen so many kids who grew up in war torn cities, living in the rubble, who looked in far worse shape. Based on that reasoning, he knew this boy was not alone here, that there had to be others among him.

"What's your name, kid?"

The boy stood his body straight and declared, "My Apache warrior name is *Bodoway*." And then he relaxed his body and added, "But my real name is Daryl

Raynor. It was my birthday yesterday."

Hollis began walking down the road, in the direction of town. "Happy Birthday, Daryl Raynor."

"I'm nine years old!"

Daryl turned his bicycle and hurried to catch up to Hollis. Walking his bicycle beside him, he said, "The Princess has been waiting for you."

Bemused, Hollis said, "Oh, she has... has she?"

"She'll be glad you made it—*everyone* will be!"

Hollis laughed. Glad? Doubtful. Surprised? Oh, yes, most definitely.

These people he saw in the satellite photo, the supposed enemy of Bravo Company... was Daryl one of their offspring?

Hollis would soon find out.

In a mock authoritative tone, Hollis said. "Take me to your leader." Daryl's brow furrowed deeply. He didn't get the joke.

CHAPTER TWENTY-ONE

"NO ONE GETS OUT ALIVE"

The only piece of furniture in the former command post was the field table, with the radio still on it, and a broken chair—the chair that Captain Radigan had thrown in a fit of rage after witnessing the attack on First Platoon. Specialist Chang was there alone, getting ready to dismantle the radio He was in charge of setting up the equipment in the newly relocated tactical command post in the library inside the school. He was underneath the table labeling the wires for an easy set up when a sputter came from the speaker. For the last half hour the only sound coming from the com was a ghostly hiss. Now a voice was calling out and he bumped his head on the under side of the table when he sat up in reaction.

"Bravo....are you there? This is Charlie, do you read?"

Chang knew the voice. It was Corporal Hargrove. The First Sergeant had told him to expect his call.

Ten meters downhill from the old CP was another tent, the First Sergeant's quarters. Inside Fitz was shaving. He had fastened a mirror to the center tent pole and hung his helmet filled with water from a hook just below it. With his face half covered in shaving cream he was about to make his first scrape across his chin when the irritating sound of someone snoring erupted behind him. He turned slowly to the source. Sergeant Percy was lying on his bunk, a motor pool training manual across his chest and his mouth open on his pillow. Fitz shook his head and went back to shaving. He couldn't blame Percy. In light of all that had happened in the last few hours, at least someone was able to get their much needed shut-eye.

Fitz thought of First and Fourth Platoons, torturing himself with images in his head of their senseless demise. As tough as he was, he fought back tears, considering that by now, if any one of them were still alive they would have made it back to camp, half dead or otherwise.

Out of the corner of his eye he caught a glimpse and turned. Chang appeared in the open flap of his tent. The specialist was out of breath from running.

"What is it?" Fitz asked him.

"You told me to get you when I heard from Hargrove," Chang said, panting.

Percy choked on his spit as he awoke and sat up. The training manual fell onto the floor. "No!" he exclaimed and wiped the tiredness from his eyes. "It couldn't be Hargrove," he went on and looked at Fitz perplexed. "Those guys could not be out of Dark Alley so soon, Top. I gave them specific orders to stay off the radio until they were clear of the Uri Etzel Belt!"

Chang affirmed, "It *was* Hargrove, sarge, I'm sure of it. He said something about a…a *blockade*."

First Sergeant Fitz was still wiping the shaving cream off his face when he charged into the old CP. Percy and Chang were a mere step behind him. As they entered a voice was transmitting from the radio speaker: "Bravo, this is Charlie, do you read?

Over."

Fitz grabbed the radio mic and spoke into it, "This is Bravo, go ahead Charlie. Over."

"Thank Christ...Bravo, I've got some bad news." There was a pause.

"Just tell me!" Fitz fired back, frustrated.

"There's a line of trees blocking the road. Definitely put there on purpose, Top. It seems someone doesn't want us to leave. How copy?"

"I read you, Charlie. Any way you can get around it?"

The reply Fitz did not wish to hear: "That's a negative. Over."

Fitz had not noticed the interference coming over the transmission. At first it just sounded like Hargrove was clicking his microphone. It was in the background and faint, but then the sound got progressively louder. It struck Chang, who'd been trained to notice such things, what the sound might be.

"Uh...Top?" Chang attempted to point out.

Fitz put up his hand to keep Chang quiet. He continued to communicate with Hargrove. "Roger that, Charlie. I'll get the map and see if I can re-route you. There's got to be some other way to the Interstate. Stand by."

"Copy that."

The clicking sound was so loud now Fitz couldn't ignore it. He turned to Chang and asked, "What's that noise?"

"What I tried to tell you, Top," Chang said, "that click sounds like one of those old digital correlators, used to acquire navigation and clock knowledge."

"I don't understand?"

"Top, do me a favor, key the mike and hold it a couple of seconds..."

Fitz depressed the button on the microphone and then released it. The strange clicking sound started again.

"An independently operating receiver can enhance a signal and measure data with another transmitting device. It's called collaborative signal processing."

"In English, Chang?"

"I think someone's trying to pinpoint our location."

Fitz's face turned ghostly white. He shouted into the mic, "Charlie, return to base! I repeat, return to base!" Without waiting for a reply, and with careless speed, he reached behind the radio and yanked the wires out of the back panel. There were sparks. The radio went dead. Fitz exhaled a long breath. He looked over at the other two men who had stepped back. Sure, it was a reckless reaction—Fitz knew that—but he felt justified in doing it. He only hoped he wasn't too late.

Corporal Hargrove's description of the roadblock was grossly understated. It had been constructed with precise engineering in mind; the trees, all identical in length and thickness, were stacked orderly. A cliff wall on one side and a steep incline on the other made it seemingly impassable.

While Hargrove was speaking to Fitz, Corporal Clemmons

took a moment to exit the Skip and investigate the incline side of the blockade. He thought the Skip might be able to maneuver around it, provided the incline wasn't too steep.

"Hey, Clem!" Hargrove shouted from the back of the vehicle, "Top wants us to head back to camp."

Clemmons heard him, but was focused on his task. He stood at the side of the road looking down. The terrain sloped far below the level of the road. A few hundred feet at least. A long way down if the Skip rolled. Trees were scattered apart. Trunks that were visible gave clue as to where the makers of the roadblock had gotten their stock.

But there was something else down there, and it made Clemmons' mouth suddenly dry. A wrecked vehicle. By the looks of it, a military supply truck. Stenciled on the door were the words: 36th SIGNAL CORPS. It figured, he thought, and squinted his eyes to see something more. Wrapped around the steering wheel he could make out the hands of a rotting corpse in a decayed uniform.

"What do you see down there?" Hargrove asked. Clemmons turned to him. "Nothing good."

"Well, get you ass back behind the wheel. We're turning around."

Clemmons shook his head dejectedly and started back. He hated the notion of having failed his comrades. "I still think we might be able to go around... if I drive carefully."

"Forget it, Clem," Hargrove argued. "Top must have his reasons for sending us back. Besides—goddamn... if we rolled, it would be a long... long walk back."

Clemmons climbed back into the Skip. "I guess you're right." He started the engine and shifted the Skip into gear.

They turned around.

After about a half mile, just as they were rounding the next bend in the road, Clemmons saw something and slammed on the brakes again. Hargrove was thrust forward. The wires were yanked from their connections at the front of the radio because

Hargrove was still holding onto the microphone when he landed on the floor next to the driver's seat. "Jesus Christ, Clem, what the fuck!" As he began to recover he noticed the look of terror on Clemmons' face. When finally he managed to sit up, he was able to see for himself what Clemmons was looking at.

It was the Sapphire King.

The robot was blocking the road ahead.

It stood like a linebacker with its arms outstretched and claws open and ready to crush anyone who dared to pass. The focal point of this mechanized fiend—amidst all the steel and mechanics—was its eye and the glowing blue ring around it. It looked alive.

Clemmons' trembling hands had a white-knuckled death grip around the steering wheel. He was breathing erratically. There was clearance on both sides of the war machine, plenty of space for the Skip to drive around, but he hesitated to give the vehicle gas to make the attempt. Hargrove was looking at Clemmons trying to figure out what his problem was. Clemmons would have tried to explain to him that this robot had just decimated two entire platoons and should not be underestimated. It wasn't worth the risk.

Clemmons threw the shifter in reverse and hit the gas. All four tires spun and tore up the road. As the vehicle drove backwards it left a thick black smoke screen of burning rubber that completely engulfed the robot.

Hargrove needed no instruction. He got to his feet and mounted the machine gun. He pulled the locking pin free from the mount and pivoted the weapon in the direction of the robot. But there was no target, not yet. All he could see was the dark cloud. So he fired anyway. He fired into it. And he could hear the rounds hitting metal within in that dark cloud.

Clemmons slowed the vehicle down and shifted into drive. He spun the Skip around and sped off at top speed, as far away from the robot as possible. Hargrove kept firing, but the bouncing vehicle made it hard for him to keep a lock on his target.

But again, their journey came to an abrupt end. In no time at all, they were back at the wall of trees stacked across the road with no where else to go.

Apart from the deep sound of the Skip's idling engine they could hear the robot coming...

Tchwonk... Tchwonk.... Tchwonk...

And they could feel the earth trembling beneath them.

"What do we do now?" Hargrove hastened to ask. "It must know we're trapped."

They had done their best until this moment to be careful, but now... it was time to do something desperate.

"Grab hold of something, Hargrove," Clemmons instructed him, "and hang on like your life depends on it!"

"What are you going to do?"

Clemmons did not answer. His actions spoke louder than words. He crushed the gas pedal to the floor and drove the Skip to the right of the blockade—straight toward the incline.

Hargrove looked back. Unbeknownst to him...

The Sapphire King processed their intentions.

Calculated their chances of success.

And then ran to intercept them.

The Skip started down the steep incline. Hargrove shifted his weight to the left. The ground was sandy and the vehicle's wide rugged wheels spun, failing to achieve a proper grip.

The danger was closing in on them fast.

When the robot started down the incline after them it appeared to lose its balance upon the loose ground. It maneuvered unsteadily, but was persistent.

Hargrove prayed for it to lose its footing all together and tumble down the incline.

The Skip had gone farther than the remains of the supply truck from the 36th Signal Corps, but was still a distance from safety. The ground turned from sandy to rocky and it gained an advantage. The distance between it and the robot increased significantly. Clemmons showed no mercy on the gas pedal, and he would not relent until the robot was no more than a mere speck to see in his rear view mirror.

Hargrove gave the war machine the middle finger.

The robot stopped all of a sudden, seemingly astonished. It just stood there with its iron feet planted firmly in the sand.

"What's it doing?" Clemmons asked. Hargrove shrugged. "It just stopped!"

"What changed its mind?"

Hargrove gave it some thought, and made light of it. "If I'd known all I had to do was give it the finger..."

They cleared the blockade on the street above them and started upwards to return to hard ground. Once the wheels touched pavement, the Skip sped off down the center of the road, leaving the robot far behind.

"I think we're safe, Hargrove!" Clemmons bellowed. But he was wrong.

The moment their movement was detected on the open road, their fate was sealed.

From its distance, now almost a mile away, the Sapphire King watched as the vehicle drove away.

And it watched as the rocket came down from out of the sky and blew the vehicle to bits.

Clemmons and Hargrove never knew what hit them. They were spared the horror.

CHAPTER TWENTY-TWO

“The Princess”

A distant rumble echoed faintly across the sky. "What's the matter, Hollis?" Daryl asked.

Hollis and the boy had been walking side by side on the road leading to Oliveri when Hollis heard it. He stopped short to give a listen. "Did you hear that?" he asked.

The boy shrugged. "It was probably thunder," he responded, and he said it so matter-of-factly it struck Hollis as odd.

Hollis stared at him. Daryl obviously did not know the difference between a build up of an electric field in the clouds and combat munitions, or in this case artillery. He thought about his uncle then, still being held in Radigan's dungeon and hoped everything was all right.

"It thunders a lot around here," the boy added.

And Hollis responded delusively, "Yeah... I'll bet it does." They moved on.

As they came over the top of the hill they were presented with a wide view of the town below. The place reminded him of home; it even had the same layout of the streets as Hidden Pond. From this vantage point Hollis could see almost all of the buildings. The tallest was supposed to have the transmitting tower on its roof. He didn't see it. Concern began to dwell within him.

Oliveri was a tiny town consisting of perhaps a half dozen traffic lights; each still directing traffic although there were no cars. The streets were empty. The sidewalks deserted. The stores all darkened and closed. All the signs of a town devoid of life. But these signs were false. There were people here, somewhere. Maybe they were hiding!

Or maybe they were gathered in an assembly! Then again, they could very well be taking positions at this very moment on rooftops with their rifles. The latter would have been of no surprise to Hollis. There was good reason for the town to be on alert, a stranger was suddenly in their midst and walking straight down the middle of their main street.

"Don't shoot, I'm not armed," Hollis muttered.

"What did you say?" Daryl asked.

"Nothing. I was just thinking out loud."

Plenty of shops lined the wide street; thick crud caked their windows making it hard to see inside them. And still, not another living soul in sight. The streets and all the buildings were empty. And the only sound was the subtle hiss of the wind blowing and the steady tap of their footsteps on the pavement as they walked.

A banner stretched across the street read: 75th *HARVEST FESTIVAL CELEBRATION.* It was peppered with holes and hanging on by a thread.

There was more of a familiar feeling that gave Hollis thought to his home town. It was not just the absence of life and energy here that had been sucked out, like in Hidden Pond, but something more vital, hope, and that was something a town could not easily recover from.

The farther they walked down Main Street, the more damage Hollis began to notice on the buildings. Perfectly round holes in the plate glass. Signs above the entrances to stores were shattered. So many pieces chipped away on the surface of the concrete facades. And he thought back to the banner, and realized those were not ordinary holes from wear, no, they were holes made from gunfire. Just a few steps more and he came to the nearest cross street and looked down and saw what looked like the scene of a battle; a light armored military utility vehicle lay on its side and was badly burned, and another one farther back was crushed flat to the street, as if it had been run over by a steam roller. No bodies however. But personnel equipment was scattered about; a soldier's helmet, a boot, someone's utility belt. The road was stained red. So much blood. Too much. A lot of men had died here. This was the scene of a massacre. Hollis turned and gave Daryl a peculiar look. He may have been mistaken about the boy; perhaps Daryl *did* know the difference between thunder and artillery.

"Let's go, Hollis..." the boy beckoned. "C'mon!"

Hollis was about to ask Daryl to describe what had happened here, but then he realized... none of it really mattered, none of this was any of his business. He had not come to Oliveri to conduct an investigation. No. Not at all. He came here to get a job done.

First things first, make peace with the natives.

"I'll be right behind you, kid," Hollis muttered and didn't look back as he proceeded toward the next intersection, the center of town.

It seemed that Daryl was trying to lose him suddenly. The boy ran ahead.

And it was obvious when the boy disappeared around the next corner. Hollis was meant to be lost.

Hollis paused at the next block to ready himself. He knew what was coming. He could see glimpses of it from this angle. Around the corner was a courtyard. When Hollis took a few steps, he saw it clearly. Designed to gather everyone in town to one central location, this park-like setting was perfectly situated. The grass was a little too high and the bushes and trees much too overgrown in spots due to a lack of maintenance, and the playground features were brown from rust, but the courtyard's overall state was intact. There was a statue of a Native American war chief in a full feathered headdress; perhaps Daryl's inspiration. Deeper in was an old degraded wooden grandstand. There chairs on the grandstand. Hollis counted nine of them. The one in the center had an unusually tall back to it; upon it sat a young woman wearing an emerald colored satin conic headdress, like the ones worn by people in medieval times, with a matching gown that shimmered in the midday sunlight as she crossed her legs. On each side of her were two older looking women in peasant garb, also from that ancient period. There was a lot to take in all at once and Hollis stood stoically, absorbing it. Daryl, who had cut through the tall grass and weeds, gained access to the grandstand and approach the young woman in the emerald colored gown. He whispered something into her ear. She had not noticed Hollis yet.

Hollis waited for it...

The woman put on a look of disbelief as her eyes began to search. Daryl pointed to where Hollis was standing and her eyes fell upon him. It took her only a second. Once the realization of Hollis entered her sights, she drew a surprised expression. Excited, she leapt to her feet. Someone nearby her gasped at the sight of him. But nobody appeared alarmed. That put Hollis at ease. They all rose to their feet. The young woman waved to Hollis, to get him to come closer. He did as she asked, and she started down the stairs of the grandstand to meet him halfway. She had to adjust the fit of her gown, and raise it slightly so the ends did not drag through the weeds as she walked. Before the two of them got face to face, the woman paused and planted her hands firmly on her hips and held her head high, as if to pose regally. Hollis noticed that burrs and sticky seeds from the weeds clung to the satin fabric. The woman pursed her lips and stared at him a long while. He could only guess what she was thinking.

"I am the princess..." she announced so eloquently. "And you... Daryl says, must be none other than the prince?"

Hollis had not expected that and didn't quite know how to respond. "It's a simple question,...well...are you?"

A grumpy looking woman in peasant clothing came between them. "Look at his clothes, Your Highness," she pointed out, "would a prince wear rags such as these?" She tugged on the loose pieces of his flannel shirt that had been torn when he jumped across the crevice.

"Now, Stella, let's not be rude."

"I watched him fly!" Daryl exclaimed and was suddenly abashed by the reaction of the others.

"True. He did make it across the bridge," Talia remarked. "What does *that* prove?" the grumpy looking woman retorted.

"No one else ever did that," the young woman cited and took a step closer to Hollis. "Say something prince-like?"

Hollis realized he was being surrounded. The others that had joined her were creating a circle around him. The only one who stood a threat was the big long-haired one who was twice Hollis' size and about a foot taller, but none of them really made him nervous. Being aware of them was wary enough.

"I was told there's a communications tower mounted to the roof of one of the buildings here," Hollis began to say. "Can you take me to it?"

"No," Talia said curtly and took her hands off her hips. Hollis was taken aback.

She repeated, "No," and turning to the others, added, "that doesn't sound prince-like at all to me."

The grumpy woman shook her finger at Hollis. "I told you—he's an imposter."

Talia looked apologetically at Daryl. "My little warrior, don't look so sad."

"Listen," Hollis said, taking a step backwards. "I don't know what's going on here...this...made for a High School play act you're all putting on..." He had seen behavior like this, knew it all too well in the town he grew up in; people living in isolation, cut off from the rest of the world, this is what tends to happen. "Or maybe you're all just *crazy*?"

That struck a chord and Talia immediately turned and broke away from the group. She forcefully removed her conic headdress and tossed it to the ground. She even looked like she was about to stomp on it.

"Your Highness—no!" the grumpy woman pleaded. She shot Hollis a scathing look.

"He's right, this is silly," Talia remarked sullenly.

Hollis was given harsh looks by all those gathered around him. Then came the sudden realization that, as usual, his mouth popped off half-cocked and made a bloody mess of an already messy situation. He swallowed hard and cleared his throat. A wish he could start over. "Listen," he said, his voice softer, "I didn't come here to cause trouble...I came here, because I'm *in* trouble."

For awhile no one said a word. The only one who gave him hope for forgiveness was Daryl.

"I'll take you," the young woman said. Hollis was not sure he heard her right.

She refused to make eye contact. She spoke into the wind. "You want me to show you where the radio tower is? Fine. I'll take you. Follow me."

"Thank you," said Hollis.

Then she turned to him, her eyes welling with tears. "Don't thank me yet."

CHAPTER TWENTY-THREE

"MISSILE CRISIS"

First Sergeant Fitz stood with Sergeant Percy on the roof of the school. They could see for miles over the treetops, and to what was happening in the distant horizon. The technology provided by the *Hawkeye* binoculars enabled Fitz to see the grim details.

Smoke was rising far away and even without the equipment he could clearly see the white contrail in the sky left behind by the missile, to the point of impact. His heart sank and he felt his hands loosen their grip on the binoculars.

"Jesus Christ... what have I done?" he muttered.

He overcame his sorrow, and with a swell of anger building up in its place his grip on the binoculars suddenly increased. If he had the strength, he would have crushed it to pieces.

"Do you think they survived?" Percy asked. Fitz passed him the binoculars in silence.

He thought about the red gun engine lying on that rock ledge, waiting there. If a good reason was needed to try and take her out, this was it. He stepped away from the roof ledge and moved toward the roof hatch to climb down to ground level. He paused. "Where's the captain?" he asked.

Percy was looking through the binoculars now. "Last I saw him, he was over by the entrance to the canyon, watching over some project he's got the men working on by that pit you told them to dig." He lowered the binoculars and turned to Fitz. "Are you going to tell him the truth, Top?"

The truth. Fitz had to think about that. "You mean, that I just sent two of his soldiers to their deaths without his authorization?"

Percy shook his head. "I mean, that we've been beaten. The truth is, Top, there's nothing left for us to do here but *retreat*. There's enough room in the rest of the vehicles to carry all of us, and the prisoners too. We should just get the fuck out of here!"

Fitz sighed. His expression was a clear indication that he did not agree. "First of all, Percy, if I mention the word retreat to Captain Radigan, in the mood he's been in, he's liable to put a bullet in my head." He paused a second to let that image get a firm seat in Percy's mind. "And second, hitting the open road may be exactly what our enemy is hoping for... if they want to wipe us out, that is. As long as we sit tight or don't get too close to their secret, we stand a chance of surviving."

"How do you figure?"

"Take a look around. See what I see."

Percy obliged him, but was unsure what he was supposed to see.

"This entire camp is practically surrounded by that rock wall. We're saddled in pretty tight. It seems obvious, at least to me, that our enemy doesn't know where we are. That's why there aren't any missiles flying in *this* direction."

"So what do we do, Top?" Percy asked. He turned away, disgusted. "Do we start praying for a miracle to happen? Do we wait for our enemy to grant us the mercy of surrendering?" And then he shouted, "Or are we just going to keep sitting on our fucking hands until help arrives?"

"No," Fitz snapped. He exhaled deeply, and as he opened the hatch and started down he remarked, "I'm *done* sitting on my fucking hands."

Captain Radigan had a way of standing out in a crowd. His stance was that of someone about to accept a medal, with his fists at his sides and his head held high; he kept everyone lower than he was. First Sergeant Fitz predicted it would be the end of him someday; that an enemy sharpshooter in combat would easily see him as the leader and take him out. Though he may have been doing his commander a favor, Fitz offered no words of caution in that matter.

Before approaching Radigan, Fitz locked his eyes on the assembly of men inside the pit. They were digging. They looked quite exhausted and in desperate need of a rest. The pit was five times larger, and deeper, than the dimensions he originally set.

No wonder they all looked ready to collapse. It would take a fireman's extension ladder for them to climb out. If the enemy were to suddenly charge in Fitz had his doubts that a single one of those soldiers could duck for cover, let alone raise their arms to fire their rifles. When one of them eyed him, they seemed to check where the Captain was to keep from being detected. They could see the anger in Fitz's expression.

"Ahhh, First Sergeant..." Radigan called out to him. The captain's voice sounded so at ease it was disturbing. "You're just in time for me to show you what's been going on here!"

Fitz ignored the greeting. His focus was on his men. "Captain, when's the last time any of these men have had some down time?"

Radigan casually glanced at them. "This is Bravo Company. Hardcore, to the last, dammit!" He sounded proud of them, but in that see-thru, obnoxious sort of way that proved he possessed no good will nor true feelings for them in any regard.

Fitz was at a loss for words, but not for actions; he made a fist and was prepared to knock the Captain off his pedestal and put him right into that pit and order the men to use their last ounce of strength to bury the sorry fucker in it.

"I want to show you something," the Captain said and pointed upwards at the top of the canyon. "See those men up there?"

Fitz relaxed his fist and looked up. It was difficult to take his eyes off his suffering men. What he saw up there on the canyon ledge, fifty meters high, were soldiers handling blocks of C4 explosives, wiring them and putting them into position. It was hard to see from his angle, but they looked like they were planting the C4 into the ground.

"I'm setting a trap," Radigan explained. Radigan had Fitz's full attention now.

"Those men are planting C4 along the top edge of the canyon wall. When they're done digging this pit I'm going to conceal the top of it, use a tarp and cover it with a thin layer of sand, so no one will even know it's there. You following me?"

"So far," Fitz replied.

"Now, when everything is wired and set to go, I'll send a team to seek out that gun engine and draw it back here. I'm leaving enough room on one side of the pit so the team can get safely back to our side. When that robot steps through the tarp and drops into that pit I'll signal our men to detonate the C4 and bring a thousand tons of rock down upon that son of a bitch's steel head. And after that, we're going to march full force into Oliveri and obliterate anything that moves."

Fitz made an agreeable gesture, in spite of his feelings for Radigan at that moment, there was a reasonable chance this trap might actually work. The Captain was not such a useless idiot after all.

But still...

"What ever happened to you plan to send our guys into Oliveri after the prisoners were sent east?" the First Sergeant asked.

Radigan shrugged insensibly. "That didn't work out as well as I'd planned." He seemed abashed, which was out of character. "It was a good call, Fitz, using the rabbit's foot with a tracking device."

Fitz admitted, "So we could re-capture them when this whole shit was over."

"Yeah, well...seems we were able to see that the prisoners were either taking off in their own directions, trying to escape, or turning back around—spooked by something, I suppose."

Fitz made a curious face. "What did they have to say?"

"Who?"

"The prisoners, sir... the ones who turned back around; what intel did they have to share?"

Radigan looked at Fitz like he had to be nuts to even ask the question. "I couldn't risk them coming back here and exposing this trap. Can you imagine if that robot followed any one of them back here before I was finished?" His burst of laughter was unrefined. "No. No Way. I positioned snipers in the cliffs on the other side of the canyon and had them monitor the movement of the prisoners, using the rabbit's foot to track them. Before the prisoners got too close, I ordered the snipers to take them out."

"You did *what*, sir?" Fitz's eyes widened.

Radigan had no emotion about it at all. "You heard me, " he said, "I had our snipers drop them in their tracks."

Fitz shook his head in disbelief and disgust. The thought of it made him almost lose his footing.

"Don't forget who they were, First Sergeant?" Fitz spat out, "*People*?"

Radigan looked bewildered, and then angry. "Thieves. Rapists. Murderers. *That's* what they were!" he stormed up to Fitz and got right in his face. "Do we have a problem with that, First Sergeant?"

Fits didn't back down. He never did and never would. The two men stood nose to nose. Fitz replied, "You're damn right we have a problem, sir."

"Well—then spit it out!" the Captain roared.

Fitz grit his teeth. "Did you see that missile in the sky about an hour ago?"

Radigan took a step back. "I did. If it was meant for us it was way off target." He turned his back on Fitz and continued to step off.

"The next one may not be."

Radigan approached the pit and faced men digging down in it. He was suddenly more concerned with them than anything of worth coming out of Fitz's mouth. "I can smell a plan in your head like a bad fart, First Sergeant."

Fitz was not amused. "I want to assemble a team—five men, one of them a demolitions expert—and go to where that red robot is and disable that rocket launcher; eliminate the threat."

Radigan gave the First Sergeant a look. "Two platoons armed with everything we had already went up against one of those robots, what chance does a team of *five* have?"

"Her location is known. From what we saw from the satellite photos, she's immobile. There's an advantage there. We can sneak up on her."

Radigan snickered contemptuously. "She's pretty far away."

"Twenty or so miles, I figure."

"I suppose this team is going to take a vehicle?"

Fitz shook his head. "Movement out in the open is too risky. We'll have to go on foot, which is going to take considerable time." He had already calculated it. "It's going to be dark soon. To limit the chance of us getting lost, we'll leave at first light.

With any luck, we should reach the red robot by sundown tomorrow."

"You said *we*?"

Fitz affirmed, "I'm leading the team."

"I should have guessed." The commander put his hands on his hips; that pose of superiority. "All right, First Sergeant," he declared officially, "you have my permission. Assemble your team. Go and do whatever you think you can."

Fitz saluted and turned to walk away.

"This trap will be ready early tomorrow!" the Captain called out to him. Fitz gave him a mild regard with a glance over his shoulder.

"When you come back we'll celebrate our victories!" Fitz started walking away.

"And after that, we'll go into Oliveri, full force..." Fitz kept on walking and did not look back.

"And we'll kill every last one of them!"

Fucking lunatic, Fitz thought.

CHAPTER TWENTY-FOUR

"A WASTED EFFORT"

"You never told me your name?" the Princess asked.

She and Hollis were walking side by side. They had turned off Main Street and were heading down an Oliveri side street, toward a part of town that was seemingly more deteriorated, further unlived.

"My name's Hollis," he said.

"*Prince Hollis* everyone!" Talia shouted, calling attention to herself, but it was only the two of them. She even held out her arms as if to present his Highness. Hollis appeared shocked. She quickly nudged him in the rib with her elbow. "Just kidding. Really, Hollis, you should lighten up. I was only playing. That's what we do here, to pass the time—we play! Haven't you ever played before? Don't they play where you from?"

Hollis smirked and supposed she was right. Making an attempt, he said, "I'm from Kansas. A small town like this one called, Hidden Pond."

"I gather it's not a very *fun* place."

"It's a lot like this place. Oliveri and my home town have a lot in common, actually. For one, it's isolated. Cut off from the rest of the world, which I've found, sometimes, to be a good thing." He changed the subject. "How many of you still live here?"

"You met most of them. Twelve of us, all together. We call ourselves *The Orphans*." As she walked her long gown made swishing sounds and the shoes that were hidden underneath tapped rhythmically on the concrete sidewalk.

She was pleasant to watch. Confident and positive. The waves of her long red hair bounced on her shoulders whenever she turned to look at him, and he encouraged her every chance he got. Even the soft features of her face were a visual delight. But he would describe her to his uncle as very child-like, almost *too* much like a child. There was an unmistakable craziness in her eyes; something amiss Hollis could not quite put his finger on—or wholly trust. But all that aside, she filled him with a sexual temptation to want to touch her. He fought his young male urge and vowed to keep his distance from her. He was here on business.

Hollis asked, "Why didn't you and the others leave when the town was evacuated? Why did you choose to stay?"

He could not be sure if he was being mocked, but she positioned her head to look up and perhaps roll her eyes. "We did not *choose* to stay, Hollis." She slowed down and eventually stopped. She moved off to the side and at a corner flower shop she leaned back against the brick with her arms tucked behind her. "We were left."

Before he asked, he tried to come up with a single reason why twelve people would be left behind. Were any of them essential personnel, vital to keeping the town functioning until the residents returned? He was thinking militarily. He doubted it though. And what about the soldiers, the ones that had been here—what functions did these Orphans provide for them?

Before he realized he was dwelling on it too long, he came to notice something. He asked, "Why have we stopped?"

"You asked me to take you to where the radio tower is... "I did."

Hollis' impulse was to look up, but he noticed Talia was directing him to look down. There was a nearby alley. He took a step in that direction and stood frozen at the entrance to the long darkened passageway between the buildings. What he saw was the tower. Yes, the tower. It was here all right, lying on the pavement, looking like a giant steel anaconda with its head propped up against a trash dumpster at the far end.

For a moment he was in a state of shock and disbelief. Anger hastened as he began to accept the realization of it. His eyes turned black. He blinked them shut and turned from Talia, conscious of her presence and an his unwillingness to reveal the otherwise inhuman transformation. He tried to fight it, but his rage often made him lose control. He was a volatile mess. "It fell?" he asked in low muffled tone, unsure if she had heard him or even if he had said the words out loud.

"No, Hollis," she answered without much emotion, "it did not fall."

He took a breath for the first time, looked at her bewildered. His eyes were back to normal. "What happened to it?"

She told him, "It was *taken* down... on purpose."

Hollis' brow furrowed. "What purpose did *that* serve?"

Talia shrugged. "You would have to ask him," she replied. "Ask who?"

"The Sapphire King."

Hollis was not a genius, but the elementary portion of his brain fit the pieces of the puzzle together quite quickly. "You mean... that *robot*?!"

Talia's suggestive smirk was the answer to that question.

Hollis thought of his uncle, stuck in that piss smelling fallout shelter in the old school. He considered having to break him out, now that there was no way Captain Radigan—who lacked human compassion—would allow him to go free as a reward for trying.

"What are you thinking about?" Talia asked.

He turned to her, his eyes and his mind so far away she'd have to scream from the top of her lungs for her to reach him.

Why would the robot do that? It was getting difficult to make sense of anything in this town. Getting a straight answer from Talia was difficult so far, about in line with trying to pull a rotten tooth from a tiger's mouth.

He said something he knew she would not understand, but thinking of all the soldiers of Bravo Company back at the camp he remarked, "A thousand pairs of willing hands, and still there's no way this thing could ever be stood back up again."

Talia responded, "All the King's horses, and all the King's men..."

"What's that?" Hollis asked.

"Humpty Dumpty," she said, and giggled.

Hollis looked at her as if she was crazy. And maybe she was.

A church bell rang out. It echoed through the vacant streets, so close it sounded to Hollis like it was right on top of them. He looked at Talia, whose subtle reaction struck him as strange. She cupped her hand over her mouth to conceal her laughter.

"It's supper time," she announced. "Come." She took his hand and he was pleased with the warmth of it and went along willingly.

The bell rang again. Hollis stopped.

"He's going to be excited to meet you," Talia told him, gently pulling on Hollis' arm. "We don't want to be late." Hollis was aloof for a second, with a significant part of his mind still preoccupied with the downed radio tower and his lack of options. "Be excited? Who will be?" he asked.

She answered, "The Sapphire King, silly!"

When that registered, he planted his feet firmly. He was not going anywhere and must have felt to her as unmovable as an oak tree. "What's the matter?" she asked.

Hollis' face had hardened. "I have to get out of here." He looked nearby for an escape route.

She must have read his expression and said to him, "No, Hollis, you must not run. If you run, he'll catch up to you. He always does. And if you try to hide, he'll find you... and when he does, he will be mad and punish you."

Hollis fought the urge to go Gunlord transformation. Talia must have felt the trembling in his hand.

"Hollis," she said pleadingly, surely understanding his hesitance, "the Sapphire King will not hurt you as long as you're with me. I promise. Just think, he has no *reason* to hurt you—no reason at all!"

Hollis looked her. Reason? He could think of a few reasons. Besides that, what good reason did a robot programmed to kill really need?

He had to make a decision, in spite of his instincts to flee.

The church was a block off main, across from the Oliveri cemetery. Nothing exceptionally unique about it. It was small. Centuries old. With four windows on each side made of stained glass panels depicting images of biblical events, like the crucifixion of Christ and the resurrection. Out in the center of the street, basking in the shade of broad oak trees that lined both sides of the road, was a fifty foot long wooden banquet table covered in linen. It was here the remainder of the Orphans were gathered. When Hollis arrived with Talia, places were being set for eleven; each of the Orphans Talia had told him there were, plus one, a surprised guest. Around the table were so many chairs, too many for all those expected to come; after a quick count, it seemed there were enough extra seats to accommodate a platoon. With that in mind, he began to picture the men and woman of the 36th Signal Corps being seated here and ready for chow.

A plump African American woman in the pure white tresses of a nurse's uniform stood off to the side, stirring a large pot at a nearby serving table. She was assisted by another young lady in a medieval peasant dress, who was collecting silverware to be placed on the banquet table. Another woman in similar clothes went around filling glasses with water from a pitcher.

The dark skinned nurse made a surprised gesture upon seeing Hollis. "Sooo," she exclaimed, "you must be the Prince!" She hurried over, wiping her hands on a towel she had tucked in the white belt at her waist. She poked a finger at Talia. "Oh, honey, he *is* cute."

Pleased with that, Talia remarked, "Oh, so someone told you about him?" She tossed a look of accusation to the woman in the peasant dress who went about placing the silverware on the table and pretended not to have heard her.

"My name is, Misses Jackson," the nurse said, and she gave Hollis a big old bear hug that nearly lifted him off his feet. She released him and he stumbled back, abashed.

"I'm Hollis," he said, recovering.

"Well, sweetie, you call me *Momma*, everybody here does. You hungry, boy?" She did not wait for an answer. Heading back towards the table, she said, "Because, sweetie, we got a stew here that will make a starving man thank the Good Lord above." She laughed whole heartedly and went back to stirring the pot.

Hollis was not exactly sure what to make of her, but he appreciated the pleasantry and smiled. Indeed he was hungry, and the smell of the food? Well, it sure did make his mouth water.

Movement toward the side of the street drew his attention and he witnessed something strange. A woman was dancing. She must have been in her early sixties. Her hair was white and tied in a bun. She wore a white gown, the kind one might wear at a formal, and it hung loosely on her thin frame. But none of that was the strange part. She twirled around and around, and she bounced and changed direction suddenly as if someone were leading her, yet her arms were positioned to an imaginary partner.

"That's Misses McGullin," Talia explained, "she lost her husband years ago.

It makes her feel good to pretend she's dancing with him."

The old woman did not seem to be enjoying herself though. Her face stiff, her eyes darting, it seemed to Hollis that she was somehow compelled to do what she was doing, as if she had no control over it. Something about her reminded him of his mother, though they did not look alike, and he turned away before it made him sad to keep watching.

Others began to converge upon the scene. They came out of nearby buildings, from around corners and out of alleys and seemed to take to their assigned places at the table. They did not sit down, but rather stood behind their chairs as if awaiting an order. By count, all eleven were present. An equal blend of men and woman, young and old; dressed in eloquent costume or some wardrobe fitting for a stately event. And here he was, the guest, donned in musty smelling clothes he had stolen from a closet in a home that by the looks of it had not been occupied in over ten years.

"You don't look like a prince," someone said to him.

Hollis turned to a man whose crossed eyes were a most prominent feature. "Yeah," he said to the man, "I get that a lot."

Their focused attention on him was not without understanding. They were all staring. In spite of how uncomfortable it made him feel he tried not to let it show that it bothered him. He maintained a smirk in the hopes it would convince them.

"You look like a villain," the cross-eyed man imposed. His persistence was vexing. "Your boots give you away. Combat boots, are they not?"

Hollis looked down at his feet. Guilty as charged. And then he looked at Talia, wondering if this might invalidate him as her prince. She went to him quickly, as if she read his mind, and said, "He *is* a prince. I can tell by looking at his eyes." She gave Hollis a wink.

"He flew across the gorge!" young Daryl exclaimed.

"Demons can fly," the cross-eyed man carried on, "that doesn't make one a prince."

"Mister Kinley,"Talia said, moving toward the man in retaliation. She shook her finger at him. "You are not a good judge."

Hollis was about to explain that whole flying thing, but thought better of it. Best to keep his mouth shut; to keep them thinking he was some mystical prince, with powers beyond their comprehension. In a few moments his life might surely depend on it.

"Well..." cross-eyed Kinley began to say as he backed off in retreat, "I hope you're right, Princess... or it's curtains for the rest of us."

Curtains. Talia mouthed the word to mock him. "Mister Kinley, now you know as well as I do," Talia jabbed at the man with her finger to stress her point, "the King would never harm any of us."

Kinley kept his head up high and got ready to proclaim something. He waited until all eyes were on him, and then he said, "Isn't that what Doctor Adler thought? And look what happened to *him*."

Talia frowned.

Momma slammed the lid on the pot with a loud clang. She moved like the wind toward Kinley and put her finger to her lips in order for him to keep his mouth shut. It got everyone's attention. "You hush up now! *All* y'all! We talked about this, and we swore to God that we would never speak of Doctor Adler again." Momma's eyes were open wide. She looked scary. "Doctor Adler didn't see things the way we do, and he..." She looked upwards toward God, searching for the right words. "The doctor made an error in judgment."

"That's putting it kindly," Mister Kinley inferred.

Momma gave a look to the cross eyed man as if to warn him not to say another word. He took heed. And by the sheer angry look in Mamma's eyes, he did it smartly.

Talia may have been the Princess, but Momma, well, there was no doubt... she was the boss.

After a moment, Momma's face softened and she smiled as she went back to the pot. She lifted the cover to the pot and took a big whiff of whatever was boiling in there. She smiled, back in character. All as if nothing had just happened.

It was quiet for a few seconds.

And then Hollis felt it. He felt it before anyone else did and looked around to notice.

Tchwonk.

Like firm thump. Like somebody underneath tapped the bottom of his foot. *Tchwonk.*

Again.

And again.

His body tensed. The tight grip on Talia's hand must have sent a message. "Hollis, don't run," she reminded him.

Tchwonk... Tchwonk... Tchwonk...

Unmistakable now. Harder. Faster. Louder.

Someone at the head of the table turned their head slightly and announced, "The King approaches!"

Cross-eyed Kinley gave a last look to Hollis. "Say your prayers," he told him.

If Hollis knew the right words to say, he just might have.

Before the king emerged from the far south end of Main Street, Hollis prepped for launch. He imagined blasting across the table and rocketing straight for the front entrance of that church. The door looked heavy. Thick. The kind to give the robot a challenge to break through while he carried on toward the rear of the church, out some back exit and onward to... to nowhere. The bridge was out. Where could he go? Leaping across the crevice the first time was a close call—death defying—tempting that fate again was flat-out suicide.

3... 2...1...

Tchwonk.

Zero.

There it was.

When the Sapphire King turned from the side street onto Main its appearance was more than the son of a Gunlord expected to see. No description from a poet, nor image from the helmet camera of a dead soldier could have prepared him for the sight of it in real life. Countdown aborted. He stood fixed. His feet unable to move. The awareness of it was like an electric shock to his senses. The robot was a big and unholy ugly thing. Industrial by design, that's what it was; an industrial strength *Frankenstein's monster*. It did not move right away. It held still, hissing, like some old time steam engine. Just a momentary pause. In a moment, it started to move forward.

The Sapphire King was heading straight for him.

Each footfall was like a tiny earthquake, intensifying as it got closer and closer. The silverware on the table began to rattle.

The miniguns Hollis expected to see were gone, but its destructive power remained quite clear and present. This machine was designed to kill; to annihilate entire platoons. This was no secret now. No soldier stood a chance. Hollis could see the impact of rifle rounds on its surface, evidence of Bravo Company's futile retaliation.

When it finally stopped, it squeaked and whined about a foot in front of him, within inches of stepping on and crushing both his feet. At this close, Hollis could hear the hum of its internal motors and the steady click, like the workings of a finely crafted watch, of components deep within its thick armored shell.

Talia, still holding onto Hollis' hand, positioned herself between them. "This is the Prince, My Lord," she calmly initiated. "The Queen told me he was coming."

Above all, the robot's one eye held Hollis' fixed gaze; a reflective sphere encased in a socket that had a blue glow, was looking directly at him. The artificial membranes fused to the back of the socket, much like a human eye, were attached to braided conduits reassembling muscle tissue that extended up between the shoulders.

They were locked into what could only be described as a giant electrical outlet. Hollis could feel the heat coming off of it.

The Sapphire King raised its claw and gently moved Talia out of its way. And then it extended its upper body to tower above Hollis, perhaps establishing its dominance.

Hollis looked into its eye. The structure of the eye seemed to transform. Lost was his reflection upon its surface, and discovered was a glistening clear liquid that soon coated the once reflective surface. Beyond belief, it seemed to Hollis that the eye had become—somehow—organic in nature. He studied it peculiarly. He was drawn to it without impulse to look away from it.

"Like looking into your soul, isn't it?" Mister Kinley stated, and added, "And not liking what you see?"

Hollis refused to acknowledge the man.

The Sapphire King took a step back. The eye rose to a significant height and repositioned to take notice of the others standing around. It backed away fully, turning toward the side of the road where it eventually parked itself, several meters away from the table. It slumped into a position of rest.

Hollis breathed a sigh. So, did Talia—she even clutched her chest and threw a look of *Dear God* to Momma who breathed a sigh of her own.

"Okay everybody... let's eat!" Momma shouted buoyantly.

Hollis stood there watching as each of the Orphans pulled their chairs out and sat down. So programmed. So adhering to protocol. The peasant girl began dishing out the stew taken from the pot. The Gunlord's son was hesitant to join them.

"Sit down, Hollis!" Daryl ushered. The young lad was so far down at the other end of the table it seemed he could have been a mile away.

Hollis kept looking at the robot and could not get comfort of the sight of it. It stood off to the side like it had no concern anymore what these humans were doing.

"Relax, sugar," Momma said. Referring to the robot, she added, "You don't have nothing to worry about with him—he *likes* you!"

"Likes me, huh?" Hollis said with a chuckle. "How can you tell?"

Momma got real close to Hollis and conveyed to him somberly, "Because he didn't *kill* you."

As hungry as Hollis was, he didn't feel much like eating after that.

CHAPTER TWENTY-FIVE

"SLEEPING GIANT"

The weather this evening was uncharacteristic for Dark Alley; the sky above Oliveri was remarkably clear. The streetlamps were turned off and Hollis observed more stars filling the night sky than he ever recalled seeing before. The air was cool, blowing gently. It was refreshing. Flickers of light from a distant electrical storm stood to remind Hollis he was still in the most violent weather band in the northern hemisphere, but there was none of that nerve shattering crack of lightning nonsense that was legendary for this region.

Hollis was sitting up. In this position, he was highest of all those nestled around him who were lying unconscious in their sleeping bags. The Orphans; the current population of Oliveri, had assembled here on the grandstand in the town courtyard as some bizarre communal slumber party ritual. He would wager it was done to keep him from trying to sneak out—he sat smack dab in the middle of all of them—but so much of how the Orphans behaved here in Oliveri was beyond strange, at what reasonable level could he judge *this*? More so, he didn't question them about it. He simply did what they asked. He was still uncertain as to his acceptance by the group, and especially by the war machine they so affectionately referred to as the *Sapphire King*. A better call was to not make waves. Like everything else he had done thus far, he would simply deal with it.

I am the Prince, he chose to accept. Pondering the illogicalness of it, he smiled inwardly.

He could still see the robot from where he was sitting. From this angle, he could see that it was on the next block where the church was, still parked on the side of the road where it had been since dinner. It had not moved from that spot. Dinner had been over two hours ago.

Its lights were out. His sensitive ears could sense nothing. No hum. No hiss. No click. For all intents and purposes the machine was as asleep as everyone else here.

The banquet table was still set. Some things had been left on it; Momma and her crew had only accomplished a minimal clean up, so there were still a few things remaining to lure the interest of a raccoon. Hollis watched the raccoon hop up onto the table with a sort of weightless effort. He saw it forage for some leftovers on one of the plates that hadn't been cleared. It was striving to be quiet, the way it careened so gingerly between the drinking glasses that stood around it. But then, it knocked one of them over. There was a break of silence in the night when the glass rolled off the edge of the table and shattered on the street. Hollis sat up even further, pitched his head to take careful note and fixed his eyes on the robot. Watched for it to react. Waited to see if even a light might turn on, hoping it didn't. And then fortunately...

Nothing. The robot did not stir.

He sighed, thinking, this might be his only chance.

He could not stay in Oliveri—no way he was going to endure this craziness any longer—and saw this as an opportunity to get the hell out. He had to get back to his uncle, break him free so they could go on their way, let Bravo Company deal with this. The robot was *their* problem, and he was not about to let it become his own.

He was about to stand up when...

"Hollis?"

It was Daryl.

The boy's tender voice gave him a start.

"What are you doing?" the boy asked. Daryl was closest to him, right next to him in fact. "Shouldn't you be sleeping?"

Hollis took in a deep breath out of frustration; his immediate plan would have to be delayed. He thought of something to say, and came out with, "Kid, one of the things you're going to learn is, a prince... such as myself... doesn't need sleep."

Even in the dark a man without the heightened senses of a Gunlord could see the broad grin that formed on the boy's face.

"You mind if I ask you a few questions, Daryl?" Hollis began. He whispered, so as not to wake anyone else. "Where did the robot come from? How did it get here?"

"Oh..." the boy replied, and needed a moment to think. After a moment he presented the answer with a shrug, "He came like you did, I guess."

"What do you mean, like me?"

"The Princess wished for him...and then he came."

Hollis couldn't make sense of the boy's vague answers and he settled on the fact that perhaps the boy was too young to have known the way things came to be. His next question was more direct. "How long does the robot power down for?"

"You mean, how long does he sleep?"

"Yes... that... *sleep*."

"Most nights, all night, until morning," Daryl had more to say about it. He cast a peculiar expression. "But these past few nights he's been going out and doing stuff."

"Yes... I'll bet it has," Hollis remarked insinuatingly. "Do you know what it's been doing—do you have any idea?"

Daryl shook his head and said innocently, "No."

"How does it get out?"

"Get out?"

"You know, how does it leave town? It can't possibly jump over the chasm."

"What's a chasm?"

"Where the bridge used to be." Hollis just looked at the boy. "There must be some other way for the robot to get out of town. Do you know, or not?" Hollis sensed his tone becoming confrontational.

Perhaps the boy did, too.

One of the others on the grandstand began to stir in their sleep. It was best to back off .

When Hollis looked back at Daryl the boy's head was lying back on his pillow. Less than a minute later the boy was making that telltale sleep-breathing sound.

No more questions.

Hollis waited a good while this time before acting. He rose carefully from the wooden platform when he sensed everyone was sound asleep and then tip toed carefully around them. He turned his eyes Gunlord black to intensify his senses for night vision.

Before he went down the stairs he paused to look at Talia. She was in the midst of dream by the looks of her. She was smiling and in a moment her brow furrowed. She chuckled and Hollis waited a few seconds to see if she would say something in her sleep. She didn't. He moved on. The stairs leading down the platform creaked as he descended.

Hollis winced. When he got to solid ground at the bottom he figured he was safe.

Now, approaching the robot was an entirely different matter. Some impulse was drawing him toward it in spite of his common sense to avoid the danger. It was more than just mindless curiosity, no, he was thinking militarily. He could not help it, the trait was inherent. He wanted to take advantage of this moment to get to know his enemy. At point blank range he was vigilant of what Momma had said, *he likes you*, and hoping the machine was not prone to changing its mind, prepared himself for anything to happen. Dark. Cold. With its bullet pock marks and leaking parts it looked pathetic.

Broken. But a killer, such as it was, deserved no sympathy.

Hollis looked back at the platform where the Orphans were still sleeping. The notion of a machine having the emotion to willfully do harm to someone seemed outright incomprehensible, but these people did not seem to think so.

Where did you come from?

Who sent you?

And for what reason?

Questions he wished he could ask it; but questions, he had to presume would never be answered.

He wanted to press his hand on the reflective surface of the war machine's eyeball, to get an actual feel for what it was made of, what was so mystifying about it.

But he refrained.

He wanted to bend back some of its armor, so he could check out its internal circuits—just to see how it ticked.

But again, he refrained.

And he especially wanted to pull on the braided fluid lines, yank on the wires and jab his finger like a dagger at the internal circuit boards, to learn how fragile they were, if indeed he ever had a to defend himself from this robot and needed to dismantle them.

But this, he dared not do.

One last time he looked back at the stage platform to ensure he was still safe from detection, and then he moved on.

Wilmington's Nuts n' Bolts was the name of the local Oliveri hardware store.

It was down from the courtyard, between the post office and the firehouse, on Main Street. There was no need for Hollis to use his Gunlord strength to break the door down, he found it was unlocked. He went in quickly and moved hurriedly through the isles in search of something. He knew what he needed; he just had to find it. Fortunately the store was well stocked. He found a large spool of rope thick enough to hold his weight and reeled a long enough length to stretch across the crevice. He threw it on his shoulders. It must have weighed a hundred pounds. He needed his Gunlord strength for that and to carry it with him all the way. Next, he needed something he could use as a grappling hook. A crowbar hung on a rack in the tool department, but Hollis could not think of a way to securely fasten the end of the rope to it. While passing through the automotive section he came across a cross lug wrench. Holding it firmly in his hands, he figured it might just work. Before he exited the store he grabbed a pair of tin snips, a utility knife and some duct tape.

He was back on the street.

His heart was racing as he ran down the tree lined road toward the crevice, and he was excited about the prospect of leaving, but not about actually returning to Bravo Company's camp, or even having to speak with Captain Radigan about his failure to complete the mission. He would have some explaining to do, and with that, once again, he had sincere doubts that the sinister captain would grant him and his uncle their freedom. He was out of options and would have to see.

At the bridge, he tied one end of the rope to an existing iron piece that was anchored firmly in the ground. He tied the other end to the axis of the cross lug wrench.

Only a man with great skill and strength could ever hope to throw that lug wrench, with all that rope tied to it, clear to the other side; it was the sort of thing the son of a Gunlord was qualified to do. He summoned the will and his eyes turned black. The lug wrench was thrown and it landed well past its intended target. It landed well into the street on the other side. Immediately, Hollis began to reel it in, picking up the slack to make a tight rope he could crawl across. Luck would have it the lug wrench caught firmly to a similar piece of the broken bridge on the opposite side.

Hollis spat into the palms of his hands to get them moist and then quickly moved into position to use the monkey crawl method to move across.

He had no fear, or doubt, only the drive to get safely to the other side.

At about halfway across he chose to look down and was reminded of the rotting corpses in a pile at the very bottom of the crevice. In those few seconds he took note of something, none of the bodies appeared singed, which would have made sense if they had been on the bridge at the time it had been blown up. He considered this, that they must have died in battle on the streets of Oliveri, he even recalled the scene on the road off Main Street with the overturned and crushed trucks and the streets stained with blood; so, the robot simply swept their dead bodies off the street, carried them all here and tossed them in.

Soon Hollis continued on, and he eventually made it to the

other side. He breathed a sigh and rubbed his sore hands from the burns he received from the rope. Impressed with himself for making it across, he stood up, but did not look back. All he wanted to see—all he cared about now—was the path to freedom that lay ahead.

That was the moment he was hit.

He had taken only one step when he was struck square in the back... by the beam of a searchlight.

He frowned and stared down at his shadow cast on the road. Never had he looked at a more pathetic sight.

"Hollis?"

It was Talia.

Fuck...

Hollis didn't want to turn around. He sensed his feet were glued to the ground. He knew what this was. This was the affect of shock to his system. He had encountered this once before and he knew just what to do to overcome it, to free himself from this psychological captivity; he had to calm down, clear his mind. Easier said than done. But then all there would be left to do is simply run—run away. No wait, there was something else, his conscience to deal with, that moral goodness his mother instilled in him? That was troublesome.

"Hollis, look at me." Talia's voice sounded weak and despaired. *Damn it...*

He turned around.

On the other side of the crevice was much more than he imagined. The Sapphire King was standing there with its spotlight aiming at his face. It was difficult to make out because of the glare, but what he could see was Talia being held in the robot's right claw, suspended over the edge of the crevice. The implication was obvious.

"I need you to come back, Hollis, please." Now her voice sounded urgent.

She kept looking down. She was clearly afraid.

Hollis shouted, "Tell it to let you go—no, wait!"

"The King wishes for you to stay, I think. So do I. Will you, please... come back over."

Hollis looked over his shoulder. Freedom was never so close.

A descent man would have taken no time at all to come to the right decision.

Hollis needed a moment. He looked down at his sore hands. His palms and all of his fingers felt raw from making the trip across. He wondered how they would be after a second crossing. He cursed his luck, and the only choice to be made.

Making his way back took an added toll, not just all of his strength, but his will as well. Once he got to the other side and climbed onto solid ground again, there at the iron feet of the Sapphire King, he gasped and spat at the dirt. He did not standup right away. He remained there on all fours, just breathing. He watched the robot step back from the edge of the crevice and place Talia gently on the road next to him.

"Don't test me like that again..." Hollis said, as he got painstakingly up from the ground. "If you do, you may be disappointed with the results."

"Oh, Hollis," Talia replied, nudging him affectionately, "you could never disappoint me."

He looked her. "I wasn't talking to you."

PART THREE

CHAPTER TWENTY-SIX

"UNFINISHED BUSINESS"

The expression on Sergeant Percy's face, like somebody had just spiked his coffee with motor oil, formed when some piece of equipment failed to work to his satisfaction. He held the GPS in the palm of his hand and shook it. He stared at the tiny display screen a moment and waited to read something different. The same message ran in a continuous loop: ACQUIRING SIGNAL. PLEASE WAIT. He raised his hand high in the air then, looking ready to slam the device down.

First Sergeant Fitz caught Percy before he did something he might regret. "Take it easy, there, sarge," he said, and gestured for Percy to hand it over.

"I want to smash thing against a rock," proclaimed the furious staff sergeant. "It worked well enough to get us this far," Fitz said in its defense. "How well did you *expect* it to work in Dark Alley?"

Percy shrugged and hooked it back to his utility belt.

The two of them had come to the edge of the forest and paused before moving out into the open. Fitz wasn't comfortable exposing the group. The next batch of trees to provide cover and concealment looked to be about two miles ahead. That was a significant distance for their movement to be detected. He turned and gave a quick whistle and signaled the rest of his team to come forward. Through the thick brush emerged Sergeant Becker, Corporals DeGarmos and Ferrara, and finally Private First Class Serban. These guys were hand-picked from Third Platoon, chosen specifically because of their demolition skills. Fitz needed the best Bravo Company had to offer for his plan to succeed.

"We're going to stop here a few minutes, eat and recharge," he told them. "We're going to need our energy if we're to make it to our objective before sundown."

The boys looked pleased with that. After traipsing rugged terrain; up and down cliff ledges, through narrow rocky passages and across beds of slippery slate, they were in need of a rest. Right here were plenty of large rocks to set their tired asses upon and unpack meals from their rucksacks.

They had traveled more than eight miles since leaving camp at dawn, and were nearing higher ground, closing in on the point where the missile had originated.

Fitz studied the SAT photo of the position of the war machine they referred to as *Red*, to get a fix on its exact location. By his best estimates they had another ten or so miles yet to go. But the terrain ahead looked even rougher. Nothing looked flat. There was a lot of climbing to do and none of them had that kind of training. The time was now 08::00 hrs, given their current course and pace, he figured they would likely arrive at their destination at around 17:00.

"So..."

Over his shoulder, Percy was looking at the photo, too. "What do you think?" Fitz asked.

Percy shook his head. "If we're lucky, we'll reach Red by sundown."

"Well, let's hope so... sundown is all the Captain's going to give us to get the job done. He won't wait to hear from us before he initiates his plan."

Percy sat on a rock and tore open an instant *meal-ready-to-eat*. He saw Fitz just standing there, staring out into space, and remarked, "You should take your own advice, eat something."

"I'm not hungry."

Percy read the label printed on the pouch. "You're turning down franks and beans?" He tore open the pouch and squeezed some of the brown chalky substance into his mouth.

"Smells like the inside of my boot," Fitz said as he sat next to him on the rock.

Percy swallowed hard. "Ever wonder why no one asks for seconds? You shouldn't."

Fitz uncapped his canteen and took a healthy swig.

Percy asked, "What do you think the Captain is doing right now?"

Fitz made a face. His thoughts of the captain were not flattering. "He's conducting a lottery." He turned to inspect Percy's reaction. He certainly had Percy's attention. "Or maybe he's drawing straws, to see which one of our men is going to be used as bait for his trap. Did you see it?"

"The trap? Yeah, I saw it. It's a Rube Goldberg, you know? A lot of moving parts have to work just right, otherwise it will only serve to expose or camp." He paused to choke some more food down his throat. "And then what?"

"Once that robot is out of commission, he says he'll gather our remaining forces and march into town. He seems to think that blue robot is our enemy's main line of defense. Once it's defeated, there will be no more threat."

"You disagree, Top?"

Fitz shrugged. "I don't know. I want to think so, but... that would make things too simple. I just can't wrap my mind around what the fuck is really happening here. The only thing that is obvious to me –and it doesn't even make sense—is that someone is trying awfully hard to keep their presence here a secret. I mean, if these robots where put in place in order to protect that secret, then how is that going to work when the harder they try to keep that secret, the more they risk exposing themselves?"

Percy gave a wry smile.

"You have some thoughts on the matter?"

Percy replied, "It's all I've been thinking about this whole time we were walking."

"Do tell."

Percy put the meal down, wiped his mouth with his hand and sat up straight. Fitz sat up, too, he couldn't wait to hear this.

"The reason *is* simple, Top," Percy began, "it's because they don't *care*."

A broad smile split Fitz's face. "You've been thinking about it this whole time, and all you came up with is, they don't care?" He couldn't hold back any longer, he burst out laughing.

Percy looked dead serious. "Listen to me, you asked, now let me explain..." Fitz regained his composure.

Percy went on. "You wonder what sense it makes for them to keep fighting us? I'm telling you; the answer is, they have no sense, none at all. If they cared, they never would have picked a fight with us in the first place. So... they don't care who we are. That's obvious. They don't care who we represent. They certainly don't care that they will never *ever* get away with what they've done—there's going to be hell to pay."

Percy put up his index finger to emphasize one point. "And the reason they don't care, Top, is because..." He paused for affect. "These guys, whoever they are, are out of their minds—they're fucking *crazy*! And crazy people don't have the sense to give a shit.

That part of their brain is missing that piece that gives them the ability to fear the consequences of their actions."

Fitz took all that in. Percy's logic was an absurd oversimplification. Furthermore, it was no excuse. Staring off into space, he heard some of the boys laughing and it drew his attention. He looked over to see what they were laughing at. None of them had listened in on the conversation he and Percy had; they were too far away to have heard them. In spite of the fact that they needed to laugh, he was curious and couldn't help himself. "What's so funny over there?" he asked.

They immediately stopped laughing, as though Top's voice had scared them to attention.

"Sorry, Top," DeGarmos said, assuming Fitz had overheard them, "we meant no disrespect."

"You never have to apologize to me, DeGarmos, you should *all* know that," Fitz implied.

One of the others spoke up. It was Sergeant Becker. "The guys in the company have given Captain Radigan a nickname. It's funny, that's all."

"Let me hear it," Fitz ordered.

Becker was hesitant. In a moment, he answered, "They're going around calling him CC... behind his back, of course"

"No doubt. What's it mean?"

"Captain Crazy."

Fitz was taken aback. It was the second time in less than a minute that someone said the word *crazy* and it had an affect on him.

Becker went on to explain, "They think he's like that crazy captain from that book Moby Dick, you know the one—Captain Ahab, who goes insane trying to catch that great white shark."

"Whale."

"Wha...?"

"You're getting it confused with another book, I think. Moby Dick is about a whale, not a shark."

"Oh..."

Fitz looked at all of them. "Any of you guys actually *read* the book?"

They looked at each other. A couple of them shrugged. Fitz thought that maybe one of them had read it as part of an assignment for school, back when they were just innocent kids. They got the Ahab reference right. Radigan's white whale was the blue war machine.

Fitz asked, "Any of you know how the book ends?" Again, all he got was vague expressions and quick shrugs.

"Well... the ship sinks...Ahab dies... and the whale gets away." By their looks, the boys did not find comfort in that.

Fitz thought it best not tell them anymore; like that all the crewmen on board the ship died.

CHAPTER TWENTY-SEVEN

"SECOND CHANCE"

The transceiver.

The signal amplifier. The jumpers.

And the microwave relay dish.

The four essential components of the radio transmitter that needed to work in order for Bravo Company's call for help to reach beyond the limits of the Uri Etzel Belt. After a close inspection, Hollis found the whole assembly to be in reasonably good shape, in spite of falling three stories, and much to his surprise; however, there was no way of knowing for sure unless he connected power to it. He crawled through the steel trusses of the downed tower and stood looking up at the brick wall of one of the buildings in the alley. The clue to the tower's soft landing was staring him right in the face. There were deep gouges in the wall, evidence that the tower had scraped along its side to cause a slow descent. How very fortunate.

He began to work out a plan.

"Hollis?" Talia said, as she appeared at the entrance to the alley. Damn, she had a way of sneaking up on him...

"What are you doing here?" she asked.

He gave her a congenial glance. "That's *Prince* Hollis, to you."

She smirked. "You're making fun of me." Hollis met her halfway. "Maybe, just a little."

She looked different today. She was not wearing her princess gown. She was dressed as a commoner, in ripped jeans and a purple colored T-shirt, and her hair was tied back in a pony tail. She was, to describe it correctly, normal looking and this look made him feel more comfortable.

"Are you going to runaway again?" she hastened to ask.

Hollis shook his head. "No," he addressed, which was a lie, of course. "I understand the way things are now."

Talia was standing rigid, she had her suspicions. But her tenseness didn't last and in a moment she appeared to relax. "Good," she said. "Momma is going to set you up a room at the hotel. That's where we all live there. In case you were wondering, it isn't every night that we sleep outside, under the stars."

He laughed. Indeed he had wondered about that. "It makes sense, since there are so few of you, that you would all chose the hotel, to sleep under one roof."

Talia walked closer to him. She saw what he was looking at and asked, "What are you doing here? I thought this thing was broken for good?"

"I may have been wrong about that. The tower didn't fall as hard as I thought.

You see, the tower scarped against the wall on its way down. Everything looks like it survived the crash." He was quite obviously elated by the fact. She was not, however.

He went on, "It does me no good with it lying heret on the ground, but..."

He wanted to show her something, but needed to get by her. He tried to maneuver around her without touching her, but she was standing too close to the tower and he had to squeeze past her. She stood firmly, intentionally, as if he might ask her to move. She was being playful—flirty—and he knew it, so when he moved by her, he had no choice but to put his hand on her shoulder.

He continued on, to Main Street, where he pointed to something beyond her view. She joined him in the street.

"You see those utility towers way up on those hills?" he said.

Poking above the tree tops beyond Oliveri, were the tops of a row of high tension lines used to provide power to those residents of Oliveri who lived on the outskirts of town.

"If I could mount this equipment to the top of one of those towers, I just might get it to work."

He stared at her looking where he had been pointing, and found he was staring too long, admiring her beauty. Her eyes shifted slightly to notice, and he quickly looked away.

"Do you really think you can fix it?" she asked.

Hollis shrugged. "Imagine if I can? I mean, before you know it we could be communicating with the outside world!"

Talia's expression turned stony. "Why would we want to do that?"

Hollis thought the reasons were obvious, but judging by her expression he had to think again... perhaps *not*.

She said, "We have everything we need here, Hollis. What more could anyone from the outside provide us with?" She was dead serious.

Hollis had to think fast, but his reply was sincere. "Have you thought about what might happen if any of you needed a doctor—I mean, a *real* doctor, like a surgeon?

What if Daryl got seriously hurt? You have to think about these things. Are any of you qualified to yank a bad tooth? You need a dentist for that. Talia, all of you have been lucky... until now."

Until now. He had to be mindful of the words he chose.

Talia's expression softened as she closed her eyes and appeared to contemplate inwardly. She opened her eyes in a moment and approached him, got real close and cupped one of her hands below his chin and said, "Now you see, Hollis, you really are a prince... you're already taking care of us."

Hollis dismissed the gesture and took a step back. "I need a favor from you though... a couple of favors, actually."

"Anything."

"I need your help finding a portable generator. I'm hoping we can find one somewhere in town."

She gave him an encouraging gesture. "And what else?"

"Well, the next thing isn't so much a favor from you, but... from the robot."

"The Sapphire King."

"Yes." Hollis replied, feeling a bit disingenuous. "You see, I won't be able to lug all this equipment way up that hill by myself. It's too heavy. I'm going to need somebody big and strong. I'm hoping you can put in a good word for me, to enlist the robot to help me."

Talia laughed heartily. "Oh, Hollis... My dear, *Prince* Hollis, all you have to do is ask him!"

"Ask? That's all?

"He'd be more than happy to help."

"Is that right—happy, huh?"

"Why wouldn't he be?"

He looked at the war machine now. It had been with him, standing near to the entrance to the alley ever since he came to inspect the damage to the tower. In fact, the robot had not taken its glowing blue eye off of him since his attempt to escape. Hollis was beginning to regard the Sapphire King as his personal sentry... or was a better term, parole officer?

An hour later, in anticipation of a two and half mile trek to the base of the utility tower, Hollis packed a light snack and some bottles of water which he stuffed inside a back pack he lifted from a department store in Oliveri. He had chosen specific tools that he thought he would need to assemble the transmitting equipment and put them in a canvas pouch which he slung on his shoulder. As a bonus, Daryl was eager to accompany him, and Hollis was quite appreciative of the gesture.

Most of the trees in this northern part of the town were pine trees,and they were spread out and easy to maneuver through, but occasionally there would be some obstacle to have to walk around or some uneasy challenge in the terrain which caused them to have to backtrack. But there was no fear of getting lost or losing the trail.

The power lines above their head were a guideline, and as long as they never lost sight of them, they would always get back on course. Hollis liked the smell of the forest. The fresh pine reminded him of home. He had never been homesick before, but something about this place kept reminding him of a time in his life when things were simpler, and with that, safer.

Their entire trip was a gradual uphill climb. Hollis had no problem with it, but to ensure Daryl did not get too tired, he kept the pace slow. To pass the time they talked about casual, nonsensical things.

"I always wanted to go there," Daryl admitted, in the midst of one of their conversations. "I saw pictures of it in a book, in the library. It looks like a lot of fun. A lot of kids are there. Have you ever been to *Disneyworld*?"

Hollis shook his head. "My Grandfather told me he went there once, a long time ago, long before I was born. If I remember, he told me it was in Florida."

"Who's Florida?" Daryl asked.

"Florida's not a who, it's a what—it's a state!"

"What's a state?"

"You don't know what a state is? New Mexico is a state. Oliveri is in the state of New Mexico. Don't you go to school, Daryl?" Hollis asked, and then immediately wished he could withdraw the question. Of course Daryl didn't. And there was no one Hollis ever saw in town who seemed qualified to teach him.

"Can we go there someday?" Daryl asked.

"Disneyworld?" Hollis shook his head. "I wish we could. I think most of it's under water now."

Daryl walked very slowly all of a sudden. Hollis went a few paces ahead before he realized and turned to look back. He was struck by the boy's expression of utter sadness. What else could he do at that point but lie? "You know what, on second thought; you and I *should* go there. When all of this is over—when things start to settle down and get back to normal—you and me, we'll go to the state of Florida and see if Disneyworld is still there." And for some unknown reason, perhaps because it sounded so good to himself, he added, "And we'll go on all the fun rides my grandfather told me about."

The sadness in Daryl's face seemed to disappear in an instant. He tilted his head up and the weighty gaze was lifted. With a bounce in his step he drove forward, surpassing Hollis, and carried on ahead of him. "Come on," the boy urged with a wave of his arm, "we have lots of work to do!"

"Not so fast, little man," Hollis asserted. He turned in the direction they had come from. "I think we're getting too far ahead of our third party; there's still one of us that has to catch up!"

Crackling through the trees and thumping its way towards them emerged none other than the Sapphire King, looking unquestionably different now than it had ever looked before; hardly the automated weapon intended to chew up and spit out entire platoons, or to smash rocks in a Russian diamond mine, the robot looked more like a steel plated *beast of burden*. It wore a custom made back pack, fashioned from broad sheets of thick canvas, measured in proportion to a robot that stood as tall as fifteen feet. Inside the pack was held all the pieces of the transmitter, all three hundred and sixty pounds of it. In the bend of each of its arms were hundreds of feet of coiled wire and cable. A rope was tied around its waist, with the other end tied to a four-wheeled trailer, which the robot towed behind it. Upon that trailer, wrapped in a tarp, were a portable generator and several cans filled with gasoline.

Even after walking with it for the last hour, seeing the robot this way was still astounding to Hollis, and it was going to be one hell of a story to tell Uncle Billy when he got back to Bravo Company's camp. Billy might not believe him, but here was the truth: the robot was actually helping him, in essence, aiding its enemy. Hollis did not honestly believe this robot had a measurable intelligence beyond its simple programming; it was a robot, after all, and robots do not have feelings. Yet seeing how it related to the residents of Oliveri, he could not deny that it had some degree of awareness, and so he felt a tinge of guilt toward what he was allowing the robot to do. He knew first hand how it felt to be used—to be *tricked* into doing something—and so, by taking part in the rebuilding of the transmitter, the Sapphire King was sealing its fate. Hollis made a deal with a silver barred devil, however—a fiendish creature that went by the name, Radigan—and with no other choice given to him, Hollis had to follow through.

The Sapphire King pushed over the thinnest trees that stood in its path and nudged away low lying branches like they were nothing. When it caught up to Hollis, it paused. It let out a hearty hiss from one of its exhaust ports, like a sigh. And there it waited, staring at Hollis the way it always did, this time awaiting its next instruction.

Daryl hounded, "C'mon, Prince Hollis! We're wasting time standing around here!"

The boy was right. It was time to go.

Hollis snapped his fingers and ushered the robot on, and together the three of them continued their journey north toward the highest tower at the top of the hill.

When they got there, they quickly unloaded all the equipment. Everything was laid out on the ground; the components to the transmitter, the tools, the cables and hardware were placed near the base of the tower in the order they were to be assembled. The six foot wide relay dish, weighing in at about one hundred and fifteen pounds, was step one—the most difficult and heaviest part to be dealt with first. Hollis' plan was simple; attach a block and tackle system to the top of the tower—a one hundred foot climb—and raise the dish up through the center with rope. When it rose to a point where it no longer fit in the center of the tower, Hollis would swing it out, through an open space in the trusses, and mount it to one of the main beams with thick steel clamps. He had a problem from the start, an issue he hadn't thought of until now. He literally had to be in two places at one time; on the ground, hoisting the dish up with the rope, and way up at the top of the tower to physically maneuver the dish into its proper position. There was no point if it was not done right. He had to figure something out.

The Sapphire King stood off to the side, its massive shape

lingering motionless beneath the shade of a tree and its glowing eye simply staring off into space.

Hollis thought this was a waste of useful power and wondered, if he could get the robot to pull on the rope and hoist the dish up (as long as it did it slowly and carefully) there a good chance this most difficult part of the operation could be accomplished. But Hollis had to count on the robot's cooperation and understanding of the task.

"I need your help," he said, approaching the Sapphire King.

The robot's eye turned to face him. Its body adjusted itself, as if to stand at attention, or so it seemed to Hollis, the way a soldier would. It put its arms out in a ready position.

"Very good," Hollis commended, trying his best to conceal his doubt, and preceded to explain how, with its cooperation, he and the robot would work together. By the time he was finished with the explanation Hollis' confidence grew and he was hopeful that the robot knew exactly what to do and how to do it.

Time was crucial and Hollis was not about to waste a single second of it. He scaled the tower with the block and tackled in a shoulder pack. Climbing without the need of equipment, he performed like a circus acrobat, using only his arms and legs.

When he got to the top, he assembled the block and tackle and fed the rope through to the ground. Once that was set, he climbed back down and approached the robot again. He was daringly firm in giving his orders and the robot showed no contention and complied. Hollis directed the war machine to a specific point at the base of the tower, at a mark he had made in the dirt. This was where the robot was to be stationed. Hollis offered the end of the rope to the machine and it pinched the end of it tightly between one of its claws. Without being instructed, it took an initiative and pulled the rope taught. Hollis was impressed. Maintaining a watch from far below, while Hollis was a hundred feet overhead, the robot would await further instruction. Hollis would use hand signals.

An hour later, in less time than it took the three of them to walk from the center of town to the top of the hill, the first phase of the operation was completed. The dish was in place and securely fastened, and Hollis was overwhelmed with a feeling of self-assuredness he never felt in his entire adult life. This transmitter was going to work. As he silently contemplated the next steps in the construction his stomach growled and the empty space in his gut was a like punch. He was so busy with the project he had forgotten to take the time to eat. And he thought of Daryl, too, the poor boy; Hollis had forgotten about him. With a spool of cable slung on his shoulders, Hollis looked around for the lad and found him seated on one of the robot's steel hooves. Daryl looked like he was seated upon his own private throne, the way he was leaning back and relaxed.

Hollis called to him, "How are you doing Daryl, are you all right? How about joining me for lunch?"

The boy lifted his head and nodded. When he got close, Hollis noticed the boy's eyes were filled with tears. "What's the matter, Apache warrior?"

Daryl shrugged and shook his head dismissively. Hollis pressed him. "You can tell me."

"When you're done fixing this thing..." the boy began to say as he pointed upwards at the tower, "will we... be able to call everyone back home?"

The residents of the town. *Those* people. Hollis was sure that was who he meant; the ones that had been evacuated. Daryl shed a weird look on his face, much like Talia had. "I don't understand, Daryl, why would you, or *anyone,* be opposed to it?"

"It's just that... well, I'm beginning think... that my parents are dead," Daryl said, and he said it as if he seemed to have some acute awareness to the fact.

Hollis was taken aback. At a loss for words, he just stood staring. "I think they died in a fire. Yes, I'm sure of it."

Hollis looked him straight in the eye. "Why would you say that, Daryl? Did you *see* them die... or did someone *tell* you they did?"

As before, Hollis got a shrug. This was too bizarre. But something started to make sense. Hollis could hardly believe he had not noticed the important missing piece to the puzzle until now. Daryl must have had a Mom and Dad. What loving parents would leave behind their child in an evacuation, unless... well, unless something happened to them *before* the evacuation? The Gunlord's son looked around, it was a nervous response, searching for someone better qualified than he to cross examine this poor soul. His uncle was far better at this sort of thing. Even if he knew what to say, he didn't know how to start. Perhaps this was the moment to change the subject.

And then came sounds from within the right arm of the

Sapphire King.

Motors whined. Gears clicked and the joints began to move. The robot's arm lowered toward the ground and thumped there next Daryl. The claw opened wide. What was the robot doing? Hollis kept watching.

Of its three fingers, one was closest to the ground. The other two were at top. Daryl climbed into it and put himself in what appeared to Hollis as a firm position. The fingers of the claw closed and locked the boy in. The boy chuckled. The jovial cant was music to Hollis' ears.

Okay, now what? Hollis kept his eye on them.

Daryl remarked, speaking to the robot, "But Princess Talia told me never to do this again. She said it was too dangerous and I could get hurt."

Whatever that robot had just done—whatever it had in mind—seemed to raise the boy's spirit. Hollis had to encourage it. He performed a mock gesture, looking around as if to see if anyone was close by. When he was done, he announced, "Daryl, I don't see Princess Talia around here anywhere, do you?"

That being said, Daryl leaned back and got more comfortable. This was going to be fun. Hollis could see it in the boy's face, and what he bore witness to next was astounding. With Daryl secured, the robot picked its claw up off the ground and using its upper body to pivot on its chassis, began to take the young lad for a spin. Slow at first, until it built up a max speed. A sound began to erupt from the robot's internal chamber, like the sound of an engine revving. The Sapphire King stood tall, extending its legs to their fullest, to give Daryl some significant height. It stretched its arms out wide, to offer a greater sense of speed. The boy was flying. Laughing, Carrying on like this was the greatest thing to ever happen to him. And all Hollis could do was watch with amazement, this bonding session. He couldn't help but laugh about it. The the thrill ride went on for another few minutes until, as if on cue, the robot's rapid turning came to a gradual halt, and it set Daryl down safely in the precise spot the robot had picked him up from. It opened its claw, but Daryl remained seated, panting heavily with a smile so broad it practically split his face in half. "I want to go again!" he cried.

"Some tough guy *you* are," Hollis snickered, looking at the robot's glowing blue eye as if it knew what he was referencing. No response of course, just a cold stare back at him.

Whines and clicks from the robot's arm again, this time from its *left* arm. It rested its left claw on the ground at Hollis' feet and opened even wider for someone his size to fit inside. Clearly, it was invitation.

"C'mon, Hollis, now *you* try it—it's fun!" Daryl urged.

Hollis' expression never changed. He looked at the robot and remarked dispassionately, "Sorry Daryl, but I have too much work to do. Some other time, maybe." The Gunlord's son turned without another word and retrieved the spool of cable he had tossed on the ground. Slinging it back on his shoulder, he marched with it to the base of the utility tower, never breaking stride, and took hold of the thick rope that was dangling through the middle. He was prepared to climb, but paused; so strange, he pondered. He looked back at Daryl, and at the robot especially.

The Sapphire King did not possess emotion—it *could* not—but who could deny what seemed to have just happened? The robot had performed what could only be viewed as a willful act that seemed to have a clear purpose, to cheer the boy up.

So... damn... strange.

Hollis had never before given thought to a robot being self aware; this proclamation that a construct of man could distinguish itself from others was too far fetched. A far more advanced and well designed machine could make tactical decisions, yes. He had seen that demonstrated with Terra-Dusters; one in particular named *Goliath*.

This one here was a simple mining robot. On an average day, its primary function was to break apart and move heavy rocks far below the surface of the earth, for the sole purpose of forging for diamonds. A benevolent pursuit. But then Hollis looked at the braces on the robot's shoulders, where once were mounted the miniguns, and he was reminded that this was a mining robot that had been re-designed to be someone's instrument of death. Sure, he thought, as he reconsidered, a simple mining robot... until that fateful day, when some sadistic puke of a being came upon it and saw through its benevolent design and recognized its potential for destruction, eliminated its basic programming, mounted those guns, and before turning it loose, issued it a new set of orders, to engage a specific uniformed target. It reminded Hollis of General Gutter, who, upon invading Hidden Pond all those years ago, found a young boy with whom he could exploit in the interest of his own sinister goals.

Who trained *you*, Sapphire King? Hollis had cause to ask.

Certainly no one he'd met in Oliveri was qualified to teach this robot how to kill so effectively, so efficiently.

And whoever they were, what reason could they have for wanting those soldiers from Bravo Company dead?

He was growing concerned and came to the conclusion that he'd be a lot better off if he just stopped thinking about it.

Laughter pried him out of his deep thought and he turned toward the sound. It was Daryl again. The Sapphire King was taking him for another spin, this time in reverse.

Hollis remained on the ground until the ride was over, and for just one moment... wished he was a kid again.

CHAPTER TWENTY-EIGHT

"EMPTY NEST"

Staff Sergeant Percy was trailing behind First Sergeant Fitz, checking his six as if at any moment someone, or some-*thing* might try to sneak up on the both of them. It was those storm clouds rolling in overhead threatening to release their payload that held his attention. The two of them were making their way up a long gradual slope, across a bed of granite. Percy's booted feet were aching. He thought that if it rained and the granite got wet it would be as slippery as ice and make their trek that much more treacherous. When Fitz stopped short, the poor sergeant nearly walked straight into him.

Their view from this height, and through the clear sky, was fifteen miles to the far away creeks, slopes and desert flats.

Without saying a word, Fitz communicated with a single hand signal; he pointed to a protrusion in the metasedimentary shale of the rock wall they were heading towards. The protrusion was like a shelf well above their heads. And keeping his voice low, he said, "Red is up there."

Sergeant Percy immediately took out the SAT photo from the cargo pocket of his BDU pants and used it to get a bearing. He checked his surroundings and concurred with Fitz, they were in the right spot.

Fitz pointed slightly to the left of the shelf. "I see shreds of fabric on those jagged rocks. You see them? These machines drop down in parachutes, is that right?"

"Yeah," Percy affirmed, "That's what Chang said, that they probably were flown in by a cargo chopper and then released from the air."

Fitz kept looking at the wall, trying to decide something. In a moment he turned to Percy. "It looks like an easy climb. Those rocks leading up to it, it's like a stair case." He watched Percy remove his cap and wipe the sweat drenching his forehead with his sleeve. He asked, "You OK, Percy?" Percy looked like he needed more than just a rest. "Take a drink of water."

Percy sighed. "I'm not ashamed to admit it, Top... I'm getting too old for this shit."

Fitz grinned, but was apathetic. "Try to hang in there, old-timer. The sooner we get this job done, the sooner things might start going right for us."

Percy put the cap back on his head and nodded affirmatively.

"Now, go back to that patch of woods and collect the rest of our team. I want them up on point. If I'm not here when you get here, wait for me."

Percy asked, "Where are *you* going?"

"I'm heading up there," Fitz replied. "On your own?"

"Someone should go up there and at least get a good look at what we have to deal with."

Percy disagreed and made a face. "Are you sure you want to do that, Top? I mean, wouldn't you rather wait?"

"Wait... for what?"

"For someone *younger* to do it?"

Fitz looked at Percy askance. "Just go get the others...y'asshole."

Sergeant Percy headed back, and to allow First Sergeant Fitz enough time to conduct his investigation, he walked in no particular hurry. He pondered the rough field of rocks he had to cross that lay ahead like a wide street of cobblestones, it was going to be murder on his already aching feet. But at least the storm cloud had passed. Percy had to walk two and a quarter miles to reach the dense forest of silver firs where the rest of the team was held up. On his way he observed rodents hop up and down between the rocks and wondered how many rattlesnakes might have called this section home. It was the last thing he needed, to take a wrong step and surprise—be bitten by one and have to suffer the affects of its poisonous venom.

When he came within a few meters of the tree line, he stopped. He could see the men were seated, one on a boulder and the others on the ground. He could hear them, too, and he eavesdropped on their conversation...

"I didn't know you were getting married, Sergeant Becker," Corporal DeGarmos said, sounding surprised.

Sergeant Becker had his arm raised high and a heart shaped diamond ring pinched between his fingers. The sun breaking through the tops of the trees made it glisten. "It's not mine, Corporal," Becker responded. "This fine piece of jewelry belonged to Sergeant Hennessey, from First Platoon. He wanted me to hold it for him until he got back."

The others were silent a moment. Without knowing for sure, everyone presumed the platoon sergeant's fate; of all those in First Platoon, the most capable of making it back to camp alive was surely

Hennessey. Had he gotten his limbs blown off, no one in Bravo Company would have been the least bit surprised if he crawled back on his belly. But still...

"I didn't even know he had a girlfriend."

"No one did," Becker explained, "he kept his private life a secret, so it was a shock to me when he started spilling his guts about her. He met her on the beach in Coronado on the first day of his leave last July. Not a young woman, he told me, and not too pretty in the face, but he said that she sure knew how to fill out the top half of the bikini she wore."

They all laughed. That was Hennessey, all right, a bona fide breast man. "Hennessey told me the woman's name, Luisa. She was Latino. Had a kid, too, a boy that kept getting into trouble. But he was a good kid, Hennessey said, one that deserved a good father. I recon he was going to be that good father." Becker put his arm down finally. "He wrote her address down on a piece of paper, and that's when it hit me. He didn't think he was coming back. He made me promise that if anything happened, I would get the ring to her and tell her what he had planned to do."

"Are you going to do it, sarge?" Corporal Ferrara asked. "I don't know."

"What do you mean, you don't know?"

"I mean, I don't *know*. I don't like making promises I can't keep." He passed a look to all of them. "Especially since I don't think I'm going to make it back either." They all locked eyes on him, glaring with disapproval.

Sergeant Percy, still standing off and listening, had finally heard enough. He clapped his hands together loudly. "All right everybody—on your feet!" he commanded.

Startled, they all sprang to attention at the same time.

Percy wanted to scold them for not keeping guard, to let them know that if he had been the enemy they might all be dead now, but under the circumstances he let them slide. "Gather your shit, people, we're moving out," he told them.

"Are we close, sarge?" Private Serban asked, his voice pitched with a kind of child-like elation.

Percy nodded. "Yep. We think we've found Red."

"Where's Top?" Becker asked.

"At the objective, waiting for us now, so shake a leg."

The team gathered their gear and Percy led them back toward the cliff. No one bothered to look back. If they had, they might have seen that Sergeant Becker had purposely left Hennessey's diamond ring there on the rock where he had been sitting.

When the team arrived at the base of the cliff, Fitz was descending from a line he had dropped from the jutting rock shelf high above. When the first sergeant finally touched down he was out of breath. He had a look on his face that made Percy uncomfortable. Fitz announced, "I've got bad news... Red's not up there."

Percy was the most surprised. "What do you mean? I thought we were in the right place—I was *sure* of it!" He went and pulled the SAT photo out of his pocket and began to unfold it.

"Don't bother, Percy," Fitz said. "We *are* in the right place—and it *was* up there—but it's not up there *now*. There's evidence all over the place. Bits and pieces of it... plus some other equipment I can't account for."

Percy fought to keep his composure. "Damn it... Top, I thought she had a broken leg and couldn't move?"

Fitz shrugged. "Either she crawled away... or somebody dragged her." He used both hands to help visualize what he about to say. "There's a gap in the rock wall up there, about yay big, maybe enough room for that robot to squeeze through."

Sergeant Becker remarked ponderously, "She knew we were coming."

Fitz shook his head. "I doubt that, Becker," he replied, "otherwise I think...we'd probably be dead."

"That's comforting," Percy remarked sarcastically. Then came the million dollar question. "So, what do we do now?"

"We should head back to camp," DeGarmos suggested. "We should tell the captain."

Becker grunted, "Fuck that Ahab son of a bitch!"

"Keep your voice down," Fitz cautioned and took back control. "Everybody, calm down." He looked at Percy. "Sorry, Percy, but we need to keep going."

Percy sighed disgruntled, but he knew it, too, and gave a nod. Fitz said to the group, "We're going after her."

No one said a word.

"The trail looks fresh; a stream of oil that might lead us straight to her. We have to try. The risk of not taking out that rocket launcher of hers is too great."

Each of them grunted in agreement. They all knew what they had to do. In jest, Sergeant Percy remarked, "Top, I'm convinced... war is for the young."

Fitz smirked. Sadly, that was true, and literally... It was absolutely absurd.

CHAPTER TWENTY-NINE

"THE DAY BEFORE DOOMSDAY"

Hollis sat at the very top of the tower, well above the tree tops and at level with the peak of the rock formation that surrounded Oliveri. He wasn't so high that he was lost in the clouds, but he imagined if he reached up he might be able to touch them. The air smelled different up here than on the ground; fresher and so much cooler. He sucked in a lung full of it and was invigorated. He appreciated the serenity for a moment and then climbed a few rungs down. Here he did a final check of the transmitter assembly. He gave the wires a firm tug; they were fastened to terminals and fixed securely. Good, he thought, so he had done his job right and was confident that he could leave it alone and let it do what it was programmed to do. Far below, on the ground, he could hear the faint growl of the portable generator that provided power to the transmitter, the chug of the motor like a distant voice calling up to him, *all systems go*!

Hollis rested his hand on the turn switch connected to the outer panel. It was in the off position now. A quarter turn clockwise was all he needed to do. Because he was familiar with the radio receiver in the CP back at Bravo Company's camp, he could visualize the amber light on the face of the radio. It would turn to green once a link was established. And if the unit radio operator was vigilant, and caught sight of it, he could start transmitting long distance almost immediately.

Captain Radigan's voice squawked inside head, he hated the intrusion; reciting the words: *when I call in for an air strike, there won't be as much as two pieces of wood nailed together, a tree standing... or anyone left alive.*

He wondered how much time he had to get out of town once the call was made? A common man would have hesitated before turning the switch, to consider the consequences of his actions. Another man—a descent man—might have given second thoughts to what he was about to do. But Hollis had too much of his father in him, and no time left to recall the measure of his mother's guilt. So, the Gunlord's son turned the switch.

With just a click, the transmitter hummed to life. There was no need to speculate; it was working perfectly.

He looked down at the ground. Despite Daryl's insistence to play, the Sapphire King was standing perfectly still and looking up. This time the robot projected a look of accusation; a suspicious penetrating leer. *Did it know?* Hollis questioned. *Was it* possible, the robot had some notion to what purpose this transmitter served and what was *about to happen*?

Hollis recalled how the robot had torn down the tower in the first place, back in town. What was its motivation *then*? Talia said it had a reason for doing it. *Reason.*

What was it about that word? But if indeed it had a reason, why was it allowing him to reconstruct it now? And something else didn't make sense now that he thought of it— how could it have torn down the tower without the means to get up there to the roof of the building and lay its claws on it? The robot must have had someone assisting it. Of course, there was the possibility that the red robot had fired a rocket at it and blasted it off the roof, but there was no sign of that. There were no scorch marks or melted parts from the intense heat of the blast. More and more questions with no one willing to provide answers. Without another thought to it Hollis prepared to climb down.

His job was done.

He reached out to a cross rung and shifted his weight to descend. Years and years of caustic rain and no maintenance was the direct result of what happened next.

Hollis began to plummet toward the ground. For when he grabbed onto the cross rung it broke free with zero resistance, as if the whole time the metal bar had simply been floating there in mid air. No chance to grab onto the rope that was still dangling through the center, Hollis was falling with the speed that would surely shatter his bones once his body made contact with the ground. He watched helplessly as the top of the tower grew farther and farther away. His arms and legs flailed, hoping to make purchase with something. There was less chance of that as the structure of the tower grew wider and wider as he fell. He knew he was going to die. This was it. In that instance, he heard a scream. It sounded like Talia. And then he hit something—something *solid*—as solid as the ground, but he was still at a significant height, still far from the bottom. His body went into shock from the sudden jolt and his mind was too confused to make sense of it. He could not conceive of what had happened, nor what would happen next. The hardened platform beneath him shifted, became wobbly, and Hollis forced himself and all his Gunlord strength to hold on and keep his balance. Dizzy from the impact, he had the sensation of being pulled sideways. And then he felt the grips of unconsciousness...

"Listen," she said sleepily.

A gradual awareness swept over him. He was drawn into a dream-like state.

The sound of a guitar played.

"God, that sounds so beautiful," she said.

She was right, it did, and he continued to listen.

"When's the last time you made an effort to notice these things?" He was unsure how to respond.

"No one *owns* this world, you know?"

He glanced around. He caught the scent of freshly cut grass and it reminded him of home.

"Do you even know what day it is?" she asked.

He did not see her face clearly, even if he squinted his eyes, nor did he recognize the voice, but he knew what she was getting at.

One hand of hers emerged from the shadows, stiff and crackly, holding a freshly cut red long-stemmed rose, went it closer to him it turned into an Uzi. She aimed it at him. She said, "It's the day before doomsday!"

Hollis opened his eyes. At first, he was amazed that he was still alive. The last thing he could recall was that he was plummeting. The next thing he noticed was the passage of time; the sun was much lower, the shadows on the ground longer. He was lying on his back, unsure of his condition. He felt a tingling sensation all over his body, but he wasn't sure if he could move. And then he heard Talia say something. "Are you all right?" she asked. His eyes focused in on her. She and Daryl were standing over him. She was using a wet towel to dampen his forehead.

"How long was I out?" he asked.

Talia replied, "A long time." She was dressed in the jade colored princess gown, the one she wore when Hollis first met her. Hollis tried to sit up. Now he could see her lips moving, trying to tell him something more, but all he could hear was the sudden ringing in his ears. He struggled to get to his feet. He put out his hand as a signal for her to give him room to recover. Both Talia and Daryl kept back. Hollis staggered clear of them as he moved to gain balance on his wobbly legs. He moved intently toward one of the concrete pedestals at the base of the tower. He pressed his weight against it and held there a moment. His head ached, like a full ammunition canister had been dropped on his head from the height of a hundred feet, or something awfully close to that. He felt the dried blood in his hair. He breathed deeply and tried to place the missing pieces of the puzzle together; he did not suppose he had somehow survived the more than one hundred foot drop from the top of the tower. To even consider that in the least was ludicrous. He looked over at the robot. It was standing nearby, its eye focused upwards toward the top of the tower, as if it was receiving a message from the working transmitter up there.

"He caught you, Hollis!' Daryl called out.

Hollis turned to Daryl as the boy drifted from Talia to join him at the base of the tower. "He saw you falling and climbed up to catch you," the boy went on to say.

The idea was preposterous. There was just no way... *it*...

Or *how*...

Or even *why*?

"I saw it with my own eyes, Hollis," Talia confirmed. "The Sapphire King saved your life."

The guilt came as sudden as the ringing in his ears, and was a far more uncomfortable feeling than his aching head. What the hell happened? It was hard to imagine the robot possessed the readiness and capability to do such a thing, let alone, the—dare he say it—*reason*. Hollis felt it was kind of creepy that the robot kept such a watchful eye on him all the time, but now he was eternally grateful.

"How long did you say I was unconscious?" he strained to ask as he pushed himself off the concrete pedestal and towards the generator.

Talia shrugged, and replied unsurely, "An hour, I guess. Why? Is that important?"

Exhaustion could account for most of that. He hadn't slept well in days and perhaps his body just gave in to the opportunity to recharge.

Hollis crossed the short distance to reach the portable generator. He stood over it a moment and considered his next move, contemplated it carefully. The generator was still chugging away, providing ample power to the transmitter high above. Soon he reached down and turned the switch off. The motor choked and then went silent. Hollis' finger was still resting on the switch when he turned to the Sapphire King and remarked, "One hour, Captain Radigan, that's all you get."

He imagined that even his emotionally idealistic uncle would have thought he was crazy. And to avoid any chance of reconsideration for what he just did, he gave the generator's control panel a swift kick, smashing it beyond repair.

The robot stopped looking up. It turned to look at Hollis again. Indeed, the Sapphire King protected all those who were under its reign.

Some of the weariness still lingered, so it was due to Talia's insistence that Hollis take time to recover some more before they all headed back to town. The three of them sat under a tree, Hollis was in the middle. Hollis played a game of tic-tac-toe with

Daryl, drawing in the dirt with a stick. What astounded Hollis was that the boy had never played the game before, nor even heard of it. After losing a few times, though, Daryl got the hang of it and it wasn't long before he got bored and didn't want to play anymore. He sprang to his feet and scurried over to where the Sapphire King was, leaving Hollis and Talia alone. In that moment, Talia saw an opportunity to ask, "Why did you smash the generator, after all the work you did?"

He looked at her sullenly, wondering why it took her so

long to ask.

She raised her shoulders as a gesture of innocence. "I mean, I figured you a had a good reason, and you would tell me when you were ready, but I wasn't sure how long that was going to take..." She giggled, adding, "and I'm not a patient woman. And you mentioned the name, Captain Radigan. Who's he?"

One question was easier to answer than the other. "Captain Radigan is the name of the commander I was... *traveling* with."

She was taken aback suddenly. Her face turned ghostly white and she quickly scooted away from him, as if someone had dropped a live grenade between them. Hollis had no idea the can of worms he opened. "You never told me you were a soldier, Hollis!" she exclaimed, horrified.

"No," he answered smartly, and then repeated it with more emphasis, "*No*!"

"But this Captain Radigan... he's your commander?" she persisted, aghast. At once she turned and posed a look to the Sapphire King, as if expecting it to *do* something.

Hollis said firmly, "I was his prisoner, Talia." He focused his gaze on her, determined to keep her calm. "And if you want to be technical, I'm a fugitive." He had no time to assess the damage his mouth had made and thought it best, to ensure his safety, to confess, but perhaps not *all* of it.

"I *was* a soldier...," he corrected himself, "but I'm not one anymore."

He thought about his uncle, still held captive. He thought about the choices he had made and the lack of options he had left.

Talia appeared to relax a bit, but kept her distance. "Are you a good man, Hollis?"

He answered gruffly, "I'm beginning to wonder."

"Why are you a fugitive? Did you do something bad? Did you hurt someone?"

I hurt a lot of people he would have had to admit if he was to confess to her more than he needed to.

He thought about it, and prepared a simpler and more direct explanation.

OPERATION: RIVER HEAD.

The words ran like a marquee in his mind, and conjured images he had for so long been fighting to suppress...

Now showing:

An elite team of operatives moving through the thick trees. An ambush.

Bullets intended to penetrate thick armor ripping through tender flesh and bone.

And only one man capable of sustaining such damage—a Gunlord's son!

"I was a member of a military team," he began, "a special team that carried out covert operations." He cleared his throat. "Covert operations are missions that the government sends you on that are so secret, so... undermined, that the government can deny their involvement in if things go wrong." Hollis paused to see if Talia was following. He continued, "Well, on this particular mission, things went *very* wrong.

There was this body of water that divided two warring tribes, and a sovereign island between them that stood a strategic advantage should either tribe gain control of it. Our team was assigned to sneak in and install monitoring devices on the island and then evacuate the villagers who lived there. But when we got there we found we were too late. A third party that we were aware of but weren't expecting was already occupying the island. We were supposed to return to base—scrub the mission—but our team leader, who was the son of a prominent general, sought to impress his old man. So instead, he ordered us to attempt to remove that third party by force. Our team was outmanned and outgunned. I'll spare you the gruesome details, but suffice is to say, we were all but wiped out. Those few that survived the initial ambush were tortured to death; our captures, having little regard for human life, behaved in levels of such depravity it would have made even the stoutest holy man lose faith in God and humanity. I was the only one who managed to get out alive. I reported to my superiors what happened and the reason why it happened, but by that time it didn't matter. Our government couldn't deny their involvement. The operation had been exposed and had gone public. It was all over the news. Before long, the whole world knew. My superiors couldn't blame that general's son—he was dead anyway—and so they found someone else to blame. I was tried for treason. Evidence was fabricated at my court-martial and I was sentence to death."

Talia breathed a sigh, "Sentenced to death," she repeated thoughtfully, and tilted her head upwards as if she was trying to figure out something. She said in a moment, "Thus ensuring *everyone* died on that mission."

Hollis' brow rose in reaction. He was amazed, she got it. He said, "I was a loose end."

He went on. "Anyway, Captain Radigan was transporting me to Fort Bradley, where I was to be executed. The vehicle I was being transported in broke down a few miles from here. There were other prisoners with me. Radigan made me a deal: if I got here to Oliveri and managed to get the transmitter working, he would set me free. You see, he needed the transmitter to work so he could call for help." He didn't bother to explain about his uncle, nor reveal any other details that might incriminate him. He considered his explanation the closely adapted *abridged* version. "And now, instead of being free, I'm a prisoner here." He looked over at Daryl and the robot, adding, "Like the rest of you."

"No, Hollis—no, no, no." Talia retorted. It was a reaction he wasn't expecting. She got to her feet quickly. "Here, in Oliveri, you're free." She referred to the Sapphire King with a nod, "And protected! You can do whatever you want here. Can't you see that?"

"You're all prisoners here, Talia... you just don't know it."

She grunted in defiance. "You could not be more wrong, Hollis." She approached him, poked her finger at his chest and told him, "You think I don't know the difference between freedom and captivity? You don't know anything about me... or any of us."

The way she was talking, so out of character for her, it seemed she was a different person. "I can prove it to you."

Hollis' eyes shifted away from her conspicuously.

"I mean it. We'll go back to town right now, and I'll show you something that will make you think differently. Can you walk?" she asked.

"Back to Oliveri?"

"Yes... or does the Sapphire King have to carry you?"

He smirked at her, envisioning the robot cradling him in its arms all the way down the hill. "I can walk," he assured her.

"Good." She held out her hand to help him to his feet. "Let's go."

CHAPTER THIRTY

"UNWELCOME VISITORS"

Buck Baker was hard at work inside his barn. It was only late afternoon, but the dense cloud cover made it look like nighttime. He burned gas lanterns throughout his work space, in order for him to be able to see what he was doing. He was so into his work that he lost track of time and it actually did become night time. At some point he paused to look at his hands. His sore aching hands were so covered in grease he could hardly see his skin. He reflected about that a moment, how far things had come. In just two short years he had gone from farmer, to caretaker, and now robot repairman. The last time he looked and smelled like this—like someone who had crawled out of a grease pit—he was just a teen, part-time gopher and clean-up boy at the *Wilbur & Coleman* factory, outside Fort McClellan, Alabama, where his father served as a drill instructor in the old Army base there. That was a long, long time ago, before the country was divided into East and West and all the wars were fought overseas, places far away. The factory built automated harvesting machines from assembly lines. The workers there were kind to him, fatherly almost, and in their spare time they taught him a thing or two about assembling harvesters, which was where he acquired much of the skills he was practicing now on the Ruby Queen.

He decided to take a break, in the very least clean his hands back at the house and maybe get something to eat—*and oh*, to check on his dog. The golden retriever had been barking a moment ago and Buck had envisioned the ole girl caught the scent of a squirrel under the porch and switched to her predator mode.

Buck climbed down from the top of the seven foot step ladder he was using (the Ruby Queen was so thick that even now while she was lying on her back he found it hard to reach across her wide chest) Nearly seven feet taller than the Sapphire King, her clubbed hooves extended past the open barn doors like a long legged man on a short mattress.

"I'll be right back," he remarked to her incidentally. "I'm taking a little break.

Don't you worry though, when I come back, I'll finish up... and by this time tomorrow you'll be able to walk straight out of here."

He stepped out. Halfway between the barn and the house he paused.

Something didn't feel right. He even sniffed the air, something about it didn't even *smell* right. What was it? He looked around, but saw nothing unusual. The porch light, powered by a generator in the basement, was on, but the kitchen lights were off. Strange, he thought, he had left them on. *Old age*, he concluded, that must be it—bitch snuck up on him and was making him jumpy. He pressed on.

When he passed through the back door and entered the kitchen he did not bother to turn the light switch on. Concerned that he might mark the wall with his greasy hands, he instead moved through the dark toward the sink. While he washed his hands he got that uneasy feeling again. Undeniable this time. He reached blindly for the dish towel, where he knew it hung on the plastic dish drain. He began to dry his hands. He did not bother to turn around. He knew he wasn't alone. He just kept his head facing forward at the window above the sink. There, in the reflection of the glass, he saw a figure seated at his kitchen table and three others standing in line against the wall behind him. Buck turned his head to the left, to view his only escape route. The back door was still open and he could see clear across the yard to the barn. One of the figures behind him must have read his mind and remarked, "Where do you think *you're* going?"

Fitz needed to squash the old man's intentions promptly. "Don't run," he warned him, "trust me, you'll never make it to the door. Have a seat."

Finally, the old man turned to look upon the strangers in his kitchen. The man's yellow dog was seated on the floor next to Fitz. Fitz was scratching behind the dog's ear; the dog seemed to like it, its tail was wagging. The old man had a look on his face as if to regard the dog as a traitor. Perhaps it was, Fitz thought, but among those in the room right now, there was doubt to him who the good guys were. "What's your name, mister?"

The old man replied, "the name's Buck, Buck Baker." Once his ass was planted, he was sitting directly across from Fitz. The two stared at each other awhile.

The old man was visibly shaken. His hands resting flat on the table were trembling.

"Tell me, Mister Baker, what were you doing inside your barn?"

Buck looked around, seeming to take careful note of the weapons each of the other solders brandished, and then said, "Nothing." He slouched in his chair.

Fitz smacked his hand loudly on the table, frightening the dog away and jolting Buck to sit back up straight.

Fitz repeated the question, emphasizing each word, "What... were... you...*doing*...inside...your...barn, Mister Baker?"

Buck's mouth was open before he even made a sound. "I-I had found the robot on the ledge of a cliff, about three miles from here. It looked like it had been there for a long time. I assumed anyone who had been missing it would have found it by now. I brought it here to take it apart."

"Take it apart. What for?"

Buck shrugged innocently. "To sell it for parts."

"To who?"

"Marauders."

"Thieves... and murderers, then?"

Buck inhaled deeply, nervous. "I give them things they could use and in return... they let me live."

The old man was growing confident, Fitz didn't like that. Fitz stared at him a long while. "How did you get it here?"

"I dragged it."

"How? Explain."

"I tied chains around it and towed it with my tractor."

"And it didn't resist? It didn't try to stop you?"

Again, Buck shrugged. "It has no power. Nothing working at all. I've been hammering on it all day, drilling, cutting. It's completely off line."

Fitz continued to study the old man. He began drumming his fingers on the table, a confusing, irritating sound that grew louder and louder as he drummed them faster and faster until at once, he stopped. "What about the other one?"

"What other one?" Buck asked, looking around questioningly at the others. "There were *two* robots, Mister Baker, did you know that?."

"This was the only one I found, I swear."

There was a long silence. It seemed as awkward for the old man as it was for everyone else in the room. Fitz just kept staring at the man. He was studying him.

Drawing a conclusion. "All right, Mister Baker," the First Sergeant eventually said. "On your feet. We're going back to the barn."

"I-I can put it back together for you, if you like. I can put the robot's leg back on?"

"That won't be necessary," Fitz said as he secured his rifle and stood up. He pointed toward the door. "After you, sir, if you don't mind."

They crossed the yard from the back porch, heading toward the barn. Buck was in front, leading them. The rest of Fitz's team followed in column formation. There was a particular bounce in the old man's step, as if he was especially eager to get back to the barn. At some point, Sergeant Becker caught a whiff of something and called attention to it. "Smells like something was burning here," he remarked, and turned to address Buck, "What have you been cooking out here, old man?"

Buck's response was immediate, and his answer so to the point it was like he had rehearsed it, "Couple of my cows was infected with blackleg," he replied. "I had to put them down, and then *burn* them, so's they wouldn't infect the others."

Partially concealed by the overgrown brush against one of the corral fences was a dark, charred mound of.... something. It *could* have been cows. Fitz did not truly care one way or the other. He was just as eager as Buck to get to the barn, but not for the same reason he suspected.

"What's going on?" Fitz asked.

Sergeant Percy appeared from the shadows. He had been posted at the barn and assigned to keep watch of any movement inside. "Nothing," he reported. "It hasn't moved. It's just lying there."

Fitz said, "The old man says it's offline."

Percy checked Buck out. Gave him a quick once over. Then he turned back to Fitz and asked quietly, "Do you believe him?"

Fitz bit his lower lip. "No," he answered. "But we're desperate. We need to get inside this barn and disarm that rocket launcher."

Percy nodded. "Roger that, Top."

Fitz signaled his men to gather close. They gathered around him. "We're going inside," he told them, keeping his voice low. He didn't like the looks on their faces. They looked too eager. Too willing to ignore the danger. It was times like these Fitz hated the responsibility of being in command. "I want everyone to be on their guard. You see that thing move, you run. You hear me?"

They each gave a thumbs up and nods of *loud-and-clear*.

DeGarmos had the C4 in his back pack. Fitz checked it. He then turned to Buck. "Mister Baker, you stay close to me."

"No problem," he replied quickly.

And to his men, Fitz said, "OK, let's get this done."

CHAPTER THIRTY-ONE

"CONSCIOUS DECISION"

The fifteen or so soldiers lying in a heap at the bottom of the crevice were in the advanced state of decay. The skin and soft tissue that still remained had not yet been eaten away by bacteria or insects, or removed by crows. The partially skeletonized heads, with their empty eye sockets and jawbones cracked open wide as if they were wailing, were locked in an eternal gaze upwards toward the top. Where once a bridge stretched across from one side of the cliff to the other, now there was nothing but jagged protrusions of steel reaching out to each other. Back at the bottom, plant life flourished all around the carcasses due to the chemical discharge released during the decaying process, enriching the soil with nitrogen. Though the uniforms these soldiers wore were drastically faded they were still clear enough to make out from above where a head peeked over the edge to view them.

Billy Duncan stepped back from the edge. He had seen enough to draw a conclusion. He focused now on the rope that stretched across the crevice. The side opposite his appeared to be tied a bit more securely, so it seemed obvious there on the other side was where the rope had originated. He looked closely at the cross lug wrench entangled in the piece of the bridge nearest him. This, he conceived, was how the rope was thrown across. With luck, it was fastened well enough to hold the weight of someone willing to get across to Oliveri.

"It doesn't look safe, does it?" cited a voice from behind him. Billy turned quickly to see a young man in uniform emerge from the line of trees on the side of the road. A specialist by rank, the boy moved toward Billy, but not in a straight line. He was staggering and looked ready to collapse. Billy had a mind to catch him if he started to fall, but his suspicions about the boy made him wary. This boy had to be one of Captain Radigan's soldiers. When he was close enough, Billy read the name stitched above the breast pocket of the boy's BDU jacket, DONOHUE.

"You're the only prisoner to have made it this far," Donohue said. "And wearing the uniform of a Bravo Company soldier." Donohue made a scolding look as he turned slightly away. "I wonder what Captain Radigan's end game was? What the hell was he hoping to accomplish?" The boy seemed to be just thinking out loud. Billy ignored his rant.

"How many more of you are there left?" Donohue asked.

Billy replied, "I'm the last one. Your captain just kept sending us out, one by one."

"I know. And I've been spotting them and turning them back around, to deliver a message. My guess is, they never made it back."

"How do you even know who I am?" Billy asked him.

"You happen to be one of the few prisoners I recognize," Donohue answered. "You came in with that other kid... the Gunlord's son...?"

"Hollis."

"Whatever." Donohue stumbled backwards, shrugging to keep his balance.

Billy could see he was in bad shape. Malnourished. Could barely keep still. And in desperate need of water, no doubt. Billy could offer nothing, nothing but a sympathetic gesture which Donohue mistook as a motion to mock him.

Donohue let out a hiss through clenched teeth and forced himself to stand up straight. He saw the rabbit's foot dangling by a string from the button of Billy's breast pocket and yanked it off before Billy could block him. "You won't be needing *this* anymore," the boy told him. "It's a tracking device."

Billy sighed deeply. "And here I was, thinking it brought me good luck." Donohue threw the rabbit's foot into the crevice.

Billy turned his attention back to the rope.

Donohue said, "That rope is somebody's formal invitation... although, it doesn't look very inviting. Could be a trap."

Billy had nothing to say in response.

"I went back and forth," Donohue admitted, gesturing to Billy as if he had walked the length of the cliff edge. "I was looking for another way to get across.

Without any rock climbing gear, this was it. This was the only *best* chance to get into town."

Billy nodded, to confirm his belief. "I have to get over there," he said. "I've got a strong feeling that my nephew is over there, and he might need my help."

"There's something else over there, too," Donohue revealed, "it stands about fifteen feet tall and fights like a boxer with the power of a diesel locomotive."

Billy had only a slight indication what he meant. He was

not provided any details about what had happened, he was just instructed to simply get to Oliveri and attempt to turn power on to the transmitter there, but he was well aware, even as he walked all those miles through the woods to get to the point where he was now, that a greater danger lurked beyond his view, but he had to do everything in his power to try and save his nephew, Hollis, from it.

"Someone would have to be pretty brave to go across that," Donohue said. "I was going to say, *stupid*."

Donohue laughed. "So, which one of us is going first?"

CHAPTER THIRTY-TWO

"CONFESSION"

Hollis and Talia stood in the middle of the street; he looking disheveled with his torn clothes, bruised and scratched face, and she so fresh in her princess gown with her face smooth and pure. He was slouched and looked forlorn; she was standing up straight and smiling. They were the quintessential odd couple, *odd* being the definitive word.

They faced a five story white building set back from the road. All of the windows on the ground floor were smashed, like someone used the place for target practice. Hollis took note that none of the surrounding buildings had been vandalized in such a way, so why was this place singled out? The grounds were overgrown. The plastic letters once mounted to the stucco face at the top were broken or missing.

Someone had targeted them as well. The original blue color of the building showed behind the missing letters, spelling out the word: HOSPITAL. It's only endearing quality was the park-like setting in the center, a courtyard with a concrete fountain and a statue of the Blessed Mother, both of which looked like ruins in and among the tall weeds and overgrown shrubs.

"Are you going to tell me why you brought me here?" Hollis asked. He had asked her more than once since their trip back from the hills where she was taking him. She refused to answer him. And now that they were at their destination she was still hesitant to reveal anything. Hollis looked back at the Sapphire King. The robot kept its distance from them, seeming to allow them their space. Daryl had been sent home, told to find Momma and tell her where they were and that they would be back soon.

"Did Daryl ever tell you his Apache warrior name?" Talia asked.

Hollis was not in the mood for riddles; his mind was still dealing with the repercussions of what he had done to the generator at the tower. All he said to her was, "I don't remember."

"Bodoway," she reminded.

He thought, if only it'd been a multiple choice question...

"It means fire maker," she went on, and began to move away from Hollis and toward the sidewalk at the opposite side of the street. "Daryl is eight years old now— almost nine—and when he was just seven he liked to light fires. One day, in the middle of the night, he lit a fire in his house while his parents were sleeping. The fire got out of control and spread quickly throughout the whole house. He managed to get out safely. He was lucky. He ran out his front door. The fire made its way up to the second floor and he stood there on his front lawn and watched as the house burned. He swears to this day that he saw his parents run out the back door of the house, and then run into the woods behind his house. He believes they hid in the woods until the soldiers came and told everyone in town they had to evacuate. He said, they ran away as a form of punishment. But they didn't. They were sleeping upstairs at the time. They never got out and were trapped inside."

At the sidewalk, Talia pointed to the hospital, at a specific end of the building. "See the windows on the fourth floor, Hollis, the ones with the bars on them?" She kept her arm up until she was sure Hollis was looking. "Daryl's room was the one on the end. All the boys' rooms were on that side." Still she kept her arm up, but this time she redirected her pointer finger. "And those on the other side, on the right, were the ones for the women. *Mine* was there, on the corner. Do you know what was so good about the corner rooms, Hollis? They have two windows on each side, which makes them nicer than the others when the sun goes down. It's a very pretty sight. I shared that room with Cora and Momma."

Her admission stunned him for a good few seconds. When he finally said something, it was, "I thought Momma was a real nurse?"

Talia looked at him. "Momma's no more a real nurse, Hollis... than *I* am a real princess."

He continued to stare, bewildered, but the inner voice of reason told him he should have already known this.

Talia explained, "When the soldiers came to town at the end of the civil war, they told the mayor, Mister Potts, that everyone needed to evacuate because it wasn't safe for anyone to live here, that is, not for now. They said rogue Americanist units were likely to pass through remote towns, like Oliveri, and cause trouble. Their job was to make sure everyone got to a more secure place. And because the town had no communication with the outside world, Mister Potts agreed to cooperate. In fact, *everyone* cooperated." She added, "I had never seen an Americanist, you know that? Had no idea what they were about. Maybe I was too young to remember, but the Second Civil War had no affect on me." Back on track, she said, "Anyways, I don't think anyone really wanted to stay here. I think they all just needed a good reason to go. The soldiers said it would only be temporary, that once the danger was over they were free to return. Just a few weeks, they said. But weeks turned into months. Months turned into years. And now, after more than two years, no one has bothered to come back. There was nothing left here worth coming back to, I suppose."

Talia removed her conic headdress and let it float gently to the street.

"So, nobody made much of a fuss about the details. The government gave everyone pay vouchers—money to live on for awhile—and right away people packed up their belongings in their cars or their pick-up trucks and drove straight on out of here. All the critical patients in the hospital—all the ones that were really sick or couldn't physically move—were taken good care of. They were carried out and put on buses or flown away in helicopters. But not the ones on the fourth floor, no...no, they were an issue. They couldn't be easily transported, or maybe it was just that they weren't worth the trouble. So, the mayor decided to let those patients remain here, or maybe he got some extra pay vouchers to come up with an easier plan. The soldiers agreed to watch over us, assuring that all of them—that all of *us* —would be safe until everyone returned."

Hollis suddenly needed to sit down, not just because he needed to process the information Talia just fed him but because his legs felt ready to give out. He saw a wooden bench on the opposite side of the street and made his ways towards it, but it may as well have been a hundred miles away.

"I can imagine what you must be thinking of us right now?" Talia posed as she watched him walk away from her.

"To be honest," Hollis replied, "it explains a lot."

He finally made his to the bench in spite of his of his lack of strength, and then collapsed upon it.

"Are you all right, Hollis?"

He took a deep breath and nodded before answering. "It's been a rough past few days. I guess it's all catching up to me." He redirected her. "The soldiers that were here, Talia, you never told me what happened to them?"

She gave a reluctant gesture as before, like she was about to tell a secret she vowed to keep. But then a strange calmness came over her. She looked suddenly at ease, as if an inner voice told her, *it's all right, go on ...tell him.*

Hollis chanced a look back at the Sapphire King again. The robot had not moved, but now it was looking at him.

Talia spun in place. She tried to perform a graceful pirouette, like she was a ballerina, but she was not good at it. When she stopped, she raised her right hand in a mock salute. "One of the soldiers was named, Charlie. Corporal Charles Taylor Rice, *Sir*!" She dropped her arm to her side in a snap and stood rigid, like at attention. "He became my friend. And in time, we became *more* than friends. He said he loved me."

She relaxed her body. "He said, when this whole thing with the war was over he was going to marry me and we would move to his hometown, some place called Louisville, in Kentucky."

That part needed no convincing. Talia was a beautiful young woman, and even though she was a little whacky, she was still quite sweet. And her willingness to be in charge and responsible for all those on the fourth floor (what the military would deem *leadership qualities)* made her even more appealing. Charlie was a lucky man. Certainly the luckiest man in Oliveri.

But Hollis could not shake the feeling that this love story had a tragic ending. "It wasn't long before some of the other soldiers got mad at Charlie. They got jealous. They said it wasn't fair that he had a girlfriend and they didn't. So, Charlie's commander gave him an order. He said Charlie had to share me." She turned to Hollis. "*Share me*, can you guess what that meant?"

With no expression on his face, Hollis simply nodded. He entertained a heroic notion; he wished he could have been there back then; if this Charlie guy truly loved her, Hollis would have made sure that the other soldiers minded their own business—or else!

Her voice fell weak as she continued, "I'm a good girl, Hollis, but after awhile I couldn't take it anymore. I went to Charlie and I begged him to help me—to make them stop. I'll never forget the look on his face. And I'll never forget what he said to me, or how it made me feel. He said..." Talia held back a second, choking on her own words. "He said, a whore like me doesn't deserve his help.

"I began to cry. I clung to him and he tried to push me away, but I wouldn't let go. I held on tight. That was when he hit me. He hit me so hard I was lifted off my feet and fell backwards." She paused significantly to look at Hollis and to try to judge his reaction. He was surely paying close attention. Hollis had never taken his eyes off her the whole time she was speaking. "When I got up, I ran away. I ran right out of town.

The bridge was still standing then, and I was able to leave Oliveri. I just kept running. And running. And running. Until I could not run anymore. I was in the middle of the woods when I passed out, probably from exhaustion. When I awoke, it was dark out.

And the Sapphire King was standing over me. He took me to the Queen. The Queen saw that I was hurt and asked me what was wrong. I told her, and I asked her if she would help me."

"Wait. What?" Hollis had to interrupt a moment. "The Queen. That's the red one, right—the one with the rocket launcher? Are you saying she can *talk*?"

"Yes, Hollis, she *can* talk. And she told me she would help me. So, the Sapphire King followed me back to town. And the Queen blew up the bridge, so no more soldiers could come to harm me."

Hollis interrupted again, "You mean, so none of the soldiers that were already here could escape."

Talia shrugged. "I went back to my room, in the hospital, where I laid awake in bed and waited."

Hollis asked, "You didn't see that the Sapphire King was tossing the soldiers over the cliff? I saw the bodies at the bottom."

Talia shook her head. "By the morning, all I knew was that the Sapphire King took care of my problem."

Hollis felt in no position to pass judgment. For all he knew, those soldiers got what they deserved. How it affected her was a terrible and unalterable consequence. For a moment, though, he felt embarrassed to be a man, and ashamed of ever feeling attracted to her, for wanting to be with her physically.

Tchwonk... Tchwonk... Tchwonk...

Hollis turned around. The Sapphire King had begun to walk away on its own.

"Where's he going?" Hollis asked.

"Probably going to see the Ruby Queen," Talia answered. "They can read each others minds, you know. She may be calling to him." She started to laugh, which was a pleasant change to her mood.

"You find that funny?"

"No, not him going to see the Queen, silly..." she said. "*You*."

"Me? What's so funny about me?"

"It's the first time I ever heard you refer to the Sapphire King as *he* and not *it*."

The Gunlord's son had to ponder that a moment.

"Talia," he asked, "you said before that the Ruby Queen can talk." Talia nodded. "Yes, she can."

"Can *I* talk to her?"

Talia shook her head. "She will only talk to me." *Naturally*, Hollis thought, and disregarded the notion.

"To me," she reaffirmed, "and to Buck Baker."

Hollis withdrew with a sudden jerk and asked, "Who's Buck Baker?"

CHAPTER-THIRTY-THREE

"BAIT AND SWITCH"

Inside Buck Baker's barn, Fitz's team took positions, covering all sides of the massive robot lying in the center. Red was mostly concealed under a canvas tarp, but some parts of her stuck out and were exposed. Her appendages, for one; they were designed differently than Blue's, for starters, she had only one claw. It was on the right, elongated, like a crocodile's snout, and had teeth made of long steel spikes to grab and hold tight heavy cargo. At the end of her left arm was a drilling apparatus; a type of gear cluster with diamond blades useful in boring into rock, the sort of thing a mining robot *should* have.

The First Sergeant walked all the way around her to get a full perspective and physical sense of what he and his team were dealing with, but perhaps more so out of pure curiosity. Up toward the top, covered under the tarp was of particular interest to him. Sergeant Percy and Becker showed initiative and acted without being told, they took out their survival knives and began cutting the lines that held the tarp in place, and then each took a firm hold and removed the cover. No need to guess anymore. There it was. The rocket launcher; a twelve tube, shoulder mounted nest with six remaining white- tipped *Hydras,* each capable of reaching and obliterating a target at nearly seven miles

away. Fitz had to consider the fate of their endeavor to travel all this way. Had they not, there was a chance the remainder of Bravo Company would have perished.

Fitz continued his examination.

The Ruby Queen's eye was similar to that of the Sapphire

King's, in that it was a chromium sphere encased in a shell. Its lights were out.

So far, so good.

Her basic structure was similar to the other robot that had wiped out two of Bravo Company's platoons; but of course, she was designed and constructed in the same manufacturing plant, so this was of no surprise. There were other notable differences.

Red was bulkier, more heavily armored, built to take a pounding from gunfire, while it seemed Blue was designed for close combat, armed with speed and agility; Red was accustomed to settling her scores from a distance.

Her severed leg was in position next to her other one. Had the old farmer been lying and planned to re-attach it? The notion did not sit comfortably with Fitz. And the first sergeant noticed the work ladder that reached to Red's chest, the array of spotlights concentrated on a specific open panel up there.

Fitz had not been keeping a close eye on Buck Baker as he should have. So enthralled with this robot he lost focus. In spite of his doubts that the old man was being fully cooperative, he never considered he had been lied to about the robot being off line. And not in a million years would Fitz have suspected Red and the old man were allies.

But he was wrong.

And in the most literal sense, *deadly wrong*.

As Fitz was about to join Corporal DeGarmos on the right

side of the robot and retrieve the high-yield chemical explosive contained within the young man's ruck sack, he heard the old man say something...

"Ruby, my dear, these men have come to harm you."

All at once, the Ruby Queen came to life. Her reaction was instantaneous, her movements precise; as if she had choreographed them ahead of time. Her eye rose like a crane, shining bright red. She quickly spread her hulking arms out. In the narrow confines of the barn she dispatched Degarmos and Serban, each standing on opposite sides. Both were crushed to death against the barn walls on their perspective sides, so intensely that the wall boards splintered from the violent impact. The crane mechanism that supported the eye gave a quick scan.

Sergeant Becker saw the eye as a target. He moved closer to get a clear shot. He raised his rifle, but the Ruby Queen's reaction was quicker. She slammed that rock drilling gear cluster straight against his frail human body and began to turning the blades. The blades tore into his meager flesh. When they bored deep enough, his body spun wickedly off the ground, like a top, as the gears drew it in towards drew him in and ground him into tiny pieces.

Sergeant Percy was the smartest one. His first response was to flee. He made every attempt to get past the robot and exit through the open barn doors. But he underestimated the speed and mobility of the robot's one good leg. On his way out the door he was hit square in the back and catapulted twenty feet into the air before coming to rest in the field, within view of the pile of bodies Buck had said were cows. But these bodies were not cows. Barely holding onto consciousness, Percy could make out the charred remnants of Bravo Company uniforms.

Fitz was the only threat in the barn now. The Ruby Queen tried to raise her arms in the hopes it might capture the man as he backed away from the top of her toward the rear of the barn. He searched for some other way out—a back door—but there was none. He fired his rifle in vain. It was a soldier's response. He kept thinking, if he could just strike one of the rockets still in the launcher it might detonate. The Queen's arm kept hitting the beams that ran across the hay loft, blocking its path to the man. Debris fell from the ceiling. Boards landed onto the Queen's steel chest plate. The beams finally cracked and the loft collapsed. Though Fitz was unharmed, the collapsed loft allowed the Queen a greater freedom of movement and when she dug through the debris Fitz was eventually caught. He was grabbed by his ankle by the tip of the crocodile-like claw. It dragged him out into the open and then got a better grip around his waist. It hoisted him in the air so the red glowing eye could get a real good look at him. Fitz struggled to get loose, but the spikes had already dug themselves deep into the meat of his torso. He was going nowhere.

The fight was over almost as soon as it started.

Buck Baker had kept himself clear the whole time. Crawling on his stomach, he found a safe position to watch the events unfold.

When it was finally over, he stood up confidently and went to address Fitz. But movement out of the corner of his eye drew his attention elsewhere. He saw the other sergeant outside. The man was attempting to flee. The sergeant was crossing the yard and hurrying to get to the farmhouse. The rifle Fitz had been wielding was lying at his feet. Buck picked it up and moved with it toward the exit.

Sergeant Percy was almost at the house. The back door was still open and he could see into the kitchen. He thought if he could jut get inside he might manage some sort of an escape. He was limping, struggling for breath, but gaining ground. He was so close he could see the dog looking at him, shivering frightfully under the kitchen table. He got as far as the porch before a round entered through his back and exploded out the front of his chest.

Buck Baker had shot him and prepared to fire a second shot until Percy collapsed onto the porch steps. The old farmer lowered the rifle and gazed at it fondly. To him, it was like an old friend he had not seen in years. "Like riding a bicycle," he remarked to himself.

CHAPTER THIRTY-FOUR

"Escape Plan"

Hollis had not moved. He was still seated on the bench, facing the hospital, looking and feeling distraught after what Talia had recently told him. Talia was still seated with him, though at the opposite end. The young woman was still unsure how her esteemed prince took to all that she had confessed and was anxiously awaiting for him to break the awkward silence.

"Last night," Hollis began, "when I tried to leave—to cross the chasm using the rope—"

"I remember," she responded, cutting him off. She presumed where this conversation was leading and looked away, feeling ashamed.

He continued, "I had just gotten over to the other side when you and the Sapphire King appeared. You were being held in his claw. He held you over the edge of the cliff. And I thought—*if I don't come back, that son-of-a-bitch is going to drop her.*"

Hollis noticed Talia was avoiding making eye contact with him. "He had a secret to keep, didn't he?"

"I guess we all have secrets, Hollis," she said, her voice barely above a whisper. "For each of us, it's just a matter of how far we're willing to go to keep those secrets safe."

"And if he let me get away," Hollis said, "I might end up telling someone, and that posed a threat to the little world he's made for himself here. He could just as easily have yanked that rope free while I was crossing back over. My death would have kept his secret safe. He's a robot—just a *robot*!—why should he give a shit? But he didn't do it. If he had, I'd be just another body at the bottom of the chasm, left there to rot.

"I realize now that dropping you was the furthest thing from his mind... his *programming*. Of course he didn't need me back alive. It was you. *You* wanted me back."

"Do you hate me?"

Hollis breathed deeply through his nostrils. "No. I don't hate you. And I guess I can't even blame you. It was a good trick, and I fell for it." He smirked at her. She took that as forgiveness.

"He saved my life," Hollis muttered. "He's more than just a robot, Hollis."

Even though everything logical told Hollis that was impossible, he could not deny what he had seen with his own eyes. "I'm beginning to believe that," he hastened to admit. He went to see where the robot was, and then he remembered it had gone to see the Queen.

As before, a moment of silence passed between him and Talia, until Hollis finally said, "I have something else to tell you... a confession of my own."

She looked at him.

"I never told you the whole truth, the real reason I needed that radio tower to be built and why it was so important?"

"You told me you made a deal with Captain Radigan."

He shrugged. "There's more to it. You see, Captain Radigan was the commander of a military company that was passing through this area. Yes, he needed that transmitter working so he could call for help, that part was true... but what he really needed was reinforcements."

"Reinforcements? I don't understand," Talia remarked innocently.

Hollis was damn certain she knew exactly what he meant. "The Sapphire King screwed with the wrong people, Talia. Captain Radigan's men were attacked in the woods not far from here—men were killed!" He didn't bother to ask her if she knew about it. He suspected she did and now was not the time to catch her in a lie. "Radigan wanted payback for what the King did, payback in a measure beyond your imagination. He was going to call in for bigger guns, armored tanks, helicopter gunships... hell, even jet fighters that would drop their ordinance before you even heard them pass overhead.

Oliveri would be gone. It would be reduced to a dark spot on a satellite photograph where a town *used* to be, but isn't anymore."

Talia held a concerned look on her face. That last part seemed difficult to process.

"Radigan doesn't care who might get caught in the crossfire, or how many innocent people might get killed."

"We have to stop him," Talia urged.

"It's not that simple, Talia."

"Yes, it is! The Sapphire King will find him and stop him!"

"No, Talia, it won't matter." He moved closer to her. She needed to understand. "That's what I'm trying to tell you. Others will come no matter what the Sapphire King does to Radigan."

"The Sapphire King will take care of *them* too!"

Hollis sighed. "Oh, I'm sure he'll try."

"He has always protected us."

Hollis looked at her solemnly. He was beginning to realize there was no way he could make her understand, simple reason seemed to have zero affect, so rather than waste any more time and keep trying, he redirected the conversation. "Talia, is there some other way out of town?"

She took a deep breath, but gave no indication.

He pressed her. "The Sapphire King can't get across that chasm. He's demonstrated some notable skills, no doubt, but flying isn't one of them. How does he get out of town? Is there some other way—some secret passage?"

Talia stood up. She tucked her long red hair behind her ears and posed expressively with her hands on her hips. "Hollis... "

"Yes."

"Prince Hollis..."

"I'm listening."

"All you had to do was ask."

"Okay, well... I'm askin'."

She held out her hand for him to grab, but he stood up on his own. He felt better for having rested on the bench and was able to manage, but she locked up her arm into his and began to lead him away. She pointed northwesterly. "We're going *that* way," she told him. Back out of town, he presumed. He went willingly.

They walked to the outskirts of town, passing an old service station along the way. It was getting too dark and they were fortunate enough to find a gas lantern inside the office to light their way. Another mile past the station brought them to the end of the paved road and down another covered with gravel that eventually came to a dead end.

They had gone nearly two miles by this time. There was nothing around. Some signs of life, chirping crickets and the occasional nocturnal animal darting through the underbrush. A patch of woods lay ahead and a convenient path carved through it.

Flattened vegetation and deep tracks made in the ground gave clear evidence of the Sapphire King's heavy traffic this way. Up ahead, through the line of trees, Hollis could glimpses of the rock wall that surrounded Oliveri and what looked to be a cave carved into it. Just another few hundred feet further and they were standing right in front of it. No, he came to realize, not a cave—a tunnel! With his enhanced ability to see as well as an owl at nighttime, Hollis saw clear through to the other side.

The opening was massive enough for an SV-P9 to pass through, the FAF's biggest and mightiest autonomous super tank, the *Terra-Duster*. No tight fit here for the Sapphire King, nor for anyone—or anything else, for that matter.

Talia spread her arms wide as if to present it. She explained, "This whole thing was a project started years ago, before the war, an alternate route to the Interstate; but the mayor ran out of money... or reasons, to finish it. The Sapphire King finished it himself. He's the one who dug the rest of the way, clear through to the other side."

And why not, Hollis took into consideration...isn't that what the robot was originally designed to do... what a mining robot is *supposed* to do?

"This is good," Hollis said, declaring his approval, and announced, "Now we can all leave."

Talia's brow furrowed. "What are you talking about, leave?"

"You have to leave, Talia. We all do. You, me, the others in town. There's no other choice."

She snickered ingloriously. "And go where?"

Hollis shrugged. "Anywhere—I mean, anywhere but *here*. This place is not safe anymore. It's going to turn into a war zone."

She began rubbing her temples. The mere thought of such a thing seemed to cause her head to ache. She stepped away from him.

"Now, when we go back we have to tell the others," Hollis explained, "we'll tell them what I just told you, and we'll high-tail it out of here. I wouldn't bother to pack anything. There's no time for that. We should all just go right away, and do it before the Sapphire King comes back. We can go straight to Bravo Company's camp. I'm positive they won't turn you away—that Radigan is an asshole, for sure, but the others in his unit are sane enough to grant you protection."

Talia stepped farther away from Hollis. She turned her back to him. "We won't go." She sounded pretty certain.

"Did you hear anything I just told you?" he contended. Her lack of sense was disturbing.

"We won't abandon the Sapphire King," she insisted. "That would make us no different than the people in this town who left *us*!"

Hollis shook his head. He sat on a boulder, almost as an expression of defeat. "Talia, let me ask you something... something important..."

She turned to him.

Impatient and clearly annoyed, Hollis finally asked, "What sort of future do you envision with that robot?"

Talia thought about it a long moment and then replied, "There are people in this town, Hollis, that believe... if it wasn't for that robot, we would not *have* a future."

He would have gained nothing by saying it out loud, so instead he only thought it: I guess, then, you people truly *are* crazy.

Talia leaned against a nearby tree forlornly. She forced a smile and then said pitifully, "I want things to be the same. I want them to go back to the way they were."

"After what happened, Talia... things will never be the same again." There was a crack of thunder, or at least it sounded like thunder. "We should go back," Talia suggested.

Without any hesitation, Hollis agreed. "Okay," he said, and hopped off the boulder and onto his feet. He was ready to go.

CHAPTER THIRTY-FIVE

"CONSEQUENCE"

The steel spikes forged within the jaws of the Ruby Queen's claw were long and prevented the claw from closing completely, thus it spared Fitz from being squeezed in half. It was quite effective, however, in holding him captive. He was locked in, still conscious, and bleeding badly. He'd been pierced by the spikes and his blood was draining down the sides of his legs, dripping off his boots and making a pool on the ground above which he was suspended.

"I have re-established my dominance," the old man said as he passed close by.

If only he had walked within reach, Fitz would have slapped the overly confident, pampas ass grin off the old man's wrinkled face.

Buck still had the rifle in his hands, the one he had shot Sergeant Percy with.

He tossed it away and went to pick up the work ladder that had fallen over during the recent commotion. He reclaimed his tool belt on the ground next to it and deliberated for just a moment before he climbed up the ladder; back to work, as if the wholesale slaughter of these soldiers was nothing more than a minor setback.

"What did you think was going to happen?" Buck asked. He was already too busy to give Fitz anymore than a careless glance back.

Though Fitz was in excruciating pain, he managed to squeeze out one word.

"Why?"

Buck made a face as if the question was ridiculous. "Why. Why... why... why..." Buck kept repeating the word. "You wouldn't understand," he said. Something he did with a pair of wire cutters was specific. When he was done he went on, "You really don't know what you're dealing with here, do you?" He turned to look at Fitz finally, at his captive audience member. What else could Fitz do, but have to listen to everything this treacherous old farmer was saying? Buck rambled on. "An entity built with a sophisticated artificial intelligence that enabled her to adapt to her changing environment—to *evolve*.

"You can release him now, Ruby," Buck dictated, "he'll do no harm to you anymore."

The Queen opened her claw—it squeaked open—and Fitz slipped loose from the spikes that had impaled him. He dropped like a sack of wet laundry into the pool of his own blood.

"I imagine the robot was left alone in an abandoned mine somewhere," Buck hypothesized. "Left to her own devices, maybe for years. Aware of her existence, but having no purpose. In time, she found answers to her questions. Solutions to her problems. Now, I don't know who put these weapons on her. Some damn fool, I suppose. But that doesn't matter now; trying to stay in one piece in a world that's constantly trying to dismantle you, those weapons seemed to come in handy. Eventually she came to realize her purpose, and it was simple, and pure... it was to survive. Imagine that?"

Fitz saw his weapon lying on the ground next to him. He also had his sidearm, which the old man neglected to search for. But the old man was not the intended target. No. The target was the robot. And given what affect bullets had on it, it was pointless to attempt to draw and shoot.

"The trouble with you and all your men is that you were trespassing, that's all," Buck remarked.

Blah, blah, blah. That was all Fitz may as well have been hearing.

Until Buck said something worthy of responding to. He said, "If you and your men were crossing the Serengeti Plains of Africa and were attacked by a lion defending its territory, would you blame it? I hardly believe you wouldn't have expected it."

Fitz's response was expressed with as much force as he could muster. "If that lion had slaughtered any of my men, I would have hunted that beast down and killed it!"

"Yes, I'm sure you would have. And you would have done it without conscience. I would expect nothing less from a soldier. You see, that's the issue I have with you and your kind, your mind is so narrow it can't let any other option pass through. Kill or be killed. That's all you know. Well, let me tell you, I'm here to preserve these two. Yes, I said *two*. I lied when I told you I knew of only one. I'm here to make sure both of them have a chance to get away. It's gotten too hot here lately. They need to move on to a place more secure. I'm going to see to it that they do... just as soon as I re- attach this lady's leg."

Fitz's own legs were useless. He could not feel them anymore and wondered if, in fact, they were still attached. He could not crawl, but his arms still worked. He could still reach. And what he reached for was Corporal DeGarmos' rucksack. Inside was the M115 high yield chemical explosive, otherwise known as C4.

He took a deep breath and thrust out his arm, but his reach came up short.

The Ruby Queen made a sound; a deep beat that bounced off the walls of the barn, like the thump of a bass drum. It was followed by a series of clicks and high pitched beeps.

"Hear that? That's a sign of intelligence. She's trying to communicate," Buck said. He began to wield a hand held cutting torch. Sparks spat from it as it seemed to Fitz as if the farmer was welding an access panel shut. Fitz was in no position to clearly see. He didn't really care what the man was doing, just as long as the man's attention was drawn away from him and what he was trying to do.

Fitz grabbed the rifle and used it to extend his reach. He coiled the rucksack straps around the muzzle tip and pulled on it. The sack did not budge. That was because Corporal DeGarmos was still attached to it, and the young man's two hundred and fifteen pound lifeless body was like an anchor. Instead, Fitz managed to drag his own body closer to it, leaving a trail of blood and his severed legs behind. Buck Baker still had plenty to say, and his voice droned on, playing to Fitz like a demented soundtrack to the final moments of his life. "You may recognize the format," Buck shared, "you being a soldier and all. She's speaking in Morse Code."

She most certainly was not, Fitz thought. He knew Morse Code, and this— whatever *this* was—was not it. The crazy old fool had no idea what the robot was trying to say, or if in fact it was even trying to say *anything*. It may have just been making noises.

"She could be talking to you. She could be saying, *good riddance*."

Fitz unzipped the rucksack and removed its contents.

"Talia claims she can hear the Queen speak as clearly as English. Now, I know you don't know who Talia is, but I think she's wrong. She's a simple minded young woman who truly doesn't get it. No matter. What I think is, if this machine could speak clearly, she might want to express how much she cares to go on living. She wants to leave here and experience life and learn what living is all about. And she will. She and the Sapphire King will find someplace safe."

Fitz replied, "I'd like to teach her a thing about life..."

He was growing weaker and could hardly even speak anymore.

Without looking back, Buck replied, "Oh, really. You? A soldier? What the hell could you possibly teach her, aside from death and destruction—the only thing a soldier really knows?"

There was a momentary pause. A split second realization when Buck stopped speaking and turned to Fitz. His eyes focused on the device the soldier held in the palm of his hand—a detonator.

It was then that Fitz answered, "Consequence."

CHAPTER THIRTY-SIX

"FITZ'S SIGNAL"

There had been a chain reaction. The initial blast of the C4 ignited the warheads of the remaining missiles within the Ruby Queen's shoulder mounted launcher. Their yield broke through the Ruby Queen's protective armor and ruptured the hydrogen fuel cells cradled at her core. The result was an explosive discharge that far exceeded anyone's expectations. It could be heard for miles and shook the earth with enough force to knock a man standing a thousand feet away flat on his back. The barn was reduced to splinters, with pieces still falling from the sky even after several seconds.

Back at Bravo Company's camp *there came a rumble.*

"Holy crap!" exclaimed Lieutenant Lewison, and he turned immediately toward the entrance to the canyon where the captain was. All those around him had heard the rumble too. Without another seconds haste, he sped off.

"Sir!" he shouted with a youthful excitement, "did you hear that?"

Captain Radigan turned to him slowly, unimpressed. "Did I hear it? Fuck man....I *felt* it," he remarked. For a moment he just stared. It seemed he was looking right through Lewison as his thoughts began to settle into his fiendish mind what he was going to say next. "Go ready the bait," he said.

And by bait, he meant first and second squads from Second Platoon.

"Shouldn't we wait to get confirmation from the First Sergeant?" Lewison proposed.

Radigan scorned him with a look. How dare he question him? "That explosion was all the confirmation I need, Lieutenant, now do as I say."

"Right away, sir." And again, Lewison sped off.

Fully armed and prepped for combat, these two squads from Second Platoon were given a specific task; they were to proceed north, through the canyon, venture into the outlining forest toward Oliveri and make contact with the enemy robot. They were ordered not to attempt to take it down, but instead to run away from it. Their mission was to lure it back to camp; get the robot to chase them through the canyon toward the trap where the captain was in position and ready to detonate the C4 once the robot fell into the pit. Should they reach as far as the point where First and Fourth Platoon were attacked— and they had not yet encountered the robot—their mission changed; they were ordered to advance north, beyond that point, to Oliveri and if possible engage the *human* enemy believed to be held up there.

The pit Radigan's people had dug at the entrance to the canyon was sufficient enough to swallow a house. Camouflage netting had been laid across the top and coated lightly with sand and leaves to further conceal it. Even now, in the dim light it was hard to see. In the dark of night, it would be near invisible.

Radigan stood looking at it. His confidence in it thrilled him and he smiled an evil smile. He thought aloud so Lewison could hear him, "this whole nightmare is going to be over soon."

Lewison did not share the same confidence. He simply nodded with all due respect.

CHAPTER THIRTY-SEVEN

“SEVERED LINK”

SYSTEMS FAILURE.

Data blackout duration: 10 seconds...

15... 20...

30 seconds...

Robotics systems integration sensors back on line.

Limited mobility due to catastrophic force.

Running damage assessment...

Gathering information...

Analysis completed:

- yield loss percentage - 10 percent
- circuit conditions negligible
- impact to primary systems: category 2

Identifying alternate structural solutions to recover loss.

Systems now operational.

The Sapphire King sat up and looked around. Dazed and confused; the robot acted like a man who had been hit so hard he was knocked senseless.

The robot knew it had been tossed; it currently sat a significant distance from the very spot it remembered it had been standing. The shock wave from the blast had sent all of its twelve tons soaring through the air.

Attempting to re-connect with L1 unit.

Nothing.

`Connection failed.`

The King tried again. Nothing else at the moment mattered.

`Connection failed.`

The signal from the Ruby Queen could not be re-acquired.

Panic set in—or rather, the robot equivalent to it. The Sapphire King got to its feet quickly and began to move toward the source of the blast. Slowly at first, and then it broke into a sprint.

Sensor alarms throughout its chassis warned the central program unit to slow down. Exertion could risk further damage. The Sapphire King ignored them and kept on running. It had a need.

There was barking from Buck Baker's dog still in the house. The roof of the house had caught fire and the flames were spreading rapidly.

The Sapphire King emerged from the tree line and entered into the smoldering mess that was once the Buck Baker Farmstead. Pieces of the barn lay about, still on fire. There was a deep crater in the earth where the barn once stood. The Sapphire King proceeded gently; it did not want to crush anything of importance. It was searching for something specific.

The dog ran from the open back door of the house. It paused when it saw the robot. It looked left and right, as if trying to decide which way to go, and then it ran off into the night.

Torn pieces of human remains and the tattered uniforms they wore littered the ground and were stuck to the trunks of trees that had not been knocked down by the blast. These were not what the robot sought, but were distinct articles that were stored in its memory nonetheless.

And then...

Half buried under loose dirt was a piece of the Ruby Queen's extension arm— the crane mechanism—that gave the Queen's eye mobility. The Sapphire King reached down with its claw and carefully pulled on it, uprooting the arm and the Queen's optical unit still mounted to it. The King held it in front of its own eye, to examine it closely.

The Queen's eye was void of light. Lifeless. And it became clear to the King that it would not be able to re-connect with the L1 unit. Not now. Not ever.

The Sapphire King was now a singular entity, and for the next few seconds it contemplated that existence. Lost. Without purpose. It was confused. Confusion fell into despair. Despair turned into something it had never 'felt' with such intensity before... *rage*... and a desire for revenge.

It rested the Queen's eye back on the ground and stepped away from it.

Looking once again at the shredded military uniforms it quickly established accountability. And soon it began to conceive a method of restitution for what had been done.

Those responsible were going to pay.

CHAPTER THIRTY-EIGHT

"STEP ONE: BACKTRACK"

Before its untimely "death", the M36A2 (fondly referred to as *The Skip* by the men and woman of Bravo Company) had taken its share of beatings throughout its service in the FAF. Allocated to the unit early in the year 2025—three years into the Second Civil War—the fast, all-terrain vehicle had been put to use almost immediately after its inauguration. Federal soldiers were pinned down on the front line by Rebel Americanists during a skirmish in Soda Springs, Idaho, and Bravo Company was tasked with getting them the first aid and supplies they so desperately needed. The newly assigned Skip was called upon for this mission, despite having never been tested for its reliance. En route to the frontline, the faithful hauler took damage; the fenders and windshield were pelted unmercifully by small arms fire, its frame pitted almost beyond serviceability, and the undercarriage bent due to the close proximity of an implemented explosive device. But it continued on, eventually reaching those soldiers caught in the skirmish. Upon its return, the M36A2 was deemed a worthy asset to the company.

Blood stains on the driver's seat were left unclean to serve as a memorial to the driver of the Skip who sacrificed his life on that fateful day to accomplish his mission.

At this moment, the Sapphire King stood over the stricken vehicle, peering down at its burnt, twisted chassis lying upside down in the middle of the road with its charred wheels pointing up at the sky. Having taken one of the few roads that lead from the town of Oliveri, the vehicle met its tragic end when it attempted to convey its two human crewmembers to the Interstate, a presumably safe and open road that would lead them straight out of Dark Alley and back to civilization. The Ruby Queen and one of her guided missiles made sure it did not succeed. But the Sapphire King was not at all interested in that. It did not care in which direction the vehicle had been going. What mattered was where had it *originated.*

All the robot needed to do was turn in the direction it came from, and then it began to run... in search of who sent it.

CHAPTER THIRTY-NINE

"STEP TWO: QUIET OBSERVATION"

There were six armed guards posted on the main road to keep watch over the convoy vehicles parked there on the side of the road. Corporals Jackson and Grillo were assigned to relieve them for chow in shifts. Jackson was a human tower with dark skin who grew up in Detroit's eighth district; he was tough as hell with never much to say unless it was important. Grillo was a chatter box from Brooklyn who never knew when to be quiet; he was lanky and almost a full twelve inches shorter than Jackson. Even now, as the two of them were making their way toward the main road Grillo was cackling about something Jackson had no interest in hearing.

"...and so I said to Burns, you have no right to stash your shit in my footlocker. My stuff ain't for you to use as your personal storage closet, you know? He just gave me a look, like I wasn't a good friend. Can you believe the nerve?"

Jackson just shrugged. Could he believe it? Of course he could. But he also couldn't care less.

It was going to take them less than a half hour to huff it from the school grounds to where the vehicles were parked. They were nearly ten minutes short of their trek when Jackson thrust his arm across Grillo' chest to halt him. "You smell that?" he asked.

Grillo sniffed the air like a dog. A look of shock and recognition came across his face.

The two took off like lightning. The road sat higher than the level of the ground they had been walking on, but from their low vantage they could see smoke rising up into the sky. They reached the incline at the base of the road and made their way up the slippery slope. The ground was loose and it was a struggle, but once they got to the level of the road they were stunned by what they saw. The destruction. All of the vehicles were smashed. Burning. Overturned. Some sustained a pattern of damage; their roofs caved in, such that they looked like a giant-sized black belt in martial arts had given each of them an earth pounding karate chop.

Jackson and Grillo immediately looked around. *Where were the posted guards*? They broke into combat stances with their rifles drawn and maneuvered through the smoldering mess with caution. The flames crackled loudly. They choked when the smoke passed in front of them. This was insane!

Grillo found one of the guards lying on her back in the middle of the road, her arms outstretched. She was conscious and her wide open eyes looked back at him in terror. The Brooklyn born corporal knelt beside her. He knew her. Her name was Ford. She was a PFC. He placed his rifle on the road next to her and began to administer first aid, applying pressure to an open wound to her chest. The young woman was bleeding from a gash in her scalp too, that was leaving a stain on the road beneath her head that was spreading. Instinct and training had Grillo insisting, "You're going to be all right!" She was trembling, but otherwise did not move. Penalized with fear? It was impossible to make a diagnosis, so he asked her, "Can you get up?" She shook her head slightly.

Her lips began to move. She was trying to say something, but no words came out. He noticed her eyes kept shifting purposefully. She was trying to draw his attention to the side of the road, but when he looked there was nothing to see. There was too much smoke.

Jackson stood a few meters back meanwhile, maintained his combat readiness, looking around in jerking motions; one direction to the next, in case the enemy was still close by. He took notice of something he saw farther down the road. Over there is where the other guards were, all thrown into a heap. At a glance none of them looked alive; their bodies looked too bludgeoned, their eyes locked in death stares.

"Jackson, get your ass over here and give me a hand," Grillo shouted. Jackson hesitated. He kept looking around, refusing to drop his guard. "It's gone," Grillo insisted.

How the hell do you know? Jackson thought. It was the robot he was searching for. But he couldn't find it. It was difficult to see anything through all this smoke, even something as big as that mechanized Cyclops.

"*Butcher*—goddamn it!" Grillo shouted.

Butcher was Jackson's nickname. Hearing it seemed to snap the dark man out of his warrior mode. Still reluctant to drop his guard, he turned to look at Grillo and Ford, seeing them now for what they were, his comrades in need of help. He flew to them.

"You and me have to carry her," Grillo told him. "If we don't get her back to camp, she'll die!"

Something was not right. Jackson had a bad feeling about it. Why had Ford been so clearly spared and none of the others? Why wasn't she thrown into the heap?

One of the oldest tricks in the combat handbook. He was sure of it. Leave an enemy injured and watch in secret as help arrives to carry him or her back to safety—and then follow them to their hideout!

The decision had to be made, and as a result, a risk had to be taken.

With his two strong arms, Jackson hoisted Ford onto his shoulders. He cupped his hands under her arm pits. She made a guttural sound as he adjusted her position. Grillo grabbed her legs. They knew she was in terrible pain and they also knew the extent of her wounds, for they felt the wetness of her blood immediately soak into the fabric of their uniforms. If they didn't hurry she was surely going to die. There was no time left to think about it. They moved.

Jackson could not shake the feeling they were being watched.

CHAPTER FORTY

"STEP THREE: ANNIHILATION"

It was thirty minutes later. Captain Radigan was standing with Lieutenant Lewison well past the entrance of the canyon, about 200 meters in, where, at the first bend, they watched the squads from Second Platoon head out to find the robot and lure it back to camp. The squads moved quickly, silently, double timing in two column formations. In a short time they were barely specks in the distant horizon.

Lewison said, "Judging by how fast the machine moved when it attacked First Platoon, we'll have about ten seconds before it falls into the hole. Ten seconds, "he repeated, "from the moment it turns this last bend and becomes visible to us." He showed the captain the detonator in his hands. "We'll have to time the detonation just right."

Radigan planned to be watching from an office window, in the safe confines of the school. He was still feeling confident and both of his hands trembled with excitement. Any such nonsense going on behind him was hardly a concern. In the distance, Radigan kept hearing a soldier from Bravo Company shouting something at the top of his lungs; something about the vehicles on the side of the road. It was not enough to break his concentration, but as more and more soldiers began to join in, their concerns could not be ignored.

Suddenly there was a high-pitched scream. Rounds began to go off.

What the fuck was going on back there?!

Radigan turned to see. An evening mist had moved in during the last hour and made it difficult for him to make out what was happening back there; he moved closer to the edge of the pit, along with Lewison, and the two of them were squinting their eyes in the hopes of trying to make out what was going on.

There was an explosion. Someone's grenade had gone off. The flash was concealed in the low lying cloud cover. There came a loud and raucous bark of orders, more gunfire and screaming.

The *woosh* of someone's shoulder mounted rocket. Another explosion.

Woooosssssh. Ka-boom!

Woooosssssh. Wooossssh. Thump... Ka-pow!

Radigan's blood ran cold. His knees went weak. *Dear God...*

The sounds he heard next were mechanical. Clicks. And clanks. The *psssst* of hydraulic pistons. The whir, screech and chug of an engine in the state of execution.

The tchwonk... tchwonk... tchwonk... of heavy footfalls.

A body soared above his head. It was a soldier. *God almighty*! It was the body of Specialist Chang; with his arms outstretched and legs spread wide he spun in the air like a ninja throwing star. The trajectory of the throw sent him hurtling toward the side of the canyon wall where he struck with a splat. The bulk of him dropped from the height of twenty feet. He fell right upon the camouflage netting. His weight could not be sustained and the netting collapsed, sending him and all that camouflage the rest of the way down into the pit. Radigan could do nothing—nothing but peer down in horror and helpless despair. The pit was now exposed.

A soldier emerged from the mist and staggered toward the pit. His arm was bleeding and he was holding it tight to his side as if to keep it in its socket. He stood at the opposite side of the pit across from where Radigan and Lewison were standing. He held a 9mm pistol in a death grip in his seemingly useless arm. "The robot, sir," the soldier strained to say, "it... it came... from *behind* us!" The man collapsed to his knees.

The captain's face turned red with fury. His failure *again*. The enormous impact of realizing he had underestimated his enemy took an immediate toll on his psyche.

A portion of the mist was swept away by a sudden gust of wind, allowing the captain to see everything now without hindrance. The massacre of his men. His whole world and everything he had ever hoped to accomplish was dissolving before his eyes. The robot stood looking at him, looking back at him—staring at him with that one blue glowing eye—and Radigan got the message, that his fate was eventual. Was the robot going to save him for last? The soldiers in the company were still fighting hard, but not hard enough to defeat it. With its focus still on Radigan, the robot was distracted and was struck broadside by a rocket. It stumbled. There were sparks. Pieces of it flew off. The robot was injured. It turned toward the soldier who fired the rocket and rushed toward him. It stomped on him with its heaving foot, ground him into the dirt and then kicked his crushed remains off into oblivion. And then at once, it turned back to Radigan. It knew who he was. It knew he was the leader. It had been trained to know. It did not want to lose sight of him. But first, there were others close by that had to be dealt with.

Captain Radigan was fixed in a state of paralysis as he stood watching. There was no stopping the robot. None of his men had the means, the skills or the firepower to make any difference. It was like the robot was invincible. The violence he had witnessed the robot execute through the lens of Corporal Hammond's helmet cam a mere twenty- four hours ago was nothing compared to the measure of which he was seeing now.

Radigan's hope was lost. His career... and everything that ever amounted to it... whatever dignity he had left... was gone... all gone.

Admitting to himself that the First Sergeant Fitz was right all along was akin to a self inflicted slice across his throat with a jagged edged knife.

Lieutenant Lewison was holding the detonator to the C4 planted in the tops of the canyon walls. The captain attempted to grab it from him, but Lewison pulled his arm back and side stepped out of Radigan's reach.

Radigan looked at him astounded. "You fuck—give me that detonator!" Lewison looked back at him, equally astounded.

Some of the soldiers of Bravo Company were accepting their loss of the battle; carrying injured, some of them began to migrate toward the pit. They were bunching up at the entrance to the narrow walkway between the canyon wall and the pit, because they had to maneuver in single file.

"Did you not hear me, Lieutenant? I said, give men that damn detonator— now!"

"Sir," Lewison pleaded, "our men are trying to get away. If you detonate the C4, they'll be trapped on the other side with that *thing*!"

Radigan drew his side arm with the quickness of an Old West gunslinger and pressed it to Lewison's forehead. The lieutenant's face went ghostly white. "I will blow your damn head off, Lieutenant, if you make me ask you again!"

A noble man might have thrown the detonator into the pit and told the son of a bitch to go fetch it. But not Lewison. He wasn't that kind of man. Knowing Radigan was not bluffing, he handed the detonator over. Radigan looked ready to shoot Lewison regardless, but in a moment he stepped back and holstered his weapon.

The exodus of injured men and women was in full swing now.

"I have to stay alive..." Radigan admitted despicably, "to avenge them!" With the detonator firmly in his hand, he pressed the button.

There came a tremendous explosion above their heads.

CHAPTER FORTY-ONE

“REUNION”

Hollis and Talia hardly spoke a word to each other during their journey back from the tunnel. Hollis' insistence on leaving Oliveri for their safety and Talia's refusal to abandon her king had formed a wedge between them. Whenever Hollis brought the subject up, Talia would break out in song, she'd sing *London Bridges*, made worse because she sang it loud and out of key. Hollis held no allegiance to these people in the town; as much an emotional bond as he had with Captain Radigan's soldiers, but he was not without conscience. When he and Talia got back to town and everyone was together as a group, he would try to convince them to leave. Their life was worth at least one more attempt. If they still refused, so be it, but he would ask Talia to let him take Daryl. Daryl was too young and unknowing to suffer the fate of those older than he who had poor judgment and a complete lack of common sense.

More than this, Hollis' concern was of his Uncle Billy. The matter of freeing his uncle from his captures and then escaping the ill fate of a general whose vengeance upon him was misguided, was foremost on his mind. Once he and Talia reached within a block of Main Street, he began to devise a plan of breaking Billy out. He hoped it would be easy. And he would try—emphasis on *try*—not to harm anyone in the process.

Something struck the two of them as odd, and they both stopped in their tracks. They saw Daryl. The young one was staggering wearily in the middle of the road. He was all by himself. Even stranger, his hands were up against his face, covering his eyes, as if he might be crying. What scared them both was that he might be hurt. When he lowered his hands, he saw Talia and immediately ran to her. He clung to her desperately and held on like he was never going to let go.

"What's wrong?" Talia asked him. The boy kept his face pressed to her belly.

Talia looked to Hollis for support.

Hollis drew near to Daryl and rested a hand on his shoulder. "Daryl, tell us what happened?"

Daryl shuddered to speak. His face was still pressed tightly against Talia so when he finally did speak his voice was muffled. "The soldiers..." he began to say.

Hollis turned to Talia; there was a sudden exchange, a look of panic. "They've come back!" the boy cried.

Hollis' heart sank and his mind filled with the most disturbing image; he pictured Radigan's men having made it to Oliveri. The trouble he had imagined and warned Talia about, now real—and present. How Bravo Company managed to get over the crevice was anyone's guess, but he supposed he would soon find out.

If Daryl had said an asteroid was on a direct course toward Earth, it would not have sounded more grim.

Regarding the hopelessness of it, Talia said quietly, "The Sapphire King isn't here."

And Hollis knew just what that meant, and was ready to admit *that was a good thing*.

Unsure himself, Hollis said, "Everything's going to be all right, Talia."

Hollis pried Daryl loose from Talia. "Daryl, look at me," he said, and sandwiched the boy's face between his hands. "Tell me where the soldiers are?"

Daryl's eyes shifted slightly and he raised his arm up in order to point. He pointed toward Main Street.

Hollis released the boy and took a step back. His face looked enflamed; not from anger, but from the rush of adrenaline. He fought back the transformation, his eyes turning to Gunlord black, because he didn't want to frighten the boy anymore than he already was, or to shock Talia with the realization he was not quite human. In one exhale of a breath, the Gunlord's son took off, racing toward the center of town.

Hollis had no idea what he would do once he got to Main Street. He didn't hear any shots being fired—or any yelling, or screaming—things he was sure he would have heard if Radigan's men had behaved the way he expected and stormed in, guns blazing.

Rounding the last corner, Hollis skidded to a halt, and he was both bewildered and relieved by what he saw.

The Orphans were safe, at least for now. They were gathered in a semi-circle in front of the church, all in one piece. A brief scan, he saw them shoulder to shoulder, and peering down at something. Hollis stood still a moment, watching them from a distance. When Momma broke rank she left a space and in that moment Hollis could see what they were looking down at; two men in uniform were on their knees, their heads covered in sandbags made of burlap, their hands looking as if they were bound behind their backs. Soldiers all right, Daryl wasn't lying, but only these two—hardly a threat by any measure.

The long-haired Native American man—the one Hollis had never gotten the name of—was coming up from behind the two soldiers wielding a wooden baseball bat. He raised it high above his head when he came within swinging distance of one of the soldiers. Hollis had a clear notion what was about to happen, but before he could act on it, Long-hair swung the bat down upon the first of the two soldiers. Hollis heard the sickening thunk of the wood against the soldier's skull. A death blow, without a doubt. The other Orphans began to applaud. It was absurd. The stricken soldier tipped forward and fell flat on his burlap covered face.

Long-hair raised the bat a second time, taking an immediate side step toward the other soldier still on his knees.

Hollis' eyes turned Gunlord black and he launched himself at the scene as if his feet were jet propelled, arriving in time to breach the bat's impact on the second soldier's skull with his forearm. The bat broke in half. Hollis was unharmed of course; his Gunlord strength enabled him to sustain the fierce blow.

"What the hell are you doing?" Hollis hollered at Long-hair. Long-hair did not answer. Stunned, the tall, burly man took a step back. Hollis turned toward the soldier, who seemed to react to his voice. "Hollis?"

The soldier's voice was shockingly familiar. "Uncle Billy?" Hollis quickly removed the burlap sack covering Billy's head.

With Hollis' back turned, Long-hair raised the broken part of the bat he still possessed. It looked like a sharp wooden stake now and he was prepared to drive it straight into Hollis' back. The man held an expression on his face, like nothing would give him more pleasure. But Hollis caught the man's shadow pass before Billy and he turned at the last second. He turned to face Long-hair with his black eyes leering, daring the man to even try it. Long-hair showed no fear—or maybe he was just stupid. He lunged with it. Hollis caught the broken edge of the bat in mid-thrust, caught it with only one hand, tore it from Long-hair's evil grasp, and yanked it free. And then threw it far away. With both fists, Hollis struck Long-hair's chest with the power of a speeding car and sent all of his three hundred and fifteen pound body flying to the opposite side of the street. He lay there unconscious. Or perhaps dead. At the moment Hollis didn't care which.

He turned toward the others. Some of them gasped. One of them even shrieked. Hollis stood still, glaring at them a moment.

"Your eyes," he heard someone say. He didn't even realize at the time it was Billy who said it.

"Hollis," Billy said firmly now, "your *eyes*."

Hollis realized he was looking at the Orphans with his black eyes. They were all seeing him like this for the first time. He sensed their fear. Recognized it. And soon he was able to manage his state, re-take control of his condition. He turned his eyes back to normal in just a few seconds.

Yes. He was normal again. But he knew it was too late. He was certain *they* didn't think so.

Momma, dressed in her nurse's uniform and bright white sneakers ran across the street to see if Long-hair was all right. At the same time, Hollis knelt down behind Billy and untied the knots to the rope that bound his wrists. Once Billy's hands were free, he went immediately to the soldier lying face down, Specialist Donohue. Billy carefully removed the blood-soaked burlap sack and checked the young sniper's neck for a pulse. There wasn't one.

Billy's teeth were clenched tight when he said, "All these people approached us just as we were walking into town. They acted so..." Billy seemed disgusted to have to say it, "so *happy* to see us—so friendly. And then two of them came up behind us and cracked our knees with bats—that long-haired one, and him, over there, and that guy..." Billy jerked his head toward the crowd. "the one in the suit."

Cranky Mister Kinley, the cross-eyed man. Hollis gave him a look that expressed no mercy, and Kinley cowered right away behind one of the women. He dropped the bat he had hidden behind his back and it bounced off the pavement and rolled away from him to the edge of the street.

"You're a monster!"

It was Momma who said that; not Momma the nurse, but Momma just another patient from the hospital.

Hollis turned his full attention to her. She was kneeling beside

Long-hair who was sitting up now and had a quivering lower lip, like he was a child about to cry. "A MONSTER!!!" the woman cried out again.

Hollis kept staring at her—she looked so viscous—and regarded her words without much significance. "I've been called a monster my whole life," he replied, and fought back the urge to laugh about it. "Now I wonder, Momma, how many people throughout *your* life have ever called you..." He bit his lip. He wanted to say *crazy*, but the trace of consideration within him kept him from saying it. "These men are not your enemy," Hollis told her. "But they are *soldiers*," someone said.

Hollis whipped his head around in time to see Talia enter upon the scene. She was holding Daryl's hand as the boy walked along side her. Though he recognized her, there was something different about her face. She looked different.

"I'm sorry, Talia," Hollis confessed. He was pondering the awful treatment she had endured. "What those soldiers did to you back then was wrong. I understand your hate. Believe me, I do. And I'd be the first one to admit they deserved to be punished. But *these* men here did nothing wrong. They're not bad."

"How can you tell, Hollis?" she asked, approaching them. "How can you tell which soldiers are good and which ones are bad when... they all look the *same*?"

Up close now, Hollis could see the pure and innocent childlike expression he was so used had now turned to stone, even the bright colored princess's dress had lost all its charm and elegance. Something else, too, she did not look at him; with every turn of her head she purposely avoided making eye contact.

In a moment she leaned in toward Billy who was still on his knees. She peered at him quizzically, like he was some curious specimen—a strange bug on the ground—and Hollis heard her ask him a question he would not ever forget, not for the rest of his life. She asked Billy, "Are you *Charlie*?"

Billy made a face and shook his head. "No."

Talia stood up straight. She planted her hands on her hips and posed regally. With a quarter turn of her head and a slight angled pitch, she regarded the dead soldier lying next to Billy, at her feet. "Maybe *this* soldier's name was Charlie?"

Gone all right, Hollis quickly accepted. Completely.

Hollis did not know what else to say.

But Momma did—and she did not hesitate to say it. "Your Highness, please...

I'm begging you... tell that monster to leave. He's not one of us."

The moment came when Talia finally looked at Hollis, and for a split second Hollis thought he could see a bit of the old Talia there, but he was mistaken. The second she opened her mouth, Hollis knew that her wits had boarded a rocket and left the planet. "Momma's right," she said, "you better leave." With a curious tilt of her head and a vacant stare she appeared to answer a voice in her mind. And after a moment she stated quite evidently, "I would hate to see what the Sapphire King would do to you if I told him... you weren't my prince anymore."

It was the last thing she would ever say to him. And it was the moment Hollis knew.

The moment everything became clear to him...

Who was the true ruler of Oliveri; it was not the Sapphire King. It never was.

The robot's strings were being manipulated by this young, angry and vengeful woman. *She* was the puppet master. The robot, as it always had, was simply doing what it was told by the one person it had recognized as the leader. It followed their orders, like it was programmed to do.

The word popped into his head yet again. *Reason.*

Indeed there was a reason why the men of Bravo Company were attacked, but what that reason lacked was justification, for its desire was carried out by an individual who was not mentally sound.

Hollis looked determinedly at Daryl. Talia must have read Hollis' mind, because she repositioned the boy behind her, out of Hollis' line of sight.

Hollis turned to face the others. There were no friendly faces anymore.

Scowls. Indecent gestures. If he had met them days ago, like this, he would have been leery of them.

This was the end.

The end of what had been some sort of a...

—*what would he consider it*?—

an association, at best.

"Who the hell's Charlie?" Billy asked, looking up at Hollis.

Hollis did not need a moment to reflect, nor did he have any doubt bout it.

Charlie was the man who fatally broke Talia's heart.

He was, as Hollis clearly put it, "The enemy."

CHAPTER FORTY-TWO

“EXIT”

Now Billy didn't know what the heck was going on here. He didn't know the details and he sure as heck didn't expect anyone to give him a brief summation. But he was quick to surmise, and even quicker to consider the strange young woman's advice and the eminent danger. "We better leave, kid," he said to Hollis, and glanced around at the others glaring back at them, thinking that perhaps they were wondering what was taking them so long to come to the same conclusion.

The baseball bat to Uncle Billy's knee rendered his left leg practically useless; therefore Hollis had to reach under his arms to get him to his feet, and then support his weight by allowing him to lean on him so he could walk. Hollis was going to have to practically carry him all the way to the tunnel. It would be a chore. The tunnel wasn't exactly around the corner. Along with Billy, Hollis could feel the weight of the Orphans staring at them as he and Billy headed north on Main Street toward the edge of town. He didn't look back. Hollis just kept his eyes forward and his concentration on Uncle Billy, keeping the older man upright and moving. He felt sorry for them, though. Trouble was, he didn't know what he was sorry for.

"Who are those people? Billy groaned. "Are they crazy?"

Hollis cleared his throat and replied, "These days, Uncle, who's to say? One thing I know for sure, they're not innocent... not anymore."

They stopped to rest a few times before reaching the tunnel, mostly for Billy's benefit. Billy didn't have much to say. Hollis did most of the talking; he shared his experiences ever since leaving Bravo Company's camp. When they got to the entrance to the tunnel they rested one last time. Hollis placed Billy upon the very boulder he sat on himself when he spoke to Talia earlier that evening. Billy looked off in the distance, making that peculiar smirk that Hollis was all too familiar with, that look as if Billy was about to say something profound—that is, something profoundly sarcastic. Billy remarked, "You know something, Hollis, you're lucky to have me with you. If I wasn't around all the time, who the hell would be there to save your ass?"

Hollis started to laugh. In moment he was laughing hysterically, but then he got control of himself and quieted down, and got to thinking about it seriously. It was a sobering moment. They had a strong bond, him and his uncle. The more he thought about it, the more he reflected on his tragic life and what a damn shame it was; the result of being the son of a soldier designed to kill as efficient as a surgeon uses a scalpel was constantly putting that bond and his uncle's very life in jeopardy. It wasn't fair.

Hollis looked into the tunnel. "C'mon, Uncle Billy, let's get out of here. I don't want to stop again until this town is way behind us."

Billy could not agree more.

After entering the tunnel, the first thing Hollis took notice of was that their path ahead was littered with rocks and boulders. A road hadn't been formed yet. He and Billy had to maneuver around them. It was like a troublesome obstacle course that seemed to stretch clear to the other end. The second thing Hollis noticed came at the point they were a third of the way through, the severe cracks in the tunnel walls and along the curved ceiling; something made sense to him suddenly, why the town had abandoned the project to make an alternate route to the interstate—this tunnel was not safe! If there had been a small quake, or perhaps even the sheer force of gravity itself, this entire tunnel could collapse. When the danger was actually realized, Hollis forced Billy to pick up the pace. The exit to the tunnel was a few hundred feet away. They were moving well and without a hitch, until the very moment they came to the end and were about to exit the tunnel. A massive shadow passed in front of them. It was the Sapphire King. The robot came upon them suddenly and stood blocking their way out.

The robot appeared different now. It looked beaten up. Everyone of its moving parts squeaked and rattled, like expressions of pain. Its upper half was twisted slightly, posing its right side foremost. And what could be clearly seen was that the fearsome robot's arm had been torn or blown off at the shoulder. The only things left of it were jagged extending pieces of metal, not unlike the bridge that had been blown up. There was the often *pop* of sparks from live wires making contact with its chassis.

The Sapphire King took one step into the tunnel and maneuvered its way toward Hollis and Billy. The glowing sapphire eye was staring. It drew forth within a foot of Hollis and held there. As before, Hollis watched up close as the chromium sphere churned into a carbon-like state; some kind of mystical metamorphosis. He felt Billy attempting to tug him away from it. But Hollis stood his ground. It would seem to anyone standing nearby and watching that Hollis had nothing to fear. To them he would have looked like a careless fool. He was sure his Uncle Billy thought he was nuts. But what no one could have known was that Hollis and the Sapphire King had a bond of their own, a bond formed of two misfits—or were they truly monsters?—whose unfortunate role in life was to be someone's puppet for war. Right now they had something very much in common, they were soldiers that had seen and done more than their share and had equally declared themselves done with it.

The Sapphire King turned away first. It focused on Billy for a few seconds, long enough for Hollis to see that it had taken note of the military uniform Billy was wearing. And then the robot turned to face Hollis again, as if to approve, or in this case *allow* that man to pass.

Hollis got a sense that the robot wanted to step in, so he shifted himself and Billy out of its way. The Sapphire King continued on past them.

Tchwonk... Tchwonk... Tchwonk...

It was dark, and although Hollis could see fairly well in the lack of light, he had not been paying attention and had actually failed to notice what was in the Sapphire King's trailing left claw. He didn't notice it until something grabbed his wrist with the strength of a vice and he heard the voice of man he utterly despised. Hollis jerked his head up to see who it was. And he saw that it was Captain Radigan!

The captain moaned and cried out, "Don't let it take me!"

Hollis felt no pity when he saw the horrified look on the man's face; what he did feel was himself being dragged along as the robot walked, because the captain refused to let go.

The Sapphire King gave a firm tug and broke free the hold Radigan had on Hollis and then it continued on, walking as Radigan whimpered... *help me... help me... help me...*

Hollis, his brain filled with apathy, just stood watching as the Sapphire King carried him away.

Eventually the robot reached the other side and it tossed Radigan's crumpled body onto the ground outside the tunnel. When it was satisfied that the sorrowful officer would not try to run away, it turned immediately back to Hollis, in such a manner it looked to Hollis as if the war machine was about to say something. But of course, it could not. The Sapphire King did not have the structural means to utter even the slightest sound. But nonetheless, there it was, looking at him intently. In a moment, it did something with its claw. Something distinctive. It began to wave. Not like a '*take care, t was nice to know you,* kind of wave. This was a sort of sweeping motion, the way an adult might shoo a child and make it go away.

Could it be...? Hollis thought incredulously. *He's telling me to leave*?

If the current situation wasn't so dire, he might have laughed about it.

The Sapphire King raised its claw and tapped the tunnel ceiling. Some rocks began to fall in front of it. It tapped a second time, harder, and even more rocks fell.

This made the message clear.

Afraid that the whole tunnel might crumble down around them, Hollis picked up his uncle and carried him straight out of the exit. When the two of them were a safe distance from the opening they stood back and watched.

The Sapphire King went from tapping the ceiling to pounding it. Now huge car-sized rocks were falling. Dust was filling the tunnel making it hard to see. Cracks spread wide along the sides of the walls and stecthed throughout the length of the tunnel. The ground shook. The entire mountain above appeared to have shifted. And it was only a matter of minutes—minutes was all it took—before the whole damn passage through to Oliveri was clogged by fallen debris. The intense rhythmic thumping sound of the King's claw against the ceiling could no longer be heard.

The way into Oliveri was sealed. Although nothing could stop an invasion from the air, there was no way a soldier—or anybody—would ever be getting in on foot.

Hollis stood with his uncle in silence for a long while. Eventually, Billy said, "So... what do we do now?"

Hollis kept looking at the collapsed tunnel. "We get as far away from here as possible," he replied. And then he turned to Billy and said something he was more than happy to express. "We've been set free."

Lightning Source UK Ltd.
Milton Keynes UK
UKHW010720120821
388748UK00001B/26